THE SINISTER COUNTDOWN HAS BEGUN. . . .

Sam Boggs: Once, he had blown up buildings but refused to waste people. Now he has been drafted for the deadliest mission of the century—and the CIA threatens to waste *him* if he turns it down.

Ilsa Vogel: Lithe, beautiful, she is Sam's vital link to the past. But once the chain is broken, will she survive to play a part in his future?

Klaus Dietrich: Brilliant, fearless, once Ilsa's lover and Boggs's best friend. Has he vanished only to surface as the brain behind the Omegas? Boggs doesn't know, but he's determined to find out.

From Europe—where underground connections lead into a labyrinth of terror—to outer space, Boggs is slated for a deadly rendezvous with a bomb, a beautiful woman astronaut, and the power behind . . .

THE OMEGA THREAT

THE
OMEGA
THREAT

Mark
Washburn

A DELL BOOK

For Jonathan Eberhart and
Jon Lomberg—Boggsophiles

Published by
Dell Publishing Co., Inc.
1 Dag Hammarskjold Plaza
New York, New York 10017

ISBN: 0-440-16669-1

Printed in the United States of America
First printing—August 1980

CHAPTER 1

Ten minutes before lift-off I began wondering if any sane person would allow himself to be strapped to the tip of a four-and-a-half-million-pound firecracker.

It seemed unlikely.

Yet there I was. Nobody thought to give me a sanity test before sealing the hatch and rolling back the gantry. I probably should have brought a note from my psychiatrist.

"T minus nine minutes and counting," the Mission Controller announced. He had a Texas twang in his voice that didn't comfort me; Texans were notoriously crazy. On the other hand, he was the one on the ground. He wasn't going anywhere. They weren't going to accelerate *him* to a breezy eighteen thousand miles per hour and toss *him* clean over the horizon. Maybe Tex wasn't so crazy after all.

The two astronauts seated just above me were also supposed to be sane. They were U.S. Grade A, quality inspected, prime-cut hero material, cloned from Steve Canyon. They both had square jaws and steely gray eyes and the kind of metallic monotone voices that make you think you hear static during the pauses, even when you're in the same room with them.

At the moment, I definitely was in the same room with them—the flight deck of the Space Shuttle *Columbia*. I was positioned directly between the astronauts, a few feet aft—or below, considering our vertical lift-off configuration.

Vertical lift-off configuration. God, I was already beginning to talk like these space cowboys.

The astronauts kept themselves busy during the last minutes of countdown. They were constantly checking the position of dozens of different switches and trading data with the people in Mission Control. I listened to the little blurts of conversation and wondered how the hell anyone could even keep track of everything.

I personally had nothing to do except listen to the thump of my own heart, and I didn't even need to do that since someone down on the ground was monitoring it electronically. Through the pilot's viewport I could see the listless movements of some high, thin cirrus clouds drifting through the blue Florida sky. Very soon we would be drilling a hole through those clouds.

There was a hold in the countdown at T minus six minutes. Someone had discovered a glitch in the linear low-frequency accelerometer. That sounded pretty serious to me. I certainly didn't intend to go blasting off into the cosmos without a reliable linear low-frequency accelerometer. I'm no fool. I held my breath and waited for someone in authority to realize the gravity of the situation and scrub the launch. After only a minute, though, they announced that everything was once again "Go," and the countdown resumed.

It occurred to me that there are profound flaws in a

society in which a linear low-frequency accelerometer can be fixed in sixty seconds flat, but a simple carburator repair takes two weeks.

The countdown droned onward. The recitation of gizmos and widgets seemed endless, a computerized catechism. The multiplexer interface adapter was "go." So were the servoactuator elevon-electro command hydraulics, the differential-pressure transducer, and the MPS liquid-oxygen overboard bleed disconnect. I was actually getting bored by the whole thing.

My big moment came at T minus two minutes and forty seconds. The countdown checklist included literally everything on the spacecraft, electronic, mechanical, and human. Like a spear carrier in a five-hour production of *Hamlet*, I licked my lips and prepared to deliver my one and only line. I listened for my cue.

"Spacecraft Commander."

"Go," said the man on my left.

"Pilot."

"Go," said the man on my right.

"Mission Specialist."

"Go," I said.

That was it. A second later the countdown had moved on to other components, such as the pulse-code-modulation master unit and the dedicated signal-conditioner. I liked that one; it was good to know that our signal conditioner was dedicated. No fainthearts on this mission.

Except for me.

I was listed as a passenger, but technically speaking, I was sitting at the Docking and Payload-Handling Station. I wouldn't have anything to do with docking, but handling the payload was going to be my number one concern.

Because I *was* the payload.

CHAPTER 2

Basically, I'm an earthbound sort of person. The piece of the earth I was usually bound to was a dozen square miles of sand known as San Vincente, the least of the Lesser Antilles. It's just leeward of the Windwards, a little windward of the Leewards. I liked it there and had no plans to leave.

Most of my neighbors felt the same way about the place. Life was easy and uncomplicated there; we had no multiplexers with which to interface. The most pressing issue on San Vincente was the Great Caribbean/Caribbean Debate. It was not the sort of dispute that was likely to lead to civil war, but some people felt strongly about it.

"It's *Carib*bean, dammit!" Tony Avellino dropped an ice cube into his glass, splashing gin and tonic over the chessboard, and reiterated, "Ca*rib*bean! Nobody but a barbarian would say 'Carib*be*an'! You want people to think we're a bunch of jerks down here?"

Across the chessboard, on the white side, Eric Sorensen raised an eyebrow and calmly wiped a drop of gin from his queen's bishop. "Frankly," he said, "I don't particularly care what people think of us. Let them think of us as simply a small, sunny isle, one out of hundreds dotting the tropical waters of the Carib-*bea*n."

"Ca*rib*bean!"

"Ca*rib*bea, and if you're not careful you're going to lose that rook. It's your move, Avellino."

"I know it's my move. And what the hell do you know about it, anyhow? Who knows from tropics in Stockholm? Tell me that, smart guy. You never even seen the sun till you were forty years old, and you wanna tell *me* about the tropics? I was working Havana when I was nineteen. That's Havana which is in Cuba which is in the middle of the goddamn Ca*rib*-bean Sea!"

Tony fumed silently while he studied the chessboard. What he saw there didn't cheer him.

"Sammy!" he shouted to me. "Come over here and explain things to this dumb Swede."

"This dumb Swede," Sorensen said patiently, "is three moves from mate."

I was content to watch from a safe distance. I try to avoid hot political issues. I was much more intrigued by the discovery that Tony Avellino, improbably, possessed one of the world's finest collections of early Fats Domino recordings.

We were on the glassed-in veranda of Tony's mansion, overlooking that body of water which was under discussion. One wall was dominated by a massive stereo cabinet made of polished teak. The stereo equipment was brand-new, but all of the records turned out to be golden oldies. I'd expected that Tony would be an opera buff or maybe a Tin Pan Alley freak, so I was surprised to find stack after stack of old 45's—

Fats Domino, Chuck Berry, Little Richard, Jerry Lee Lewis, pre-Vegas Elvis, even Buddy Holly and the Big Bopper. It was difficult to picture Tony Avellino as a paleozoic rock-and-roller. There was no *bop bobba rebop* in *The Godfather*.

But then, it was also difficult to picture a former Swedish finance minister playing chess and arguing about the pronunciation of *Caribbean* with a retired mobster from Cleveland. We had an odd mix in San Vincente. The place was not so much a melting pot as a wok, where disparate little bits and pieces sizzle side by side.

The Great Caribbean/Caribbean Debate was typical of San Vincente. Someone decided that we needed a national anthem, God knows why. A contest was organized and several of our musically inclined residents took a stab at it. The two finalists were a reclusive German industrialist and a retired cocaine smuggler who referred to himself as The Last Hippie, TLH for short and just plain old T to his friends. T's anthem had a catchy reggae beat and was easy to dance to—I gave it an eighty. The German's sounded suspiciously Wagnerian and made me wonder what he had been doing from 1939 through 1945. Both songs attracted supporters and either one would have been adequate as an anthem. The final choice would rest on the resolution of the Caribbean question. T's rhythm scheme depended on Ca*rib*bean, while the German had managed to rhyme Carib*be*an with "Periclean."

The whole subject of a national anthem arose because San Vincente had recently become an independent nation. That status was questioned by some, so it was important for us to play the part correctly and act like a real country. We needed a national anthem to go along with the other trappings of nationhood, such as our flag and our local currency.

The story of San Vincente's struggle for independence is somewhat less inspiring than such stories ought to be. We had no George Washington or Ho Chi Minh; but we did have a Board of Directors.

San Vincente was invented by a crusty old Texas oilman named Horace J. Piro, a soldier of fortune who currently called himself Bill Bushman, and a Swiss banker named Basil Rheindorf. A few years back a similar group tried to engineer a separatist movement on the Bahamian island of Great Abaco. The idea was to create a legitimate independent state that was wholly owned and operated by people who, for various reasons, were no longer safe or welcome in their native lands. It would be the perfect place to operate money laundries and international investment scams. Robert Vesco and Meyer Lansky would have loved it.

The Abaco scheme never materialized, but Piro heard about it and decided to try it himself. Together with Bushman and Rheindorf, he chose San Vincente as his target. San Vincente was the perfect choice because nobody was really sure who owned it. Spain, France, Denmark, the Netherlands, Great Britain, Venezuela, and the United States could all make equally tenuous claims to it, but nobody ever really cared enough to make an issue of it. The population of about a thousand natives didn't really care, either. But Piro cared. He cared enough to spend a million dollars buying off the natives and another million to ensure that Venezuela would look the other way at the critical moment. Then Bushman moved in and organized a native resistance movement, an easy enough thing to do since there was no one to resist. A local alcoholic doctor was persuaded to lead the

movement and—hey, presto!—the Republic of San Vincente was born.

Piro money bought quick recognition from a half
dozen legitimate (if small) countries. Rheindorf handled the diplomatic niceties and established quasi-
official relations with some of the European countries
and (more important) the Swiss banks. The major
powers couldn't quite figure out what to do about San
Vincente. They didn't like it, but they had little choice
other than to accept its existence. The U.S. and the
European nations with claims to San Vincente
couldn't very well send in the marines without getting
into deep trouble with the Latin American nations,
who were a little weary of that sort of thing. And in
Latin America itself, where coups are common anyway, the various generals and colonels in charge of
things decided that San Vincente might prove to be
convenient. Switzerland, after all, was a long way off
and might be difficult to reach in an emergency. So
when the going got tough, the tough went to San Vincente.

By informal agreement, San Vincente had become a
kind of Coventry. If, like Tony Avellino, you got
squeezed out of your territory, you could always retire
to San Vincente and not have to worry about getting
rubbed out by your former business partners. If, like
Eric Sorensen, your international fiscal juggling act
collapsed on top of you, if you were smart and quick,
you might wriggle out from underneath and split to
San Vincente with a suitcase full of cash.

To keep out the riffraff, Piro imposed a modest cit-
izenship requirement of $250,000. That ensured a
classy population and also eliminated the need for an
income tax. Piro used the money to build a lavish re-

sort hotel and casino, which brought in still more
money and kept everyone happy.

All things considered, San Vincente probably had
the most contented population this side of the Carnation dairy farms. Also the most interesting. We counted
among our number a handful of ex-Mafiosi, a few
dozen high-rolling bankers and financiers, several
dope barons, a couple of mysterious figures like our
German songwriter, three former heads of state, and
one retired terrorist.

That last one was me—Sam Boggs, Ph.D., erstwhile
chemistry professor and mad bomber.

I walked back over to the chessboard and found
that true to his word, Sorensen had bumped off Avellino's rook. Tony was in bad shape, but after a minute's study I discovered a possible escape. It involved
a gutsy queen sacrifice but led to a sequence that
could unhinge the Swede's entire defensive line. Sorensen knew that I had seen it and shot me a threaten-
ing glance.

Sorensen had an extremely high forehead capped
by wispy blond hair. His eyes were watery blue and
set deep in boney sockets with brows like overhang-
ing cliffs. He reminded me of Max von Sydow playing
chess with Death.

Tony Avellino, though, was badly cast as Death.
He was about five feet four and weighed better than
two hundred pounds. He looked like a large medicine
ball. Back in Cleveland he was known as Two-Ton
Tony. It was said that he made his hits by sitting on
the victims.

San Vincente's official motto could have been,
Judge not, that ye not be judged. Despite our scarlet
pasts, nowadays we were all just folks.

My own past was decidedly scarlet. My road to exile began at Berkeley, where I was an assistant professor of chemistry back in the semilegendary sixties. I was one of those hairy academics you see in the old Currier & Ives woodcuts, protesting something called the War in Vietnam. Our protests fell on deaf ears, so some of us decided that we had to make louder noises. I began using my chemical skills to blow up draftboards and recruiting offices.

God, it sounds so harmless now—postgraduate panty raids. But at the time, my activities were enough to make me an Enemy of the State. I went underground and plied my trade as an itinerant demolitions expert. I admit that I rather enjoyed blowing up buildings, although I began to doubt that my activities would shorten the war by even a day. Eventually the heavy hitters of the underground decided that I should be using my talents to explode people instead of buildings.

At that point, I fell out of love with the Revolution. I was a chemist, not a murderer. I split to Europe and spent several years creating specialized chemical devices (bombs, in other words) for whoever could pay enough. My only stipulation was that the targets should not be human. If all you wanted to do was kill people, there were plenty of crazies around who would be happy to do the job. But if you wanted to blow a bank vault or a prison wall, Sam Boggs was your man. I became something of a legend in my own time. My clients included most of the nationalist/separatist movements in Europe, as well as the Mafia and the CIA.

Finally, I was invited to build an atomic bomb for a nameless group with plenty of money and clout. I accepted the job, mainly because if I didn't, I would have wound up as a bag of Purina Worm Chow. I did build the bomb, but my conscience caught up with me at long last and I became a fink. I ratted to the CIA and eventually managed to become a hero, in spite of myself.

That was the end of my career as a mad bomber. I had a full pardon and a half million in a Swiss bank. Although I was once again a legal citizen of the good old U.S.A., I couldn't quite picture myself buying a house in the suburbs and going to work for Du Pont. Instead, I bought a ticket for San Vincente, paid my initiation fee to Piro, and became the next door neighbor of Tony Avellino and Eric Sorensen. I was welcome as long as I didn't do anything to lower the property values. I looked forward to a long and leisurely life, sipping piña coladas and humming San Vincente's national anthem.

Tony Avellino didn't see the queen sacrifice. He moved a knight instead, and Eric allowed himself a brooding Nordic smile as he closed in for the kill. Tony stared at the lynch mob now surrounding his king and growled, "Fuck it. It's still Caribbean."

"Again?" Sorensen asked.

Tony got to his feet and waved his arm contemptuously. "Fuck it," he repeated. "Play Sammy. He's the smart one. He'll blow you away, Swede."

"Sam? What about it? Do you think you can blow me away, as Mr. Avellino put it?"

"Not without dynamite. Maybe later. I have to get back to work."

"That's what I like about you, Sammy," said Avellino expansively. "You got dedication. You'll go places."

I laughed and shook my head. "I've *been* places, Tony. See you later."

I left Avellino's air-conditioned veranda and stepped out into the muggy afternoon. It was like getting hit in the face with a soggy electric blanket. Eric Sorensen probably liked it in San Vincente because it reminded him of a sauna. I made my way down the dirt pathway to the beach, forty or fifty feet below Tony's hillside mansion. The surf looked inviting. I was wearing my standard uniform of the day—cut-off jeans and a straw hat. I skimmed the hat away and charged into the water.

After some vigorous splashing I rolled over onto my back and floated lazily in our controversial sea. Life, I reflected, was damned good.

One of the extremely good things about life shouted to me from the shore. I lifted my head and saw Carla Avellino waving to me. I decided it was a good time to hit the beach.

Carla was Tony's twenty-three-year-old daughter. Her mother had died years ago, but she must have had a bunch of beautiful chromosomes. Carla was rather short—some of Tony's DNA must have survived—but perfectly proportioned and gracefully curved. Her long dark hair flowed over her slim, browned shoulders· like a midnight waterfall, and framed a face that was doe-eyed and innocent. She looked a little like a young Natalie Wood with maybe a dash of one of Charlie's Angels, the smart one, and a hint of Hedy Lamarr as Tondalayo for spice. It was a powerful combination.

Tony had high hopes that I would marry Carla and provide him with a grandson. He admired me for my education. Carla admired me for somewhat less lofty reasons, but she had no intention of marrying me or anyone else. That was fine with me. I was still a few years on the Pepsi Generation side of forty, but I felt it was a little late for me to go into the baby business.

For her part, Carla was less interested in procreation than recreation. Also, there was her career. She was a singer, a good one, and performed regularly at the local casino. She had big-league ambitions, but having Tony Avellino for a father made stardom unlikely. Back in the States, Tony was not beloved by his former associates, and nobody in the entertainment business was likely to risk promoting the daughter of a defrocked racketeer. Carla knew the score and was more or less reconciled to life on San Vincente for the time being.

In the meantime, it was nice to have Carla for a next door neighbor. I waded out of the surf and gave her a quick kiss. She responded with one that wasn't so quick. We might have done a Burt Lancaster–Deborah Kerr scene, but just when I was really getting into the spirit of things, Carla broke clean and retreated a few steps. She was wearing only an insignificant green string bikini bottom (San Vincente has no laws concerning toplessness, or even bottomlessness) and a straw hat. Straw hats sell well in San Vincente.

"Cool it, Sam," Carla told me as I began another approach.

"You want to go into the shade?"

"Not now."

"When?"

She pushed me away again. "Why do you always have sex on your mind?"

"Why do you always walk around nearly naked?"

"It's hot."

"So am I, dammit."

"Well this might cool you off. Sam, there's some man over at your trailer. He's looking for you."

"Let him look. I'm busy right now."

"Sam, I told him I'd go and get you."

I slipped my arms around her again. "Well," I said, "you've kept your word. You've got me."

"And vice versa, too, I think. Look, Sam, I don't know what he wants, but he said I should bring you back with me. It's important. And he also said that I shouldn't tell you his name because if I did you wouldn't come back."

I loosened my hold on Carla. There was only one person whose name would have that effect on me.

"McNally," I said.

Carla's eyes widened. "How did you know that? Were you expecting him?"

"Yeah," I said. I'd been expecting him ever since the day I arrived in San Vincente. I expected him the same way I expected old age and senility. McNally was unpleasant and inevitable.

"Well?" Carla demanded. "Are you going to tell me what's going on?"

"I don't know," I said. "But I think I'm about to be drafted."

CHAPTER 3

I found McNally waiting for me in the shade of my Winnebago. He looked damp and rumpled. His jacket was draped over the door handle and he was leaning against the side of the trailer languidly flapping the front of his shirt in an attempt to stir up a breeze. He reminded me of a vice-president of a rubber factory, flown in from Akron for a look at the plantation.

Carla and I stepped out of the jungle and into the clearing surrounding my home. I stopped about a dozen feet away from McNally and took a good look. He noticed me and returned my stare. The staring went on for quite a while; I couldn't think of anything to say.

"I take it you two have already met," Carla said at last.

We nodded in unison but said nothing. Carla tried again. "You look awfully hot, Mr. McNally. Would you like something cold to drink?"

That effectively concluded our staring contest.

McNally smiled gratefully at Carla. "A beer would be nice," he said.

"Beer it is. Sam? You, too?" I nodded. Carla disappeared into the trailer, leaving me alone with McNally.

"Here on vacation?" I asked him.

"Not exactly," he said.

"Too bad. San Vincente is a great place. After you've been here awhile, you get so you never want to leave."

"I'm afraid I won't be here that long," he said, barely cracking a smile. McNally was too much of a bastard not to enjoy this. "I'm leaving on the evening plane. So are you, Boggs."

"Am I?"

"I already paid for your ticket."

"You're too kind. But suppose I don't want to go?"

"Then I'll stop being so kind."

Carla emerged from the trailer with two cans of Michelob. McNally took his with a gracious bow of his head, then chugged about half of it, dribbling some down his chin. He was never the fastidious type. I remembered his office in Washington; it looked as if it had been decorated by the Bowery Boys.

I also remembered the last time we had seen each other. That was in Washington, too, at the Walter Reed Hospital. I had just spent three months recovering from a large dose of radiation poisoning, a souvenir from my days of nuclear banditry. McNally had been my government contact and at that point my fate was more or less in his hands. His superiors were in favor of "neutralizing" me, but McNally persuaded them to let me go. I wasn't exactly a good guy, but I was no longer a bad guy, and my unique skills might prove useful in the future. If I ever got out of hand, they could always send someone around to neutralize me—the CIA was rather efficient at that sort of thing.

When McNally described the deal to me, I told him to shove it. I was retired. I wasn't going to be a stringer for the goddamned Central Intelligence Agency. McNally just smiled and told me that he'd see me later.

"Not if I can help it," I told him.

"You can't," he said. As usual, McNally had been right.

It didn't require ESP for McNally to figure out what I had been thinking. He sipped his beer for a few more moments and let me dwell on the consequences of refusing to play ball with him. There was an obvious way to avoid those consequences. All I had to do was ask Tony for the use of a couple of his friends for an hour or so. That would be long enough to deposit McNally at the bottom of one of San Vincente's scenic swamps. Then I would have another day or two of blissful freedom. And after that I'd run like hell. No sweat. I'd spent most of my life on the run.

"Come on," I said to McNally. "I want to show you something."

McNally followed me around to the other side of the Winnebago. There I proudly displayed the foundations of *la Maison* Boggs.

"What's it going to be?" McNally asked. "A sewage treatment plant?"

"Careful," I warned. "You can dishonor the great name of the Republic of San Vincente. You can spit on our flag. You can even step on my blue suede shoes. But don't say anything nasty about my house."

McNally gestured with his beer can. "*This*," he asked incredulously, "is a *house?*"

"It will be. See all those concrete blocks? The foundation. That pit over there is going to be my wine cellar."

"Wine cellar, huh?"

"There'll be a big patio area facing the sea, right beneath those palms."

"And a heart-shaped swimming pool?"

"I told you not to get smart, Mac. I'm serious about this. As serious as I've ever been about anything. I'm doing it all myself. Every brick, every nail. It may take me five years, it may take me ten. But when it's finished, it will be my home."

McNally strolled over to the foundation and gave one of the concrete blocks a gentle kick. I think he expected it to fall apart.

"Dammit, Mac, try to understand. I've spent most of my life blowing things up. Now I want to see how it feels to build something. Don't force me to start making bombs again."

McNally looked up at me. He was not a particularly good looking person. His eyebrows looked like a thick colony of lichens struggling against a fungus invasion. His long thin nose tended to trail off toward the east while the rest of his face headed west. But the unnerving thing about him was his eyes. They were a malevolent brown and had a piercing, laserlike intensity. Not the look of eagles, so much as the look of a cynical old predator owl, about to swoop down and eat Minnie Mouse.

"I'm not asking you to build any bombs, Sam. I'm not asking you to blow up anything."

"Ask, hell! You don't ask, Mac. You tell."

McNally shrugged. "It amounts to the same thing," he said.

Carla had been watching us from about a dozen feet away, by the right front corner of the Winnebago.

McNally turned to look at her. By now I was accustomed to the sight of people in general and Carla in particular strolling around in their skin, but it must have been a little disconcerting for McNally. Last time I heard, they were having blizzards in Washington.

"This is where I'm supposed to remember that I have important business on the other side of the island, right?"

McNally gave her a smile. "That would certainly be convenient," he said.

Carla returned the smile, which bothered me. I couldn't stand the thought of her actually *liking* this ogre.

"As it happens," she said, "I really do have some things to do. Rehearsal at the casino. I'm working in some new material."

"I wish I could stay to see your act."

"Maybe next time. Sam?"

"What?"

"Don't do anything stupid, okay?" She blew me a kiss and then was gone before I had a chance to say anything. She could be damned annoying at times.

"Not the typical Boggs beach bunny," McNally observed.

"Newer model, " I explained. "They come equipped with brains and everything. Annette Funicello she's not."

"Boggs, now that you've shown me your Xanadu, could we get out of the sun? It must be cooler in that wagon."

"You're getting soft, Mac," I said as I led him into the Winnebago. "You used to brag about what a he-man you were in the Congo, back in the good old days. Is the CIA limiting its dirty tricks to temperate zones only now?"

McNally paused in the doorway for a few seconds while his eyes adjusted to the dim interior of my motor home. San Vincente was an odd place to find a Winnebago, inasmuch as there were only two roads worthy of the name, and you could circumnavigate the entire island in less than an hour. I discovered it in a used-car lot shortly after I arrived on the island. The native salesman assured me that it had only been driven by an elderly missionary couple who used it as a kind of mobile chapel. I might even have believed him if I hadn't discovered two bullet holes in the upholstery of the dining nook. I didn't particularly want to know how they had gotten there. I forked over a bundle of cash and drove it across the island to my property, parked it next to my building site, and hadn't moved it since. Home sweet mobile home.

I motioned for McNally to have a seat while I went to the refrigerator for two more beers. I also turned the airconditioner on. I'd installed some auxiliary batteries to run the system, and as long as I remembered to keep them charged, everything worked fine.

I joined McNally on the built-in couch and handed him a beer.

"Okay, Mac. What's on your mind?"

McNally launched into it without any preamble.

"Somebody has put a bomb on one of the Space Shuttles," he said. "It's in orbit and we can't bring it down."

I fiddled with the flip-top of my beer can and breathed deeply. Already, I didn't like it.

"More precisely," he went on, "we *think* somebody put a bomb on the *Discovery*. At the moment, we've got it classified as a 'bomb threat.' We don't know for sure."

"Why not? Can't they just search the Shuttle top to bottom—or whatever passes for top to bottom in zero gravity?"

"Because it *is* zero gravity. The *Discovery* went up yesterday morning on a routine two-week mission. An hour later a letter was delivered to NASA. It said that there was a bomb hidden on board and that if we tried to move it or disarm it, it would explode."

"Sounds pretty standard to me."

"Down here, it would be. Up there, nothing is standard. We've got a multibillion-dollar spacecraft with seven people on it, two hundred miles above the surface of the earth. We can't just call in the bomb squad."

I had to smile a little at that. "So you called me, instead."

McNally took a swig of beer, then wiped his mouth with the back of his hand. "Boggs," he said, "If you wanted to put a bomb on the Shuttle, how would you go about it?"

"Not guilty, Mac."

"Will you relax your goddamn paranoia for a minute? Nobody's accusing you of anything. I just want your thinking on this. You were the best in the business. I want to know how you'd do it."

Technical problems always intrigue me. They're like reading an Agatha Christie novel backward. If you want things to come out so that the butler does it, what steps do you have to go through in order to bring it about? Mac's question was as loaded as the dice at table 7 at the casino, but I plunged into it.

"The first problem, and the toughest, is to get the bomb where you want it. The second problem is to get it to go off when you want it to, and not before. From what I know of the Shuttle, I'd say it wouldn't be too difficult to sneak something aboard."

"Why do you say that?"

"The Shuttle was advertised as the first step toward making space accessible for the masses. Increased accessibility means increased opportunity for mischief. You don't have to be a highly trained astronaut to fly in it. You can simply be a scientist or an engineer of some sort. Or you can pretend to be one. Also, there's the ground crew. The Shuttle lands at an airstrip just like a normal airplane, more or less. Then it's taken back to the assembly building, mated to a new rocket, and launched again. A lot of people have access to it during the turn-around procedure. And the more times it flies, the more routine it gets. Anything that is routine and repetitive is predictable and therefore vulnerable. Then there's the business of cargo. NASA is selling space on the Shuttle to anybody with enough money and a reasonably valid experiment they want to perform in orbit. One of those experiments could be a bomb."

McNally nodded thoughtfully. "We've considered all of those possibilities. The FBI is running the support crews and experimenters through a wringer. So far, nothing."

"Doesn't mean anything. Anyone clever enough to get the bomb on board isn't likely to leave a trail of bread crumbs back to his nest."

"All too true. But we're trying. What about the second part of the problem? Getting it to go off when you want?"

"Lots of intriguing possibilities here. Once the Shuttle is in orbit, it would be tough to set it off with a radio signal. The most logical way would be a timer of some sort. Did the letter specify a time limit?"

"That's the odd part. They've given us until next Tuesday, midnight. A little over eight days from now. That gives us time to get together a rescue mission. It also gives us time to sweat."

"It would seem to indicate a timing mechanism in the bomb."

"Not necessarily. The letter said in addition that any attempt to deorbit the Shuttle would immediately set off the explosion."

I pondered it in silence for a few seconds, until the answer jumped out at me.

"Of course! Zero gravity. You could design a bomb that would be armed by the absence of gravity, and triggered by any return to gravity. Simple and foolproof. That's why they can't come down."

McNally sighed. "It's worse than that," he said. "They can't even maneuver. Any significant thrust could be the equivalent of gravity as far as the bomb is concerned."

"I see you've already been down this road."

"Many times. The NASA guys tend to agree that the bomb is probably gravity-activated. So we can't even search for it. Somebody could give a push or a tug to the wrong thing and blow themselves all over space."

I got up and went over to the dining nook, where there was a pad and pencil on the table. I'd been calculating building costs, a depressing exercise. Labor was cheap (free, in fact), but materials cost me an arm and a leg, plus tax.

I started sketching a simple gravity-activated device. McNally watched over my shoulder.

There were a lot of ways to approach it, so I opted for the simplest scheme I could think of off the top of my head. The detonator consisted of a cylindrical peg in a round hole, with a contact at the bottom of the hole. Bottom was relative here, but I assumed it would be aligned with the acceleration vector, so that "down" would correspond with "aft" on board the Shuttle. At lift-off the peg would simply sit there in the hole, resting on the contact, but not connected with anything. When the engine thrust was terminated, the peg would drift upward, out of the hole. Directly above the hole I put a magnet which was wired to a battery. The metal peg would lock into the small magnet, thereby arming the bomb. It would stay there as long as the ship was at zero-G. But when it fired its engines or returned to earth, the G forces would push the peg back down into the hole, along with the magnet and wire. When it touched the contact at the bottom of the hole, the circuit would be completed and the bomb would go off. Ridiculously simple.

I explained it to McNally, who nodded and grunted in agreement.

"Depending on the weight of the cylinder and the strength of the wires and so forth, you could calculate the precise amount of G forces necessary to trigger it. I'd guess it would be in the neighborhood of one-G. It wouldn't pay to make the trigger too sensitive."

"Interesting," said McNally. "But you could disarm it easily enough. Just clip the wires."

"Good point," I admitted. I picked up the pencil again and drew in a couple of additional squiggles.

"So?"

"So now you can't disarm it. Design the whole box and place it so that the only way to get at the wires is to unscrew the whole assembly. But when you remove the screw right here, it releases a spring mechanism that slams the peg down into the hole to the contact. Boom."

McNally studied the sketch for a few moments. He was trying to think of a way around my safeguards, but I knew he'd come up dry. It was foolproof.

Mac shook his head, then finished off his beer and crushed the can. "I'm glad you're on our side now, Boggs."

"Well, that makes one of us."

"Tell me, is that design the product of your vast experience, or could any dumb shit do it?"

"I thought of it in five minutes. It might take someone else five hours. Or five days. Give me more time and I could probably come up with something even better, maybe something using an entirely different principle. But I'd bet that if there is a bomb on the Shuttle, it's similar to this."

"Then you think the threat is credible?"

"I have no idea what the threat is. But if there is a bomb, I'd take it very seriously. What do they want, anyway?"

McNally rolled his eyeballs heavenward. "The sun in the morning and the moon at night. For starters."

"High stakes, huh?"

Mac rumaged around in his pocket for cigarettes and a lighter. He got them, but dropped his sunglasses in the process. He wearily bent over to get them, then retired to the couch again. After a couple of drags on a cigarette, he was ready to talk again.

"They want us to free every radical terrorist from every jail in Europe. Red Brigades, IRA, Basques, South Moluccans, you name it. It'd be like unlocking the viper cages at the London Zoo."

"I don't get it. Where's their leverage? Blowing up

an American spacecraft isn't really going to hurt the Europeans."

"Oh yes it will. On this mission, the *Discovery* is carrying the Spacelab, designed, built, and paid for by the European Space Agency. Half a billion dollars. Not to mention the fact that two of the scientists on board are Europeans. An Italian and an Englishman."

"I guess that complicates things a little."

"Eleven different governments are running around in circles. Nobody knows what to do, but everyone has an opinion. Incidentally, they also want all U.S. forces to get out of Germany."

"Something for everybody. Who is 'they,' anyhow? Any ideas?"

"Very definite ideas. They were thoughtful enough to sign the letter. Have you ever heard of a group called the Omega Alliance?"

"It's a new one on me. Sounds sufficiently ominous."

"It's new to us, too. We're afraid it might be a kind of all-star team, made up of survivors from Baader-Meinhof, Black September, the Japanese Red Army. Nice folks, all of them. I suppose it was inevitable that they'd finally get together. Tell me, Boggs, if you were still in the bomb business, would you have joined them?"

It was an ugly question. McNally had never trusted me completely and had never bothered to hide his contempt for my past activities. I couldn't really blame him.

"No," I told him. "I wouldn't have joined. I was never much of a team player. But that's not the real reason. You have to understand that things are different now. Back in the sixties, we were still naïve enough to believe that all we had to do was throw the

rascals out. Stir things up a little, scare some of the
big shots, wake up the populace. Our role model
wasn't really Che Guevarra, it was Robin Hood. But
the radicals today are tougher and more cynical than
we were, and they don't have any sense of restraint.
My bombs never seriously hurt anyone. I had a romantic notion that you can't fight evil with more evil.
I don't think your Omega Alliance even recognizes the
concept of evil. It's simply a power game to them, and
there aren't any rules."

McNally stared at me for what seemed a long time.
I had no illusions about him. He was on the side of
truth and justice, but he was playing the same game
as the Omega Alliance. Power. The ultimate prize in
the Cracker Jack box of life.

"The Omegas are bad news, all right," said
McNally. "But there may be more to it. Nobody had
ever even heard of them before yesterday, and suddenly they're in a position to demand the wholesale
release of every terrorist in captivity, along with the
complete removal of American military presence on
the continent of Europe. That kind of clout doesn't
grow overnight. The KGB may be involved in this."

"Those nasty Russians again."

"You'd be well advised to take them a little more
seriously, Boggs."

"Every time somebody sneezes, you guys accuse the
Soviets of germ warfare. Sorry, Mac, but I'm no
longer enthralled by the romance of international es-
pionage."

"I think you're still a romantic, Boggs," McNally
said after a moment. "I think you still want to wear
the white hat. But they only come in shades of gray
these days. We need your help, Boggs. You don't
really have any choice, but I'd prefer that we had

your willing commitment. Even if it means that you'll
be in a position where you may have to betray or even
kill people you've been close to."

"I'm not a killer."

We both knew that wasn't true. I'd pulled the trigger when I had to. It saved McNally's life, mine, and
about a hundred thousand others, but that didn't remove the stain.

McNally decided not to press the issue. "Maybe it
won't come to that," he said. "We don't want it to. The
person we're after, we need alive."

"What person?"

"The letter to NASA was signed by someone claim-
ing to be the 'Minister of Science' of the Omega Alliance. His name is Klaus Dietrich."

I could actually feel the blood rushing from my
face. I must have gone pale as a pillowcase.

Klaus Dietrich was a certified genius. An IQ of 190.
A mind that was quick, creative, and fearless. Klaus
Dietrich was the most hated and most respected Euro-
pean radical of his generation.

And he was the best friend I ever had.

CHAPTER 4

McNally and I took the evening shuttle flight to Caracas. He didn't even give me time to say good-bye to anyone.

From Caracas we caught a midnight flight to Paris. We were nearly alone in the first-class cabin, which gave us room to stretch out and sleep. McNally, however, wasn't interested in slumber. He insisted that I should be fully briefed before we hit the ground in Europe. So instead of dreaming or watching the moonlight rippling on the South Atlantic, I spent most of the night wading through dense government documents.

I was already generally familiar with the Space Shuttle, so I quickly skimmed the NASA documents. The Shuttle—or Orbiter, as the actual vehicle is called—was the world's first true spaceship. Everything else that had ever ventured into space had been used once and then retired to a museum. It was an expensive way to travel. If Henry Ford's first Model A had an operational lifetime of one tankful of gas, automobiles never would have caught on. Without reusable vehicles, space travel would be a dead-end street.

The Orbiter was reusable, after a fashion. It was strapped to two solid-fuel rockets and an immense bullet-shaped liquid-fuel tank. The solid fuel rockets dropped off shortly after lift-off and parachuted into the sea, where they were recovered and reconditioned for future use. The liquid-fuel tank was detached after the Orbiter attained orbit and was not reusable, although in the future the empty tanks might be used as modules for space stations. The Orbiter itself had enough fuel aboard for some modest maneuvering in orbit before its deorbit burn. After that the ship was simply an incredibly sophisticated and expensive glider, which landed, wheels down, at a specially built airstrip near Cape Canaveral. It was all still very expensive, but it was a distinct step forward; rather as if Ford's Model A could be refueled, but needed a new set of tires after each trip.

At the moment, there were two operational Shuttles, the *Discovery* and the *Columbia*. Two more were under construction, and the entire fleet would be operational through the end of the century. Stanley Kubrick's vision of Pan Am flights to the Orbiter Hilton was perhaps premature by a few years, but the day is certainly coming when you (or your children, more likely) will be able to buy a Big Mac on the way to the moon. Welcome to the future.

I asked McNally about the status of the second Shuttle.

"Optimum turn-around time is two weeks," he told me. "But the whole program has had so many bugs and delays that NASA is just beginning to get a handle on things. Normally, the Air Force would launch a mission like this from Vandenberg, but the *Columbia* happens to be at the Cape at the moment, so it's NASA's ball game. Theoretically, a rescue mission can be launched with twenty-four hours' notice, but we're not to that point yet. Right now, the best we can do is a launch next Monday."

"And the deadline is Tuesday," I reminded him. "That's cutting it a little thin."

"Boggs, the people at the Cape are going to have to work around the clock just to launch on Monday. If they hit any major snags, they won't make it, and those people on the *Discovery* will die. But we'll be working on the assumption that they'll get the *Columbia* up in time to effect the rescue. With a crew of three, they'll have room for all seven people on the *Discovery*."

"Then they're planning to abandon the *Discovery*?"

McNally curled his lips downward in a sour expression. "If they have to," he said, "then they will. They can seal it up and leave it where it is. Its present orbit should keep it up for about twenty years."

"Then what's the rush? Get the people off now and then go back later to defuse the bomb, if it's even there."

"Fine. We'll just leave a couple billion dollars worth of hardware floating around, unused and unattended."

"Hmmm. I see what you mean."

"Losing the *Discovery*, even temporarily, would knock the entire space program into a cocked hat. There are some planetary probes that just won't wait, or so I'm told. And NASA has already sold all the available experiment space on every scheduled launch for the next three years. Knock out the *Discovery*, and a lot of important work is going to be left undone."

As a scientist—I still thought of myself as one—I

could sympathize. Outer space was an ideal laboratory, and there were things you could do out there
that you could never do back on the ground, no matter how clever you were. But Mac's recitation of the
party line was a little too pat. It made me suspicious.

I thumbed through the papers and found the item I
was wondering about.

" 'Cross-range maneuvering capability of two thousand thirty-seven kilometers, eleven hundred nautical
miles,' " I quoted. "Interesting."

"Oh?" asked McNally, noncommittally.

"That makes the Shuttle a very versatile craft. I
imagine you could see a lot from up there."

"What are you driving at?"

"The real point of all this, I think. The Shuttle can
be used for a lot of purposes other than pure science.
It'd make a jim-dandy spy platform, for instance.
Could that be why everyone is so upset?"

McNally looked around him, at the three other people in first-class. They were all asleep. The stewardesses were off somewhere doing whatever it is that
stewardesses do when they're not serving drinks or
spilling macadamia nuts in your lap.

He turned back to me, looking as annoyed as he
usually did when he thought I was being a smartass.

"Of course it's a spy platform," he hissed at me. "My
God, Boggs, did you think Congress appropriated ten
billion dollars just to find out what makes the universe tick? Most of them don't know the difference
between a quark and a quasar, and don't care."

"So the Pentagon twisted some arms."

"It's all in the hearings. It's no secret. We just don't
like to advertise the fact. When the program gets rolling at full capacity, there'll be fifty to sixty missions a

year. Maybe a dozen of them will have defense applications. It's no sin."

"But it's not 'The Hardy Boys in Outer Space,' either."

"So what the hell are you looking for? A merit badge?" McNally treated me to another of his accusing, you-radical-scum-of-the-earth scowls. "Dammit, Boggs, whether you like the military or not, we live in a dangerous world. There are American spy satellites, just like there are Russian spy satellites. And there are also Russian killer satellites, with operational charged-particle beams that can pick off our satellites like Davy Crockett in a Coney Island shooting gallery. You have the luxury of sneering at all this, Boggs, but I don't. I have to deal with it."

"Look, Mac, I don't like the idea of a bomb aboard the Shuttle. But I also don't like the idea of 'Star Wars Two,' taking place right over my head. I think it would be nice if we could leave all that crap on the ground. Yeah, I know, I'm being naïve again."

"Somewhat."

"If you need my help to get rid of that bomb, okay, you've got it. I'll use my old radical connections and try to find Klaus Dietrich for you. But don't expect me to play any spy games. As far as I can see, the only difference between the CIA and the KGB is that the KGB doesn't have a softball team."

I was hitting McNally where he lived, and I expected to get a full dose of his venom as a result. But he surprised me by staying cool.

"As a matter of fact," he said diffidently, "the KGB *does* have a softball team. At their American town near Zhanov on the Sea of Azov. They train their agents there. I hear the team is pretty good, consider-

ing the lack of competition in the area. Look, Boggs,
the KGB is a fact of life, just like the CIA. We both
turn up in unexpected places. The Company has some
orbital operations, and so does the KGB. But this
time, we're clean, whether you believe it or not. The
Discovery is on a scientific mission, period. And as for
the Russians, you know as well as I do that the Soviets
and the European radicals are not exactly sharing the
same bed. The Russians haven't been in the revolution
business since they laid out Lenin. I have to operate
on the assumption that the Russians are involved,
even if we don't have any evidence that they are.
That's part of my job. But for your peace of mind,
Boggs, I tend to doubt that the Soviets are in on this
business. True radicals scare them."

That much was true. The Russians dismissed the
radicals as amateur Marxists and the radicals scorned
the Russians, considering them to be no more than revisionist bureaucrats. The KGB was not above trying
to use the radicals for their own purposes, but their
efforts were usually laughable failures. Someone once
tried to get me to blow up the PX at an American
army base in Frankfurt. I immediately realized that
my contact was a Russian, just trying to stir up some
trouble. No true radical would have wanted to blow
up the PX; it was the best place in town to get American blue jeans.

"Okay, Mac," I said, "I'll take your word for it. No
Russians. But at the first whiff of vodka, I'm out of it.
I'm not interested in games superpowers play."

McNally laughed. "Hell, Boggs, that's the only
game in town. You just don't have any team spirit."

"Truer words were never spoken." I turned off the
reading light, tilted my seat back, and tried to sleep.

✿   ✿   ✿

My eyes were closed, but I didn't sleep. When McNally first told me that Klaus Dietrich was involved in this mess, I experienced a moment of shock and disbelief. But things were happening too fast for the luxury of emotions; I filed them away and reminded myself to be shocked later. Now was as good a time as any.

Underground bombers don't have the opportunity to make many friends. When a group hired me, I tried to get in and out of town in a single day. I left the conspiratorial plotting to others. My concerns were limited to the job and the getaway. Eventually stealth, like sloth, becomes a habit; each potential friend is also a potential informer, each casual word is a clue. Paranoia becomes common sense.

But even anarchists have to trust somebody, or they go crazy. A psychologist once told me that my bombs were really part of an elaborate self-destruction fantasy. I had good reason to doubt the validity of his analysis, yet there was a hint of truth in it. The pressures and tensions of life on the run come out in strange ways. I'd sometimes find myself taking foolish or needless risks. I'd get sloppy. My psychologist acquaintance probably would have said that I was subconsciously looking for a quick and final end to the tension. I wanted to be caught.

Perhaps my subconscious really was looking forward to the peace of a prison cell, but the rest of me wanted no part of it. Yet the need to relax, to trust someone, was undeniable. If it hadn't been for Klaus Dietrich, I probably would have done myself in, intentionally or not.

Klaus Dietrich was born in Germany in 1942. His earliest memory, he once told me, was of an air raid shelter. He had no memory at all of his parents. "It's a disturbing thought," he said with an amused, ironic smile, "but there's no way to be certain that my father wasn't Adolph Hitler."

He grew up as a street kid in the bombed-out ruins of Stuttgart, surviving as a parasite on the well-fed bodies of the conquerors. By day, he begged Hershey bars and hustled in the black market; by night, he and his playmates rolled drunken GIs, stripping them of wristwatches, Ronson lighters, and back pay. Eventually civil order was restored and Klaus was sent to live in an orphanage, where he applied his street smarts to more orthodox studies. He received a Ph.D. in physics at nineteen, and picked up another one in philosophy three years later. Before his twenty-fifth birthday he had written two dazzling, highly praised books on science and civilization. Before his thirtieth birthday the West German government had quietly suppressed both works—the art of repression, once learned, is not quickly forgotten.

Klaus had become a radical. Or rather, the world suddenly realized that he had been a radical all along. His work with the Ban-the-Bomb movement had been tolerated, but when he began talking blatantly about the need to overturn the prevailing social order, the universities decided they could get along without his brilliance. In another era Klaus might have become a German Bertrand Russell; instead he became a kind of latter-day Giordano Bruno, wandering around Europe spreading heresy, one step ahead of a burning at the stake.

They caught up with Bruno, but Klaus remained a free man most of the time, despite occasional interludes in various jails. He was too smart to let them find him guilty of anything worse than rabble-rousing and being a public nuisance. His connections with

radical groups were well known, but he never let the
authorities find him with his own finger on a trigger.

In fact, Klaus disdained violence and spent most of
his time trying to dissuade the radicals from doing anything that would place them irrevocably outside the
pale. That was how I met him.

I was in Berlin to do a job for some hotheads who
thought it would be a good idea to blow up Checkpoint Charlie. I thought it was a pretty stupid idea,
but they were willing to pay me twenty-five thousand
dollars to do it. I needed the money and I no longer
gave a damn about the revolutionary wisdom of such
an act, so I settled into a comfortable hotel on the
Kurfürstendamm and cased the job.

My employers didn't care if I killed anyone or not,
but I did, so I spent several days trying to find the
best time and method to produce a bloodless boom. I
finally decided that I would need some sort of diver-
sion in order to lure the GIs away from the checkpoint
long enough to do the job. I figured that a string of
small explosions a block away would be adequate.

I was strolling around the area one evening, taking
mental notes on traffic flow and such, when a tall,
spindly fellow stepped out of a shadow and remarked,
in English, that only a damn fool would try to set off
a bomb here.

I must have blanched visibly, for he quickly
grabbed me by the arm and dragged me into a side-
walk café. He ordered two beers from a passing
waiter, then maneuvered me to a table in the corner. I
was too stunned to say anything.

We sat down and waited silently for the beer to arrive. Across the table the tall man propped up his chin
on both fists and stared at me with a benign smile. He
had rather short dirty-blond hair and blue-gray eyes

that waited patiently behind rimless spectacles. He looked underfed and anemic.

It took a few moments for me to recognize him. When I did, I blanched again.

"No names," he said quickly. He looked up and smiled at the waiter, who smiled back and slid two steins of lager in front of us. Klaus raised his beer high and saluted me with it.

"To applied science," he said cheerfully. I nodded and took a large gulp of my own beer.

Klaus wiped some beer from his chin and smiled again. "It occurs to me," he said, "that in a happier world, you and I might have met in Stockholm instead of here."

I didn't get his meaning for a moment, and when I did I had to return his smile.

"Not very damn likely," I said. "They don't give Prizes to second-raters."

"Nonsense. When I first heard of you, I dug around in a library for some old journals. I found two of your papers. They were very impressive. And your later activities give proof of your cleverness. You were not a second-rater."

"But I was never in your league."

Klaus spread his palms slightly in a gesture that seemed to suggest cosmic inconclusiveness. He had a beguiling manner about him, and I found myself liking him.

"However," he said, "your presence here leads me to wonder if you are quite as smart as I surmised."

"Really?"

"If you go ahead with this project, two things will happen. First, innocent people will die, no matter how careful you think you are. Second, you will be captured when you try to leave Berlin—remember, we are an island here—and since you are no martyr, you will inevitably betray the people who brought you here. That in itself would not be a disaster, but it would jeopardize others who are no part of this mad scheme."

"Including you?"

"Like you, I am not a martyr. And have no wish to become one."

I drummed my fingers on the tabletop. I had admired Klaus Dietrich for years and had often wished that I had been able to find some way to be his American counterpart, notorious but legal, instead of going into the bombs-for-bucks business. If Klaus Dietrich thought I was a fool to be taking this job, then perhaps I was.

"What do you suggest?" I asked him.

"I suggest a vacation," he responded. He snapped his fingers to the waiter for more beer. It arrived swiftly.

"There is a lake near Salzburg," Klaus continued, "where the fish line up to be caught. They are very German fish, you see. I suggest we go there and accommodate them."

"Can the revolution spare us?"

"The Revolution," he declared, "is inevitable. Karl Marx has said so. While you and I catch fish and drink beer, the inevitable Revolution will inevitably take care of its inevitable self."

"You think so?"

"Who are we to doubt the word of Karl Marx?"

I couldn't dispute such sound revolutionary doctrine. Klaus and I went off to the lake, leaving Checkpoint Charlie and the Berlin underground far behind us. He hadn't lied about the fish, and we also caught a couple of Bavarian girls who were almost as eager to please us as the pike. We spent six weeks there, and somehow the world survived our absence.

During the next few years I encountered Klaus Dietrich perhaps a half dozen times. He always seemed to pop up at just the right moment, usually rescuing me from some folly I'd planned. He gave me sound advice and someone to talk to, which was something I never had before. I think I gave him a chance to loosen up and stop playing the revolutionary gadfly. "Being a symbol," he told me once, "is tough work."

We also had in common the intellectual joys of science. It was a rare treat to sit down and shoot the bull with another scientist. The movement attracted a lot of weird people, very few of whom knew or cared much about the physical universe. Most of them were steeped to the gills in astrological mysticism or Ouspenskian claptrap and cared not a farthing for the beauty of the world that *is*. True, the beauty of, say subatomic physics is abstruse, but it is real, unlike the imagined raptures offered by ancient astronauts and Atlantean prophets.

The real world finally became too hot for Klaus. He graduated from being a *Sympathisanten*—one with radical sympathies—to a *Verfassungsfeind*—"an enemy of the constitution." In liberal, enlightened, democratic postwar West Germany, it actually became a crime to think the wrong thoughts. Since this was accomplished without any book burnings or torchlight marches, nobody got very upset about it. People lost jobs for having the wrong friends, books and plays were censored, and milquetoast liberals found themselves in jail for dropping an ill-chosen word in the wrong place. Klaus Dietrich went underground. I hadn't seen him in three years. Neither had anyone else.

* * *

I finally did sleep. When I opened my eyes again, it was winter. The sight of sugar-frosted French fields beneath our wing did nothing to pull me out of the funk I was getting into. April in Paris may be one thing, but February is quite another.

We touched down at Orly in mid-afternoon, local time. McNally whisked me from the plane to the Lufthansa terminal and onto another plane with an awesome efficiency. I spent all of fifteen minutes on French soil.

McNally's double-time drill at Orly was wasted. We spent more than an hour circling around in the gray aerial wasteland above Cologne before we finally made our descent to the slush at the Cologne-Bonn Flughafen. It was every bit as attractive as its name. I confess to a vague linguistic prejudice against Germany; I find it difficult to warm up to a country where towns have names like Schwäbisch Gmünd and Tauberbischofscheim. Probably those names are no worse than Kennebunkport and Punxsutawney, but at least we can blame them on the Indians.

We were met at customs by a heavyset man in a trenchcoat named Richter. He flashed some papers at the customs agent and spoke to him rapidly for about a minute. I knew only a smattering of German, but it sounded as if Richter were telling the customs man not to worry about the technicalities and regulations. The customs man started to protest, but another look at Richter's papers shut him up.

Richter shook hands with McNally and stared indecisively at me for a moment. He obviously knew who I was. He concluded that protocol did not demand shaking my hand.

"Follow me, please," he said briskly.

He led us through a series of gates, back out onto the slush-covered concrete where a shiny black Mercedes was waiting. Midwinter dusk had descended and the car's headlight beams cut through a pelting downpour of something that was neither rain nor snow and stung when it hit my face. My clothing was too light for this, and my brain and body refused to adjust to the abrupt transition from San Vincente. Maybe we pay too high a price for speed. A billion years of evolution has exquisitely adapted us to four seasons and twenty-four-hour days; *Homo supersonicus* will be a different breed. He'll jump from June to January, from noon to midnight, and never feel a thing.

McNally and I got into the backseat of the Mercedes. Richter's driver had somehow managed to get our bags from the plane to the car ahead of us, no mean feat. Richter closed his door, nodded to the driver, and we were off.

Richter turned to face me. He was in his early forties and had a predatory look about him. His ears were slightly pointed, making me think of a fox.

"Mr. Boggs," he said, "for years I have wanted to meet you. In Hannover, we nearly did meet, but your car was too fast for mine. That *was* you in the Ferrari, was it not?"   •

"I drive a Winnebago," I told him. I glanced at McNally, who appeared to be maintaining a studied neutrality. The bastard hadn't bothered to tell me about this. The roomy Mercedes suddenly seemed claustrophobic.

I felt like a lamb caged with a lion. Richter stared at me with undisguised hostility. He was trained to sniff out dangerous radicals, and he'd found one.

The staring went on just long enough to let me

know how things would be between us. Then Richter flicked an internal switch somewhere and became a model of gracious, central-European diplomacy.

"We are grateful for your assistance, Mr. Boggs. I'm certain that your special knowledge of the situation will be invaluable."

"I know Klaus Dietrich, if that's what you mean."

Richter nodded politely. "That is what I mean," he said.

"Have there been any new developments?" McNally asked him. "I've been out of touch for the last thirty-six hours."

"Nothing of any importance," Richter replied. "The Italian police have made some arrests, but they were inconsequential. Scotland Yard tracked down a false lead. Your FBI reports nothing new in its investigation."

"What makes you think Dietrich is still in Germany?" I asked.

"What makes you think he isn't?" Richter turned a cold blue eye toward me.

I looked out the window and watched the gray snow flash by. "Nice autobahn," I remarked. "Who built it?"

I felt McNally give me a sharp kick in the shin. I thought he was being unfair; if Richter wanted to bring up my past, I'd bring up his. I'd have bet Richter looked cute as a button in his Hitler Youth togs.

"In answer to your first question," said Richter, "our sources in the underground have been able to tell us nothing about Dietrich. That, in itself, is unusual. For three years we have investigated a constant stream of rumors about Klaus Dietrich. None of them were productive, but that is not the point. Suddenly, the rumors have dried up, and no one knows a thing about

Dietrich. We believe that any deviation from the norm is suspicious."

"You would."

The skin of Richter's face seemed to tighten. "Mr. Boggs," he said tersely, "circumstances have thrown us together. In the interest of international cooperation, we have assured the American government that we will in no way hinder your activities. Yet I must call your attention to certain, ah, irregularities attending your presence here. You entered our country on an American passport, but our records show that you are de facto a citizen of the Republic of San Vincente, an outlaw regime not recognized by our government. Do I make myself clear?"

He did, abundantly. I'd obligingly stuck my head in a noose and Richter's hand was on the trapdoor lever.

McNally didn't like the drift of things. It must have pained him, but he stepped in on my side.

"Herr Richter," he said coldly, "we consider Boggs to be a valuable agent of the United States government. He's here under our auspices and our protection. We take a dim view of anyone who compromises one of our agents."

"And we take a dim view of terrorists, Mr. McNally, no matter whom they are working for. But rest assured, Mr. Boggs is perfectly safe as long as he cooperates with our investigation. You have my word."

"We also have Bonn's word."

"As you say."

Richter turned around to face forward and we rolled along the autobahn in icy silence. The airport was about a dozen miles north of Bonn, seat of the West German government and birthplace of Beethoven. The gloomy weather and frozen marshes, though, made me think more of minor chords played on oboes and bassoons, rather than of the immortal Ludwig. Translucent curtains of fog drifted across the autobahn, swallowing up Volkswagens like some voracious mist-monster.

I noticed a panel truck gliding alongside us on the left. I looked around McNally and watched the fog swirling in the wake of the truck, making perfect little wind-tunnel patterns. Then the entire world suddenly went blank.

The window had turned into a crystalline network of a million spidery lines. Before I could open my mouth, the same thing happened to the driver's window, and then the windshield.

McNally grabbed a handful of my coat and flung me down onto the floor of the car. Richter shouted something in German and suddenly the car swerved drunkenly, tires squealing like a banshee in pain. I heard the muffled *putt putt putt* of automatic weapons fire.

I tried to look up, but McNally was on top of me, pressing my face down into the wet rubber floor mat. We skidded alarmingly to the left, then swung right again and bashed into something solid. There was a sound of groaning metal and then another collision that slammed me against the other side of the car. Before I could get my bearings, I found myself on the ceiling with McNally's knee in my face. We skidded down the road that way, spinning like an unbalanced top.

The motion finally came to a halt and there was a moment of errie silence punctuated by the random jingling of falling glass. I heard a car door slam and some loud German voices. I struggled to get out from under McNally, but he was as limp and ungainly as a sack of oats. I managed to get my head turned around so I could see.

Two men were trotting toward us, carrying automatic rifles and wearing black ski masks. They were ten teet away when Richter and the driver calmly shot them. They jerked backward and flopped onto the pavement, their rifles clattering on the wet asphalt. The driver wriggled past Richter, snaking through the shattered window. He had a big, ugly automatic pistol in his left hand.

I heard a car engine rev and the sizzing noise of wet tires. The driver got to his knees and held the pistol out in front of his chest with both hands. The panel truck materialized out of the mist with startling abruptness, so quick that I didn't think to duck.

Our driver opened fire, holding his ground with a blind intensity. He was still firing when the front left bumper of the truck clipped him in the chest, hurling him completely out of my field of vision. The truck swerved sharply to the right and into the bodies of the men who had been shot. The wheels spun as they rolled over them, throwing off a fine spray of pink. Richter started firing from the window, but in another second the truck had disappeared into the dense gray cotton that enveloped us. The sound of the engine faded a moment later.

Richter wormed his way out of the car and walked toward the mangled bodies of the gunmen. He didn't even pause to see if our driver had come down yet. He ripped the ski mask off the first body and stared at the bloody face for a few seconds, then nodded to himself.

While Richter examined the second body, I managed to drag myself and McNally out of the car. Mac was out cold, and there was a dark egg protruding just below his hairline. I put my fingers to his neck and had a panicky moment before I found his pulse.

Richter found our driver thirty feet down the road. His examination was even more cursory than the one he gave the gunmen. He shoved the pistol back into his shoulder holster and strode back toward the car.

"They were of the Red Brigade," he informed me. "Unfortunately, they are both dead. The truck killed them, not our bullets. I would like to have questioned them."

"Pity," I said. "A goddamn pity."

CHAPTER 5

I smoked cigarettes and thumbed through back issues of *Stern* while they worked on McNally. A young man from the American Embassy joined me in the hospital waiting room, but when he found out who I was, he studiously ignored me, which was just fine.

At length an aristocratic, silver-haired doctor appeared and spoke to the Embassy man. I got up and walked over to them; both of them turned and gave me a dead-fish stare.

"How is he?" I demanded.

"What is your relationship to the patient?" the doctor inquired coolly, in British-accented English.

"I'm his sister."

"Really?"

"How is he?"

The doctor turned to the Embassy man, who shrugged. Apparently I wasn't on the right List, so he didn't know what to do with me.

"He has sustained a severe concussion," the doctor

said, "but there is no fracture evident. There may also have been damage to the second and third vertebrae."

"But he'll be all right?"

"'All right' is not a medical term."

Jet lag always makes me cranky. So does being shot at. "What's the medical term," I asked him, "for a punch in the nose?"

The doctor seemed amused. "Would you really do that?"

"He would," a voice assured him. It was Richter, still in his trench coat. He walked across the gleaming linoleum floor, heels clopping loudly. Apparently he had been in the room with McNally.

"Mr. Boggs will trouble you no more, Doctor. You'll keep my office informed?"

"Of course," the doctor replied, with an almost imperceptible nod of his head.

Richter motioned for me to follow him. We went down a long, echoing corridor, through a set of double doors, then out into the drizzling night. There was another Mercedes waiting for us. We got into the back; in front, there was a new driver and a character who looked like Max Schmeling.

"We're taking you to your hotel," Richter said as we got under way. "Mr. Korbach will stay with you. For your protection."

Korbach turned and actually smiled at me. Two of his molars seemed to be made of stainless steel.

"What about McNally?"

"You heard the doctor. He has a concussion and is still unconscious. He may stay that way for days."

"Great. And in the meantime?"

"I have spoken with the American officials. You are to work directly with me."

I'd sooner have worked with the Flying Wallendas. But it didn't matter; I wasn't planning on working with anyone.

"What work? It's all over, Richter."

Richter looked at me in mild surprise. "Over?"

"Finished. Kaput."

"There is no need to translate," Richter assured me. "But you are wrong, Mr. Boggs. Our work is just beginning."

"Our work ended out on the highway. Along with three lives."

"I'm quite aware of what happened on the autobahn, Mr. Boggs. One of the three was a man who worked with me for five years."

"Yeah, I could tell you were really broken up about it."

Richter paused before responding. His face was partially hidden by shadows.

"If there are tears for my friend in me," he said quietly, "they will be shed at the proper time. I am sorry if you are offended by my stiff, Prussian devotion to duty. We Germans are like that, you know. How much better if we permitted ourselves the luxury of unrestrained emotionalism. But the Teutonic mind precludes that sort of behavior, I fear."

"Okay, you made your point, Richter. I was out of line."

"Each of us deals with his emotions differently. I handle my grief by devoting myself to the job at hand. You manifest your anxiety over Mr. McNally by making yourself rude and objectionable. Who is to say which is preferable? Forgive me, I am indulging in yet another German vice, the tendency to philosophize. But tell me, why do you say our work has ended?"

"Because of an American vice. Yankee pragmatism. They were waiting for us out there, Richter. They knew we were coming and why. They tried to kill us. Does that suggest anything to you?"

"It suggests a serious lapse in our security. Or yours, perhaps."

"Whatever. They're on to us. Specifically, they're on to me. I'm worthless to you now. I won't get within a hundred miles of Dietrich. They'll shoot me the minute I show my face."

Richter seemed to think that was funny. He chuckled to himself, a bone-chilling sound that made me think of an ogre cleaning his teeth.

"Then you had best be very careful, don't you think?"

"You're out of your mind if you think I'm—"

"Mr. Boggs! Do I need to remind you of your unique situation? I could arrest you this very instant. I could even shoot you while you were trying to escape, and there would be absolutely no repercussions. Or very few. The Americans are hardly in a position to protest the arrest of a notorious terrorist, particularly one who works for the CIA. Every breath you take on West German soil is illegal. If you want to continue taking them, I strongly urge you to do as I say."

"This is insane! They'll kill me!"

"That would be, in your own words, a goddamn pity."

Richter had the hook in all the way, and he was enjoying watching me thrash about. My first instinct was to bug out. We were stopped at a traffic light. I could open the door, leap out . . . and take three steps before Richter drilled me in the spine.

Richter continued in a cold, dispassionate voice. "My driver was not the first man I have lost in deal-

ing with the terrorists. He won't be the last. The terrorists are ruthless and quite dedicated to our destruc-
tion. I do not enjoy sending good, decent men out to
make targets of themselves. But I confess to seeing a
certain irony in having you, Mr. Boggs, at my disposal. You were one of them, one of their own kind.
By chance, circumstances have now placed you on my
side. As an officer of the police, I find it unpleasant
working with a man of your sort, but it is frequently a
necessity in my business. You have connections with
the radicals and with Klaus Dietrich. Dietrich may
still be in Germany. Thus, fate has brought you here,
to my side, as it were, on a difficult mission. If you
are successful, you will have performed us a service.
And if they kill you, then *they* will have performed us
a service. Here is your hotel. Have a pleasant night,
Mr. Boggs. I'll see you in the morning."

The car lurched to a stop. Korbach was out quickly
to get the door for me. He smiled at me again, but I
was damned if I was going to tip him.

My roommate, Man-Mountain Korbach, woke me in
the middle of the night. He told me it was morning. I
called him a filthy liar and rolled over. Korbach
opened the curtains, letting harsh sunlight stream into
the room, proving his point. It seemed futile to argue
that in San Vincente it really was the middle of the
night. I got up.

Korbach, I learned, came from Leipzig and had
spent a dozen years in East Germany as a double
agent before his cover was blown and he had to make
a dash for the border. He spoke English better than I
spoke German, but didn't say much in either language. He was about six four, two seventy, had a roll
of fat around his neck that looked like the collar of a

life preserver, and wore his hair in a spiky crew cut
that was about as sparse as Nevada pastureland.

I showered and shaved with a shaky hand, then
joined Korbach in the hotel coffee shop for breakfast.
A jolt of strong black coffee woke me up enough to
enjoy the breakfast of eggs, fried potatoes, and thick,
greasy sausages. If I lived in Germany, I'd look like
Hermann Göring in no time.

It seemed that breakfast was to be the only enjoy-
able part of the day. Korbach drove me to Richter's
office which was in a modern building near the Bun-
deshaus, overlooking the Rhine. Richter motioned for
me to sit down opposite his desk. He looked snappy
and full of pep, but I suppose he had a right to; this
might turn out to be the day he'd get me killed.

"I have just spoken with the hospital," he informed
me. "There is no change in Mr. McNally's condition.
But since it is little more than a dozen hours since the
incident, that is not unexpected."

"When will I be able to talk to him?"

Richter frowned. "Impossible to say. Perhaps tomorrow, perhaps not. In any event, there is no real
need for you to confer with McNally. You will be operating under my orders. I believe I made that clear
last night."

I had been hoping that McNally would wake up
and call off this madness. He was a pain in the ass,
but I didn't think he'd agree to send me out on a
pointless suicide mission. On the other hand, Mac was
always fearless when it came to risking someone else's
life.

"The Americans have received another letter from
the Omega Alliance," Richter continued. "This one
was not signed by Klaus Dietrich. It was signed by

someone calling himself Spartacus. Does that name mean anything to you?"

"Kirk Douglas leading a slave revolt?"

"Your attempts at humor are not appreciated, Mr. Boggs. From the content of the letter, we inferred that this Spartacus person is the leader of the Omega group. We have no clues to his identity. That makes the capture of Klaus Dietrich even more imperative."

"What did Spartacus have to say for himself?"

"He reiterated the original demands. The terrorists are to be freed by midnight, next Tuesday. The first contingent of American troops is to leave Germany at the same time. Spartacus also mentioned that the Omegas are fully aware of our intention to launch a rescue mission on Monday. He implied that the attempt would fail."

"Anything else?"

"Yes," said Richter. "Something that might be of interest to you." He checked a sheet of paper on his desk for a moment, then began reading. " 'Kindly inform Dr. Boggs that his services are no longer required. Proof will be provided.' "

Richter looked up at me and smiled benignly.

"Well?" he asked.

"They know I'm here," I said. "But we already knew that. If my services are no longer required, why don't you just let me go home?"

"No, Mr. . . . no, *Doctor* Boggs, it is the Omegas who no longer require your services. We still have need of you. Apparently the Omegas are aware of your . . . shall we say, *flexible* loyalties. If you had any hope of returning to your radical comrades, I would say that that hope is now forlorn, wouldn't you?"

"I suppose so."

"Now, as to this matter of proof. What do you suppose Spartacus means by that?"

"I used to make bombs," I said, pointing out the obvious. "Evidently they found somebody else to make them."

"Evidently," he agreed. "The question is, what will they do with those bombs?"

"Use them, I expect. Look, Richter, this is getting absurd. I don't know anything about the Omegas. I never heard of Spartacus. I don't know where Klaus Dietrich is. Would you explain to me why the hell I am so indispensable?"

"Nobody is indispensable, Mr. Boggs," Richter replied with a slight smile. I noticed that I was plain old *Mister* Boggs again.

"This is a strange and difficult situation," Richter went on. "It is impossible to tell how the cards will fall. But it seems to us that you may yet prove to be useful. In the meantime, your FBI is conducting a thorough investigation in America. Interpol is coordinating operations by eleven different governments in Europe. The CIA is exploring the KGB's involvement in the affair. Spartacus, Dietrich, and the Omegas will be destroyed, Mr. Boggs, have no doubt of that."

"Will they be destroyed by next Tuesday, Herr Richter?"

"That," he said with finality, "is our most earnest intention. And you will help."

"Does the public know about any of this?"

"At the moment, no. That, too, is unusual. Perhaps they think that the Western governments will be able to meet their demands better if they are not subjected to public pressure. No government lightly submits to public blackmail. Private blackmail, however, is another matter."

I was a little surprised to hear Richter say that. It sounded as if the powers might be willing to deal. I wasn't sure where that would leave me.

Richter opened the middle drawer of his desk and pulled out five thin manila folders. He slid them across the desk toward me.

"It is time for you to get to work, Mr. Boggs. We have analyzed the files of every known radical and *Sympathisanten*. We have narrowed the possibilities to several dozen individuals who seem to be the most likely to possess knowledge of the whereabouts of Klaus Dietrich. Other agents are already at work in Berlin, Hamburg, and elsewhere. My own belief is that we will find Dietrich right here in Bonn, or nearby. This has always been his base of operations in the past, and we have some reason to believe that he is still in the area."

"Such as?"

Richter gave me his patented half-smile. "We are not entirely without resources of our own," he said. "Our budget is not so big as that of the CIA, but we are effective at what we do. We have informers among the radicals. Not as many as we would like, but they do provide us with useful intelligence. Our information is that even among most radicals, Dietrich remains a mysterious figure. But the general belief seems to be that if Dietrich is in West Germany at all, he is probably in the Bonn area."

"Sounds like you don't need me at all."

"Possibly not," Richter conceded. "Nevertheless, we have you. We intend to use you. From what we know of your past activities, we surmise that you have many contacts of your own in this area. I look forward to discussing this matter with you in the near future. But for the moment, you will concentrate on the five indi-

viduals whose files I have given you. Look at them
and tell me what you know of them."

I had a sick, queasy feeling. My comrades in the
underground had been a mixed lot, to say the least.
Some of them scared me, some of them disgusted me.
A few of them were so appallingly sick that I wouldn't
even mind if Richter got his hands on them. But nobody likes a rat, not even the rat.

Reluctantly, I opened the first folder. It contained
two stapled-together sheets of paper and a photograph. Apparently, I would be getting only cursory
summations, in English. I recognized the man in the
photograph as Karl Borken, whom I had met once
several years before. Borken was a deranged anarchist
artist who liked to paint bizarre, fragmented murals
and then publicly set fire to them. If Borken was typical of the dangerous radicals on Richter's list, Klaus
couldn't have been safer if he were on the moon.

"Inconsequential," I told Richter. "Nobody in his
right mind would trust Borken with a secret."

Richter nodded. "That agrees with our assessment.
Nevertheless, he might know something."

"I doubt it. Anyway, I don't know he'd even remember me."

"Very well. What about the next one?"

The second folder belonged to Emil Rothenburg. I
stared at the photo for a few seconds and furiously
tried to think of something plausible to say to Richter.
I knew Emil well, considered him a friend. He had
been one of Klaus's old professors, and their relationship was nearly that of father and son. Nearly, because there may have been other elements involved.
Emil was a confirmed homosexual, and although I
knew for a fact that Klaus liked women, he was a tre-
mendously complex man. But regardless of the nature

of Klaus's relationship with Emil, I enjoyed the company of both. Emil was a gentle, trusting soul who
long ago was a friend of people like Einstein, Heisen-
berg, and Bohr. He was not a great physicist, but he
was the sort of man that Einsteins can talk to without
condescension or rancor.

Emil was Jewish, but he chose to stay in Germany
when others fled. The Nazis let him continue working
during the early years of the war because he was one
of Germany's few remaining nuclear physicists. In
1943 Emil decided that he could not go on working
for the fascists. He bundled up his notes, managed to
sneak into a Luftwaffe base, and stole a small airplane. He had never flown before, but he had read
books on the subject and was confident he understood
the theory of flight. Perhaps he did, but the practice of
the theory eluded him and his plane crashed in
France. He lost his left leg in the crash, but the
French underground eventually managed to smuggle
him to England, where he recovered from his injuries
and went to work for the Tube Alloy operation, the
British adjunct to the Manhattan Project. After the
war he returned to Germany to teach and write. He
had never harmed a soul in his life, if you excluded his
contribution to the cremation of Hiroshima and Naga-
saki. Emil didn't exclude it; his sense of guilt drove
him to work tirelessly for world peace. And those who
work for such a goal tend to get themselves labeled as
dangerous radicals.

I couldn't possibly betray Emil Rothenburg to the
likes of Richter. On the other hand, Richter obviously
had his eye on Emil anyway.

"Well?" Richter demanded.

"Sorry," I said. "I was woolgathering. Yes, I know
Emil Rothenburg. I don't think he ever knew what I

was, though, so don't go trying to arrest him for aiding and abetting me. It wasn't like that."

Richter seemed amused. "I rather expected you'd say something like that. Everyone is so protective of poor old one-legged Emil Rothenburg. The man must be a saint."

"No. But he's a little closer to it than you and I will ever come."

"Nevertheless, he may know something. You will talk to him. He is old and a little senile and may confide in you what he has refused to tell others. And don't worry yourself, Mr. Boggs. We'll not arrest him, whether he helped you or not. That goes for the others as well. We're after far bigger game. I hope that eases your mind."

It didn't, not a bit. I moved on to the next folder. I thought I recognized the picture, but the name was new to me. I didn't know him. In the fourth folder, I didn't even recognize the picture.

"Don't think you can play games with me, Mr. Boggs," Richter cautioned. "If you choose not to recognize any of these five, we'll give you five more. And the next five will be a rougher sort than these. More like the gentlemen we met on the road yesterday. Do you understand?"

I understood. It looked as if I'd have to lean on poor old Emil. I opened the fifth folder, not expecting to find anyone I knew. I was wrong.

"Ilsa Vogel," said Richter. "I think perhaps you do know this one, Mr. Boggs."

I stared at Ilsa's photo and felt my guts twist. Ilsa silently looked back at me from the glossy surface of the photograph.

"Yes, I know her."

"Rather well, I think. She's a lovely woman."

I wanted to smash Richter's face; I might have, but
for the rocklike presence of Korbach at the rear of the
room. It's all grist for their mill. The intelligence gath-
erers, the file keepers, the paid snoops. They think
they're entitled to know whatever they can find out,
and every glinting fragment of someone else's life becomes another tiny facet in the grand mosaic of state
security. If knowledge is power, then the state can
never be totally secure until it knows everything.
Nothing else matters.

"She lives in Bonn," Richter said, "near the university. She is no longer permitted to teach, of course,
but she remains attached to the academic community.
Currently, she is managing a small bookstore. The
store specializes in selling copies of illegal books, but
we find it convenient to let the store remain open."

"Big of you."

"In the best of all possible worlds, Mr. Boggs, the
censorship of provocative or subversive books would
be unnecessary. In the best of all possible worlds
there would be no subversive books. But we do not live
in the best of all possible worlds. We live in the Fed-
eral Republic of Germany, in a perilous time. We take
the measures which are necessary. And so will you,
Mr. Boggs."

"I'm not going to help you arrest Ilsa Vogel."

"We could arrest her at any time we care to. We
don't need your assistance for that. But you will talk
to her. Today. You will find out anything she may
know about Klaus Dietrich."

"Maybe she doesn't know anything."

Richter brushed a speck of dirt from his desktop.
"Everybody," he said, "knows *something*."

*   *   *

Korbach let me out of the car three blocks from the bookstore. There was no need to tell him to stay out of the way; I knew that every step I took from now on would be observed by someone.

The bookstore was in an older section of town. Bonn used to be a quiet university town, and it was spared most of the horrors of the war. The cities that were bombed out now tend to resemble Chicago, all steel and glass, but Bonn retains what the guidebooks like to call "Old World charm." I walked along a narrow street that was probably in use before Columbus set sail. Shopkeepers were busy clearing the sidewalks of yesterday's snow and plump *Hausfrauen* bustled around like white mice in a familiar maze. The day was clear and cold, and for a few moments I was glad to be in Germany again.

It was called Die Antwort Buchhandlung—The Answer Bookstore. I wondered what the question was. The store was no more than a small, narrow shop, crowded between a bakery and a dentist's office. From the outside it looked like the kind of place where Hansel and Gretel might have bought their schoolbooks.

I looked in through the frosted window and saw books stacked everywhere, more in the style of a Gypsy rummage sale than of a German bookstore. There were shelves everywhere, overloaded and sagging with the weight of mankind's accumulated knowledge. In the corners books were simply stacked on the floor, climbing upward toward the low, wooden-beamed ceiling in formations that made me think of the rock chimneys of Monument Valley. I wondered what they did when someone wanted a book on the bottom.

Ilsa was standing behind a counter near the front of

the store, selling a book to a long-haired young man.
She took his money and smiled at him. It was a smile
I remembered too well. I turned away from the window and looked up into the cloudless blue sky, trying
to get my heartbeat under control.

The young man emerged from the store, the bell on
the door jingling behind him. I didn't want to go in. I
told myself that I needed a little more time; five years
didn't seem to have been enough. But Ilsa was alone
inside, and I knew I wouldn't find a better opportunity than right now.

I opened the door slowly and stepped inside quietly,
but the damned bell started jangling, loud as a fire
alarm. Ilsa looked up and saw me.

She didn't react for a moment. We stared at each
other like frozen figurines on a Dresden china music
box. Then Ilsa's mouth dropped open and her brown
eyes went wide.

"My God! Sam!"

"Hi," was all I could say.

"My God!" she repeated.

I closed the door, just to be doing something other
than staring like an idiot. The bell jangled again.

Ilsa was having as much trouble as I was. She
rushed from behind the counter, then pulled up short
a few feet away from me. She started to move again,
and again stopped sharply, like someone trying to
drive a car with a clutch for the first time. Finally she
spread her arms, closed the remaining distance between us, and hugged me tightly. I woodenly put my
arms around her back and returned the embrace. We
stood there like that for a minute or more and didn't
say anything.

At last Ilsa broke away and stepped back, smiling.
She was in her early thirties now, and there were a

few lines around her eyes and mouth that hadn't been
there the last time I saw her. But her smile was as
fresh and warm as ever, white teeth shining from her
tanned face. The tan puzzled me for a moment, till I
remembered that she liked to ski; everyone else I had
seen looked pale and pasty, in stark contrast to the
people in San Vincente.

"What are you doing here?" she demanded, a hint of
laughter in her voice. She spoke English with almost
no trace of an accent, the result of the two years she
spent at UCLA in pursuit of a doctorate in history.

"I was in the neighborhood," I said, "and thought
I'd drop in." Inwardly, I cringed at the inanity of my
small talk. This was difficult enough in the first place,
without the added complication of being on a government mission.

"The last time I heard, you were in Spain."

"That was a while ago. I live in the Caribbean now.
Or Caribbean, as some folks say."

"But what are you doing here?"

"Came to buy a book. You seem to have a few."

"A few," she grinned. "But most of them are in German, I'm afraid. Or have you finally learned the noble
tongue of Goethe?"

"*Fährt dieser Omnibus zum Museum?*" I asked. Ilsa
began laughing. "Wait," I said. "I know more. *Bitte
sagen Sie mir wo ich aussteigen muss.*"

"No," she laughed, "this bus doesn't go to the museum."

"And you already told me where to get off. Five
years ago."

Her smiled faded quickly. She turned and walked
with exaggerated casualness back toward the counter.
I could have kicked myself.

"So what *are* you doing here?" she said, turning to face me again.

"That's the third time you've asked me that."

"And you still haven't answered."

"Do I have to have a reason for being here?"

"Yes. You do. You always have a reason for everything."

"Would you believe me if I told you I just wanted to see you again?"

She shook her head. "I might believe that you wanted to see me again. But I don't believe that's why you're here."

"You always did have a suspicious mind."

"It comes from knowing suspicious characters."

I wandered over to one of the shelves and stared at book titles. I always feel oddly secure in the presence of books, as if nothing bad can happen because too many people are watching.

"How is the book business these days?" I asked.

"I enjoy it. I thought I would miss teaching, and I do, but I enjoy being a bookseller."

"What happened?"

Ilsa tossed her head back, getting a lock of her brown hair out of her eyes. She leaned back against the counter, then looked down and studied her toes.

"What happened? Nothing much. I was just another victim of the *Berufsverbot*. There are thousands of us now. Civil servants get fired these days if there is even the slightest doubt about their political affiliation. You don't have to be a communist; it's enough if you merely *know* a communist, or even someone who is thought to have communist sympathies. I, of course, qualified."

She said the last with an embarrassed grin. She

could still laugh about it—the last line of defense in a world moving inexorably toward insanity.

"It's like your McCarthyism," she said, "only worse. In the States people finally realized that there weren't really Reds under their beds. Here, the threat is real, if exaggerated. We both know that, don't we? But every time some lone-wolf mad bomber blows up something, the government clamps down even tighter on the rest of us."

"I don't do that anymore," I said.

"I'm not blaming it all on you, Sam. Which came first, after all? The repressor or the revolutionary?"

"The chicken or the egg?"

"God knows. Anyway, I sell books now. Those that the government lets me sell, at least. We have a beautiful law here called Paragraph Eighty-eight A, the Law for the Protection of the Communal Peace. It could have been written by Joseph Heller. The law is to 'curb violence and its verbal preliminaries,' which means whatever they want it to mean. Historical accounts of past revolutions and leftist thought are *verboten* now because they might inspire people to think evil thoughts. I could be arrested for selling you a copy of Bakunin. Charming, isn't it? But I don't need to preach to you, Sam, do I? You already know all about it, don't you?"

"Only what I read in the papers."

"Ah, the renowned Boggs style. Just an ignorant country boy from the States.

The bell suddenly rang and we both looked toward the door in relief. A dowdy middle-aged woman entered the shop and smiled graciously at both of us. Ilsa spoke to her in German, and I ambled off to a far corner of the store. I stared at meaningless titles while the lady customer browsed.

Klaus Dietrich had introduced me to Ilsa years ago. She was teaching American history at the university then, and traveled in the same leftist circles as Klaus. But Ilsa was a dedicated pacifist at a time when pacifism was going out of vogue with radicals. When she found out what I did for a living, she nearly turned me in.

It took her a while to warm to me, but I was a friend of Klaus's, and since she and Klaus were somewhat more than just friends, she eventually accepted me. I think she came to feel a little sorry for me. I was the eternal nomad, ever on the outside looking in, and Ilsa was still naïve enough to find my situation vaguely romantic. Romantic, that is, in the sense of pop music and gothic novels. I was a latter-day Rob Roy or John Wesley Hardin to her, the stuff of Dylan songs and Disney movies. The other sort of romantic feeling she reserved for Klaus.

Five years ago I did a job in Düsseldorf that was foolishly dangerous to begin with, and got much more so when one of our group turned out to be an informer. We had planned to blow the wall of a prison and free a number of radicals who had been arrested at a rally protesting the very decrees that eventually cost Ilsa her job. The security guards let me have time to set the charges, presumably to beef up their case, and then came charging at us from all directions. That proved to be a mistake because it meant they couldn't fire at us without also hitting their own men. I managed to get away.

I spent two months hiding in Ilsa's apartment in Bonn. Klaus had dropped out of sight, as he did periodically, so Ilsa and I were alone together. Inevitably, I began to fall in love with her. But the ambiguity of the situation kept my amorous instincts more or less in check. Ilsa was Klaus's lover and my benefactor; it would have been in bad taste to try to seduce her.

It was obvious to both of us what was happening, but we kept our distance and awkwardly pretended that all was well. We spent the evenings playing Scrabble and talking about politics and history and science till exhaustion set in. Then Ilsa went to bed and I retired to the couch. I avoided her bedroom as if there were land mines planted in the doorway. Radicals are traditionally expected to have the morals of oversexed hamsters, but Ilsa and I played our parts with Victorian restraint.

It's a wonder I didn't go completely bonkers. I was stir crazy and in love. I never really knew how Ilsa felt, but it couldn't have been easy for her, either.

One night Ilsa brought home a couple of bottles of wine to celebrate the publication of a paper she had written. We drank the wine over a game of Scrabble, getting sillier with each turn. When I got a triple word score on zax—a handy cutting tool used by roofers and Scrabble sharks—Ilsa attacked me with a throw pillow, calling me a degenerate American imperialist, among other things. I fended off her charge and managed to dump her on her back. We struggled drunkenly for a while. Then my hand was on her breast and my mouth was on her mouth, and we were no longer struggling.

Suddenly she turned her head away from mine and shouted, "No! Sam, what are you doing?"

"What am *I* doing?"

She squirmed out from under me and got to her feet, her face flushed.

"We can't do this!"

"Why the hell not?" I demanded.

"We just can't!" Ilsa staggered back from me, then

turned and fled into her bedroom, locking the door behind her. I pounded on it ineffectually for a few seconds, then gave it up. I flopped down on the couch, drank what was left of the wine, and passed out.

In the morning we were overly polite to one another. We didn't mention what had happened. I was hung over, deflated, and miserable. I told her that it ought to be safe by now for me to leave. She agreed that this was probably the case. I packed up my few belongings and Ilsa gave me a sisterly hug at the door. I trudged out of the apartment and hadn't seen her since. Until now.

The woman customer left without buying anything. Ilsa joined me at the back shelves.

"Find anything interesting?" she asked me.

"I saw a copy of *Valley of the Dolls* over there. You disappoint me, Ilsa."

She shrugged. "We cater to the masses. They aren't always as discerning as we would like them to be."

"The eternal burden of the Left."

"Uh huh." Ilsa busied herself straightening books on the shelves. She was stalling, and so was I. It was time to get on with it.

"How is Klaus?" I asked her.

She turned around to face me. "Is that why you're here? To find Klaus?"

"I just asked how he was. I didn't ask where."

"No, that would have been your next question. What makes you think I would know?"

"You would if anyone would."

"Then maybe no one does. You've been away a long time, Sam. People change. Maybe Klaus and I are no longer as close as we once were."

Her tanned cheeks were turning pink, the way they

did that last night in her apartment. People do change, but they also stay the same.

"I have to find him, Ilsa."

"Why?"

"Dammit, I just have to, that's all. Don't complicate things."

"In the old days you never had trouble finding him when you really wanted to. Why not ask around? Ask the people you used to know, those who aren't dead or in jail."

"I can't. The people I used to know tried to kill me yesterday."

That was not what Ilsa wanted to hear. Violence terrified her. She always used to shut me up whenever I started talking about my work. She began straightening another shelf, then suddenly swept the books onto the floor.

"Leave him alone! Leave *me* alone!"

I grabbed her by the shoulders and forced her to look at me.

"Ilsa, I can't! You have to tell me what you know. If you don't, there's a bastard named Richter who'll get it out of you anyway."

She broke away from me, whirled around, and screamed at me. "I didn't betray him five years ago! Do you expect me to betray him now? Get out! Get out of my bookstore! Go back to your fucking bombs and leave me alone!"

She was trembling, sobbing. I felt empty and sick.

"I'm staying at the Königshof on Adenauerallee," I told her quietly. "You can reach me there if you need to." I walked to the door, turned to take a last look at Ilsa, then left. The little bell rang cheerfully behind me.

CHAPTER 6

There wasn't any point in lying to Richter, since I was certain that every word we said in the bookstore had been recorded. I met him in his office following lunch and told him that I hadn't learned anything from Ilsa. Richter didn't seem surprised by the news.

"Perhaps you didn't try hard enough," he suggested.

"Bullshit. When I left, she was in tears. As you damn well know."

"Feminine tears prove nothing. You must try again."

"Why don't you just leave her alone, Richter? You've banned her from her profession, you've harassed her at her job. Isn't that enough?"

Richter pushed his chair back, got to his feet, and walked over to the plate glass window. Outside, the sun was streaming down on the Rhine, flaring off the melting snow. The world looked impossibly bright.

"I'll remind you, Mr. Boggs," Richter said, "that we are engaged in a very serious business here. Seven human lives are at stake, to say nothing of a multibillion-dollar program and even the very future of space ex-

ploration itself. We have no time for your finely tuned
sentimentality. If Ilsa Vogel knows anything at all, we
must find out what it is. You will see her again. If you
are unsuccessful, then we shall have to bring her in
and question her here. Do I make my point?"

"How do you sleep at night, Richter?"

"With a loaded revolver on the bedstand. I find it
more reassuring than any sleeping pill. Speaking of
which, you'll be glad to know that Mr. McNally is
awake."

"How is he?"

"A little dazed. But the recovery will be complete."

"When can I see him?"

"There is no need for that."

"The hell there isn't."

Richter smiled slightly. "You're being difficult
again Mr. Boggs."

I got up from my chair and walked to where Richter
was standing. Without any preliminaries, I balled my
fist and slammed it into Richter's belly. Then I grabbed
a lapel, twisted his tie around my right hand, and
backed him up against the big window. The color
drained from Richter's face.

"You don't know what difficult is, Richter. I can
show you."

We were nose to nose. I watched Richter try to re-
gain his composure. Suddenly his eyes seemed to
harden and the thin half-smile reappeared. I knew the
game was up; I had exausted my supply of intimida-
tion. I released my hold on him.

"If the doctor permits it, you may see Mr. McNally.
Korbach will drive you to the hospital."

I nodded, then pivoted and walked quickly to the
door.

"Mr. Boggs."

I turned to look at Richter. He was calmly straightening his tie.

"I'll remember this," he said matter-of-factly.

"I wouldn't have it any other way."

I left the office and headed for the nearest elevator. Korbach, who had been waiting in the outer office, fell in step behind me.

I had probably been a fool, but it was worth it. I had forcibly reminded Richter that I was not simply another marionette whose strings he could pull at will. Richter was bigger than I, but I had surprised him momentarily. He could have battled it out with me, messing up his nice office, or he could have called for Korbach, who would have broken me into little pieces. Instead, he filed the incident under Scores to Settle, and then let me have my way. He had a cop's confidence that there would be another day. That sucker punch was going to cost me.

"Your boss looks a little flabby," I said to Korbach in the elevator. "He should get out and play some handball or something."

"Not possible," said Korbach. "It would interfere with his jujitsu lessons."

"Learning self-defense, eh?"

"*Nein.* Teaching it. He is a black belt."

"Oh," I said meekly.

"You look like Sam Jaffe in *Gunga Din*," I told McNally. He had a turbanlike bandage wrapped around his head and was propped up on two big hospital pillows.

"We have to stop meeting like this, Boggs," he said sourly. He fumbled around for the bed control, found it, and pulled the lever back. The bed whirred and

•sputtered as it cranked McNally up to a forty-five-degree angle.

"How do you feel?"

"Not good. They've got me on some kind of dope for the pain. It works, but I lose track of my hands."

"What?"

"My hands. I don't know where they are unless I can see them. Weird sensation. I've been lying here all morning playing hide-and-seek with my own hands. How has your day been?"

I didn't beat around the bush. "Get me out of here, Mac. Let's slip out the back door and catch the first plane to San Vincente. You can convalesce in the sun. My treat."

McNally actually smiled. "If the nurses there dress like your friend Carla, you might even talk me into it."

"Best nurses in the world," I assured him. "Every one a graduate of Nick Thessalonika's Hospital and Massage Parlor."

"Sounds good. We'll go as soon as we finish the job."

"Christ, you sound like Richter. That guy is trying to get me killed. He actually said as much."

"I don't doubt it."

"And you're not going to do anything about it?"

"What do you suggest? We're on his turf. And the job does have to be done."

"Even if I get killed?"

"I nearly got killed. Why should you get special treatment?"

I kicked the leg of his bed in frustration. It produced a muffled clang and a sharp pain in my big toe.

"Goddammit, Mac! They are really going to kill me. What do you think that ruckus on the autobahn was all about? They know why I'm here and they want me dead. And if they don't get me, Richter will. What good will I be to you if I'm dead?"

McNally did a Jack Benny pause. "Let me think," he said.

That was too much. I kicked his bed again, but with no effect other than more pain in my toe. I grabbed the tray holding his water pitcher and threw it against a wall. It clattered around, but didn't break. Plastic. I punted it against the far wall, then stood there panting.

"You throw a nice tantrum," McNally said coolly.

"I hold the Olympic record, Mac, for Chrissake, can't you see I'm a desperate man?"

"There are seven people on the Shuttle who are just as desperate. And they don't even get to kick anything. Tough to do in zero gravity."

"Balls."

"Okay, Boggs. You're desperate. I give you points for desperation. Your old friends are trying to kill you and you haven't got any new friends. You have my sincere sympathy. But if you try to duck out on me, I'll find you and beat you senseless, as soon as I can find my hands."

"You, too?"

McNally propped himself up on one elbow and gave me a hard, level stare. "Me, too," he said. "I'd hate to see you dead, Sam, but that's the chance we all take in this business. Yeah, I know, you didn't ask for an invitation, but you're in it now whether you like it or not. You are the best hope we have of finding Dietrich. We need you. The people on the Shuttle need you. So get your ass in gear and do what has to be done."

He almost made me feel ashamed of myself. I

hadn't felt so small since my high-school baseball coach chewed me out for loafing on a fly ball. I stuck my hands in my pockets and walked toward the door.

"I'll talk to Richter," McNally said. "I'll remind him whose side you're on."

"Great. Whose side *am* I on?"

I knocked on Emil Rothenburg's door, still feeling ashamed of myself—this time for being impolite. Emil had strict, old-fashioned ideas about the social amenities. One didn't call unannounced. Emil was the only person I knew who actually kept a supply of calling cards.

He still lived in the spacious third-floor apartment that I knew from the old days. Despite Emil's notions about propriety, his home had been a kind of crash pad for the vagrant left-wing flotsam of the sixties and early seventies. We regularly gathered there to plot the overthrow of the state while nibbling on gooey German pastries made by Emil's housekeeper.

I knocked again. Inside, I heard an electronic hum and a clicking sound as a bolt unlatched. The door swung open. I walked in and the door closed behind me. Emil was behind his desk on the other side of the room.

"Welcome, Sam, welcome!" he beamed.

I looked around for the person who had opened the door, but saw no one. Emil chuckled.

"I've entered the electronic age, Sam. I press a button here, poof, the door opens. I press another button, it closes. Not very gracious, but undeniably convenient. Especially for a crippled old man."

He *was* old. I had always thought of him as being somewhere between twelve and ninety. He was short and fat and totally bald, except for a decorous snow-

white Vandyke on his chin. He made me think of
Santa Claus's older brother, the smart one who keeps
the books back at the North Pole, while Santa handles
the firm's public relations. But five years had muted
the pixie in him; he was no longer ageless, simply
aged. He was thinner and shrunken, a dry, fragile
eighty-year-old man in a wheelchair.

"How did you know it was me?" I asked.

"There is a television camera in the hallway. I have
made this building to function with Orwellian efficiency. A disgrace, *nein?*"

"A necessity, I guess. How are you, Emil?"

Emil shrugged, a minimal gesture that caused the
shawl over his shoulders to slip. He tugged it back
into place.

"You can see for yourself how I am. I wish I could
see for myself how you are, my old friend, but even
with these glasses, anything more than a few meters
away is a blur. Come, sit on the couch. I'll pour us
some brandy."

Emil backed up his electric wheelchair, then went
rolling off toward the bookcase where he kept his
brandy. I could see worn tire grooves on the Persian
carpet between his desk and the bookcase.

Emil's apartment was essentially unchanged. There
were more books in it than in Ilsa's entire store, but
here they were lovingly arranged on the bookcases
that lined every wall from floor to ceiling. The fur-
nishings were mostly Victorian, and after a few bran-
dies in Emil's living room, it was almost possible to
forget about the twentieth century.

I sat down and draped my light, tropical raincoat
over the back of the couch. I had been cold ever since
I arrived in this country. Emil gathered up the brandy
decanter and glasses, then motored over to the coffee

table in front of the couch. Ceremoniously, he poured the brandy.

"What happened to Hilda?" I asked.

"She died," he said simply. "After thirty years of taking care of me and my home, one day she was dusting the books and her heart gave out. She died, and yet I go on. Where is the justice in that, I ask you? Where?"

"You're the only one I know who would even think to look for it, Emil. To your health."

I drank my brandy, but I noticed that Emil merely lifted his glass and sniffed. "For too many years," he said, "I drank to my own health and that of others. With the result that now I dare not drink at all, for the sake of my health. But really, it is the ritual that counts, *nein*? That is what I enjoy the most. So drink, Sam. Have some more."

He refilled my glass. His hands were spotted and unsteady. I realized that Emil would be dead soon. I think it bothered me more than it did him.

"How long has it been, Sam? Four years?"

"Five."

"You shouldn't have waited so long. I have often thought of you. I worried about you. I would hear things that troubled me. I would think to myself, that Sam Boggs is one immense fool and will one day blow himself to atoms. I am frankly amazed that you haven't. But I am also pleased, of course. I seldom see my old friends these days. I find it ironic that with my electronic security system and my television camera that lets me see my visitors before they see me, that I rarely see people I truly want to see."

"Have you seen Klaus lately?"

Emil gave me a puckish grin. His dentures were grotesquely white, an imposition on a face that was already overloaded with things to look at—the beard, the bulbous nose, the thick eyeglasses and milky blue eyes, the endless forehead.

"Have you?" he asked.

"Not lately."

"And you are looking for him?"

"I'd like to see him, yes."

"Why?"

"He's an old friend. Like you."

"Old friends. So many old friends. Why is it that there are no new friends anymore?"

"I was wondering the same thing myself a couple of hours ago. Emil, do you know where I can find Klaus?"

Emil sniffed at his brandy again.

"It is possible that I do know. It is also possible that I might not want to tell you."

"Why not?"

"Why?" Emil grinned at me again, his dentures reflecting sunlight from the window. Emil used to have a grin that was warm and inviting, but his new teeth spoiled the effect. It was as if someone had installed a neon sign on the cathedral at Notre Dame.

"You're still a philosopher, aren't you, Emil?"

"Only when it is convenient to be one."

"Like now?"

"If I am still a philosopher, then you are still a pragmatist, Sam. Right to the heart of things. That was always your style, wasn't it? And I always used to tell you that the shortest distance between two points is not always a straight line. Einstein showed that. You chemists should pay more attention to the physicists. Everyone should pay more attention to us. We may all sound like madmen, but we do know things. Many, many things."

"Such as where Klaus is?"

"You insist on a direct answer? Very well, I shall give you one. At this moment, I could not tell you within ten thousand kilometers where Klaus Dietrich is."

He said it flatly, in a way that made me certain he was telling the truth. Yet there was something else there, a hint of depths and black recesses. Emil was giving me a clue, a challenge—something. But I didn't know what.

A raucous buzzer suddenly sounded from Emil's desk. It was loud enough to wake three fire companies.

"Ah," said Emil, "another visitor is on the way up. A big day for me." He maneuvered his wheelchair back to the desk and motioned for me to come along. There was a small black and white television built into the right side of his desk. It presented a blurred image of the hallway outside Emil's apartment. I wondered how he could identify anyone.

A slovenly young man appeared on the screen. He wore a U.S. Army surplus parka and blue jeans and was carrying a package.

Emil flipped a switch on the desk. "Who is it?" he asked. Then he said it again in German. Evidently Emil was reaching the point where he forgot what language he was speaking. It was a sure sign of senility.

The caller answered in static-ridden German and I didn't catch what he said. But Emil apparently understood, for he threw another switch and the door opened.

"I thought I recognized him," Emil said. "It's the young man from my publisher."

The young man from the publisher entered the

apartment and exchanged greetings with Emil. They seemed to know each other, which set my mind at ease. I had wondered about the lady in the bookstore, and I had similar doubts about Emil's caller. Richter would not be above sending in someone just to check on things.

The package turned out to be the galley proofs of Emil's new book. The delivery boy put it on the desk in front of Emil and smiled at him. Emil thanked him, and the kid left, the door swinging shut behind him.

"My new book," Emil explained. "A short, boring tract linking subatomic physics with moral philosophy. I'm too old now to write long, boring tracts."

I picked up the package. It was wrapped in brown paper and was about two inches thick. "Doesn't feel very short to me," I said.

"It is short in comparison with how long it would have been if I had written it ten years ago. But nowadays, I am not optimistic enough to launch any lengthy projects. One day the Dark Angel will be outside my door, and all of my expensive gadgets won't keep him out."

I put the package down and stared at Emil. "The Dark Angel, huh?"

"You don't believe in angels, Sam?"

"Should I?"

"You will. The older I get, the more things I believe. I believe in ghosts and spirits and elves and leprechauns, as well as angels."

"How about devils?"

"Oh, devils I believed in long ago. I have seen them myself. Devils are easy to believe in. Angels require somewhat more time."

"And how many of them can dance on the head of a pin?"

Emil gave me his neon grin. "As many as you like!" he said. "It all depends on the size of the pin."

"Okay, Emil. I know how you stand on the subject of angels. How do you stand on the subject of murder?"

"Murder?" Emil's grin disappeared. He leaned forward in his wheelchair.

"Seven people on the American Space Shuttle are going to be murdered, Emil. Someone put a bomb on board. Klaus Dietrich may be involved."

Emil stared at me for several seconds. It was impossible to read that wizened face.

"Klaus is no more a murderer than you, Sam."

"People change."

"Yourself, as well. Why have you come to me about this? Who sent you here?"

"Does it matter, Emil? The only important thing now is to find Klaus. If you know anything at all, you've got to tell me."

Emil leaned back in the chair and sighed. "I have to tell you, eh? For the Nazis, I had to work. For the bureaucrats of modern Germany, I must keep quiet. And for you, I must talk. I will tell you, Sam, there is absolutely nothing which I *must* do. I have learned that, if nothing else, in my eighty years on this planet."

"Then you do know something?"

"I know many things. I know, for example, that Klaus Dietrich would not murder seven innocent people, or seventy, or seven million. Can the people who sent you here make that same claim? Can you?"

"Forget about the people who sent me here. This is between you and me. And the angels. Don't tell me about what Klaus would or wouldn't do, Emil. He's my friend, too."

"And that makes you an authority?"

"It makes me damned eager to get to the bottom of this thing. One way or another, Klaus is involved. Maybe not by his own choice. He could be in trouble."

"Klaus is frequently in trouble. But have you ever known him to do anything that wasn't his own choice?"

That was a good point. Too good. I kept hoping that we would find that Klaus was being forced to cooperate with the Omega Alliance. But I couldn't picture Klaus letting himself be bullied into anything he didn't want to do. Emil hadn't made the point idly. He was trying to tell me something.

"Dammit, Emil! You do know something. You know where he is, don't you?"

"I told you, Sam. Not within ten thousand kilometers."

"Then you know how I could reach him."

Emil chuckled. His teeth rattled like castanets.

"What's so funny?"

"What's not?" he asked. "You say I know how you could reach him. That is f~ my."

"Why? Because you do?"

"No," he said, "because I don't. But you do."

"What?"

"Your hearing is not as bad as mine, Sam. You heard what I said. Now you will go crazy trying to figure out what I mean. When you learn the answer, you'll laugh too, Sam. I promise, you will laugh."

I didn't feel like laughing. I didn't even feel a mild snicker within me. What the hell did Emil mean? How could I possibly know how to reach Klaus?

"You're playing games, Emil. People's lives are at stake, and you sit there playing games."

"People's lives always depend on games. Russian games. American games. German games. Why should I not be permitted my own harmless games?"

"Can you be certain they're harmless?"

"Can you be certain they're not?"

"You're doing it again, dammit!"

"And again and again. Round and round, Sam. That's how it goes, and there is your answer."

"Round and round? What the hell are you talking about?"

"I'm answering your questions, Sam. All of them. When you understand the answer, come back and we will talk again. For now, I will say no more."

I could see he meant it. I got up, gathered up my coat, and walked toward the door. I was too thoroughly confused to try to get any more out of him.

"You really ought to believe in angels, Sam," Emil said as I opened the door.

"Dark ones?"

Emil shrugged. "All kinds," he said. "Believe in them, Sam. Trust them even if you can't see them. They work miracles, you know."

I closed the door and walked out into the hallway. I stared up into Emil's television camera while I waited for the elevator. Orwellian efficiency, he had said.

The elevator finally arrived. It was one of those open cage affairs, which the Europeans love but which unfailingly scare me. An American elevator is simply a windowless room where you can't smoke. But a European elevator is a naked mechanical contraption with the gears and levers exposed. You can look out and see how far you'll fall if something should break.

The cage safely lowered me to the bottom floor. I left the building and walked out into the street, wondering what my next move would be. Richter would demand that I go back and hound Emil for something more substantial than riddles. If I didn't do it, Richter would probably do it himself. I was sure that Emil's apartment was well bugged, so there was no way to mislead Richter about what had gone on up there. Not that I was sure myself.

I walked down the street lost in thought. I was about a half a block away when the third floor of Emil's building blew up.

I was knocked flat on my face by the blast. Stunned, I rolled over onto my back and looked. Debris was drizzling down on the street, clattering on the pavement. Dazed pedestrians were trying to get up again. Someone down the block was screaming.

And Emil's building was a two-story pile of smoking rubble. There was no longer a third floor.

CHAPTER 7

Richter was off in Frankfurt, tracking down another lead, so I couldn't report to him. McNally was still in the hospital, so there wasn't any point in reporting to him. I went back to my hotel and soaked in a hot bath for an hour. I didn't feel like going out to eat, so Korbach had dinner sent up to the room. I watched him eat. He was very efficient.

I tried to start a conversation, but it was like pulling teeth—something Korbach was evidently familiar with, to judge by his stainless steel molars. That was the kind of dental work they did a couple of hundred miles to the east.

"How long were you in East Germany?" I asked him.

"Years," he mumbled.

"What did you do there?"

"I drove a truck. It allowed me to travel freely."

"What happened? How did they find out about you?"

Korbach put down his knife and fork and looked at

me for the first time. "The KGB," he said, "is very efficient. They knew about me for many months. They hoped to use me to feed false information to the West."

"But you knew that they knew?"

"And they knew that I knew that they knew. It is a complicated business."

"What finally happened?"

"My usefulness came to an end. I was forced to leave."

"Your usefulness, huh? Usefulness to whom?"

"I was never sure," he said bluntly. He picked up his knife and fork and resumed eating.

After he ate, Korbach settled back on his bed and watched television. The German version of *Bonanza* was on. Little Joe, the fool, got himself shot and had to send good old Hoss back to get Pa and Adam. "*Mach schnell,*" Little Joe told Hoss. It was easy to see why the show was so popular in Germany: Ben Cartwright was the best father figure the Germans had seen since Hitler.

I was drifting off to sleep when someone began pounding on the door. Korbach was up with surprising speed. He turned off the tube and went to the door. Before he opened it, he adjusted his shoulder holster.

Korbach opened the door a few inches. The door suddenly swung completely open, throwing Korbach out of the way. I sat up straight, wondering who was big enough to shove Korbach around.

It was Ilsa Vogel. She took two steps into the room, then stopped short. She planted her feet wide apart and stared at me.

"How could you?" she demanded in a low, dangerous voice.

I rolled off of the bed and walked toward her.

"Ilsa . . ."

"*How could you?*" She screamed. "*How could you?*"

She came at me. She pounded her fists into my chest with enough force to rock me back. I was too surprised to put up any resistance. Ilsa kept on pummeling me, her hair flying wildly. Tears streamed down her face. She looked as if she had gone mad.

Korbach finally grabbed her from behind, all but smothering her with his bulk. She flailed at him and managed to sink an elbow into his gut, but Korbach never flinched. Resolutely, he started dragging her toward the door.

"Hold it," I said. Korbach stopped and looked at me. Ilsa's struggling tapered off, and she looked at me, too. I'd never seen so much hatred in a face. Her nostrils flared and her eyes were red-rimmed and wild.

"Let her go," I said.

Korbach hesitated. He didn't look as if he believed I could defend myself against her.

"Get out," I told him. "Leave us alone."

Korbach loosened his grip on Ilsa but still looked doubtful. "I will be just outside," he said. He released her and then waited a few seconds to see what she would do. She did nothing, but stood there as if bolted to the floor, her chest heaving rhythmically.

"Take a hike, Korbach."

"I will be outside," he repeated. He backed out of the room and carefully closed the door.

With Korbach gone, the room seemed much larger. There was enough space now to contain Ilsa's rage. Deliberately, she pulled her hair away from her face and straightened her sweater. I waited until she was ready.

"Who is he?" she asked. "Did you have him beat up Emil before you killed him?"

I was shocked and angry for a second, but then I understood. "Ilsa, that's not what happened."

"Oh, you just blew him up with a bomb. You didn't bother torturing him."

"Ilsa, believe me, I didn't—"

"That's your style, isn't it, Sam? Clever little bombs? That's what you do, isn't it?"

"Dammit, you know that's not true! Not like that, Ilsa. I never killed anyone with a bomb!"

"Then he was already dead before the explosion?"

"I didn't do it, Ilsa!"

She spun away from me and stared at the door.

"Sam Boggs shows up, and suddenly bombs start exploding. And you expect me to believe that you have nothing to do with it? I'd laugh, but a friend of mine is dead and I don't feel very much like laughing."

"He was my friend, too, Ilsa. I was with him two minutes before it happened. I was with him when the bomb was delivered. It was pure luck that it didn't kill me, too."

"Really? What happened, Sam? Make a mistake? Did you make the fuse too short?"

I grabbed her, turned her around, and slapped her. It wasn't a thanks-I-needed-that slap. I meant it. Ilsa recoiled, then fell back against the door. She brought her hand up to massage her cheek and stared at me with cold loathing.

Suddenly, it was as if someone had cut all the strings holding her up. Her head sagged down against her chest. She covered her eyes with her hands and gave out a choked sobbing sound. Then she simply slid down the door, coming to rest in a nearly fetal position on the floor. I stood still and listened to her cry.

I snapped out of it and went into the bathroom to get her a glass of water. It seemed like the thing to do.

I gave her another minute to let her tears out, then handed her the glass. I had the odd feeling that I was acting out some ancient ritual, like a character in *Dune*. She had released the moisture of her body, and I gave her water to replenish it. The circle was closed, debts were paid.

Ilsa drank the water and looked up at me as she handed me the glass. Still huddled on the floor, she looked young and tragically vulnerable. I felt embarrassed to be seeing her like this. I walked away and put the glass down on the nightstand between the two beds. When I turned around, Ilsa was on her feet again, brushing off her skirt.

"I'm sorry," she said quietly.

"It's okay."

She shook her head. "No, it's not okay. I should have known you wouldn't . . . wouldn't do that to Emil. I guess I did know it. I just . . ."

"You were upset and you leaped to a conclusion that seemed to make sense. Emil was killed by a bomb. I used to make bombs."

"But I shouldn't have . . . oh, hell! Sam, what is going on?"

She looked as if she were about to cry again, but she rallied. Sniffing back the tears, she asked again, "What is going on?"

I went to her, took her hand, and led her back to Korbach's bed. We sat down and looked at each other.

"Is Klaus involved in this? Is he?"

"I think so. I'm not sure of anything, but it looks like Klaus is in it up to his eyeballs."

"But Klaus would never . . . he couldn't! He's no more a murderer than you are!"

"Emil said the same thing." In light of what happened to Emil, it was a disturbing thought.

"But why? Why would anyone do it?"

She didn't give me any choice. I'd be breaking security, but that would be the least of the crimes Richter would hang me for if he got the chance.

I told Ilsa about the bomb on the Shuttle. When I mentioned the Omega Alliance, her eyes seemed to narrow a little. She didn't say anything at all when I told her about the letters Klaus had signed.

"What about you, Sam?" she asked when I had finished. "Why are you involved in this?"

"I didn't have any choice."

"Maybe Klaus didn't, either."

"Maybe. Tell me about the Omega Alliance, Ilsa."

She gave me a sidelong glance. "I have heard of them," she said. "One hears things."

"What things?"

"Just things. Unconnected things."

"Tell me."

Ilsa got up abruptly and crossed to the other bed. She sat down, facing me.

"Whatever I tell you will get back to the people who sent you here."

"Yes," I admitted.

"Does it bother you, Sam? Being an informer?"

"Lately, just about everything bothers me."

"You have friends in the Omega Alliance."

"I know. They've already tried to kill me. That bomb in Emil's apartment was supposed to get me, too."

"Are you sure that bomb was sent by the Omega Alliance?"

I shrugged. "Who else could it have been? Emil knew something. He could have led me to Klaus, I think. The Omegas must have known that, so they shut him up."

"But—"

"But Emil was one of them? Is that it?"

"I don't know! I think so, but I don't know anything for certain. I just heard things that didn't make much sense to me. I didn't try to figure them out. Klaus mentioned the Omega Alliance the last time I saw him."

"When was that?"

"Six months ago. We met in Koblenz and spent a weekend together. That was the last time I heard from him."

"What did he say?"

Ilsa ran a hand through her hair, as if trying to straighten out her thoughts. She seemed to be balancing on a fine edge. Too many forces were pushing her from too many directions.

"He said that the Revolution was no longer possible. Not the way we envisioned it in the old days. There would be no mass uprising, no workers marching through the streets. He said that what was needed was something new, something to pull together what was left of the old groups. A final alliance. An omega alliance."

"Why final?"

"I don't know. But he seemed . . . he seemed different somehow. I don't know. In bed he was . . . oh, Sam, I can't explain it. He was just different. He wasn't the same Klaus. I mean, it was Klaus, it wasn't somebody trying to impersonate him. He had his hair dyed and wore a moustache, but it was him. He was just . . . he had changed. I don't know."

"Ilsa, Klaus has been on the run for years. It's a tough life. Believe me, I know what I'm talking about. You try to keep sane, but somehow it all begins to work on you. It changes you. Things are never safe or clear. You don't know who can be trusted. Eventually you get to a point where you have to make sense out of it or you'll go crazy. So you fixate on something, a goal, a plan, anything you can think of. It starts out as no more than a polestar, something to orient yourself. But it can become an obsession. It can become the only thing in the world that has meaning for you."

Ilsa was silent for several seconds.

"It could have happened to Klaus," I said, making the connection so she wouldn't have to.

"It did," she said. "Sam, do you know why I wouldn't make love with you?"

The non sequitur threw me. It was a question I hadn't been able to answer in five years.

"It was because of what you just said," Ilsa went on. Her voice was low and measured. "I wasn't just Klaus's lover. I was his polestar. I was the thing that kept him sane. He didn't have to tell me, I could feel it. And you wanted me to be the same thing for you. Maybe you didn't know it then, but I did. Sam, I loved you but I couldn't be the same thing for both of you. It would have torn me apart. Didn't I have a right to my own sanity?"

"Yes," I said. I stared at the floor.

"I tried, Sam. I tried to be what you wanted, but I just couldn't. I had to be what Klaus wanted, for as long as I could. But finally . . . I guess I just wasn't what he wanted anymore."

"Have you tried being what *you* want?"

"I'm trying right now. Sam? Make love to me."

She took my left hand in both of hers and caressed it. My skin tingled.

"Make love to me, Sam. Now."

"Now?"

She nodded.

"This room is bugged."

"Now." She released my hand, then quickly pulled her sweater over her head. The motion set the bed springs and her breasts jiggling. She took my hand again and held it against her right breast. I felt the nipple hardening beneath my palm.

"Now," I agreed. I got up and went to the door.

"Korbach?" I yelled.

"Yes!" he said instantly. He was obviously leaning against the door.

"Go away."

"What?"

"Go away. Stay away. You hear me?"

"But I cannot do that!"

"Korbach, if you don't get the hell away from here, I swear I'll have one of my rich friends buy you and turn you into a landfill."

He paused a few seconds to consider that. Finally, he said indignantly, "I will be at the end of the hallway. I will wait there."

"You do that. Just a second, Korbach." I yanked the TV plug out of its socket, opened the door, and rolled the television out into the hall.

"Enjoy," I told him. "Let me know if Little Joe bleeds to death." Then I closed the door and locked it.

I turned back to Ilsa. She was standing between the beds, nude. I stood there and admired her for a moment.

"Sam?"

"What?"

"Now," she said.

It didn't take us very long. Five years of repressed passion tends to come out in a rush. Afterward, we lay there and smoked a cigarette, the way they do in the movies. I told Ilsa about San Vincente and the way I lived now. She asked me if I would take her back with me.

"For a while, at least. It sounds so peaceful. So safe."

"If it were safe, I wouldn't be here now."

"But you will take me? Or do you have someone else?"

"Sort of. Not really. I don't know." I didn't. Carla Avellino was certainly someone else, but she wasn't necessarily *my* someone else. I told myself she'd understand when I returned with Ilsa in tow. I hoped she would. If she got upset enough to complain to Two-Ton Tony, I could find myself sleeping with the sharks.

"Would you mind my coming, Sam?"

"If it's what you want, it's fine with me. More than fine."

"It is what I want," she said. "For now. When will we be able to leave?"

"That's not up to me. You'll have to ask a gentleman named Richter. He's calling the shots around here."

"And he wants you to find Klaus?"

"That's it. If I don't, he's going to be pretty annoyed with me."

Ilsa sat up, pulling the sheet over her breasts. She took the cigarette from me and puffed it nervously for a few moments.

"I can help, Sam."

"How?"

"I think I can get to Klaus. Or at least get a message to him."

"Are you sure you want to do that?"

"It's what I have to do, isn't it? Those people on the Space Shuttle are going to die if we don't find Klaus, aren't they? If we can find him and talk to him . . ."

I retrieved the cigarette from her, took a quick puff, then snubbed it out in the ashtray.

"Ilsa," I said, "it's past the talking stage. You can't kid yourself about Klaus anymore. I tried, but it just won't wash now. Not with Emil dead. He's involved with people who are playing for keeps. He may even be leading them."

Ilsa pulled the sheet closer. "You mean, if we find him, we have to turn him in?"

"Or worse."

"*Kill* him?" Ilsa's face seemed to go a little pale.

"His friends tried to kill me. We need him alive and talking if we're going to find out how to disarm that bomb, but don't expect it to be easy. I'm sorry, Ilsa, but that's the way things are. You don't have to help me if you don't want to."

"But what about Richter? What about the bugs?"

"I think I can handle Richter. I have a friend with a little leverage. We could find a way for you to disappear for the next week or so. After that, it won't matter."

"Why?"

"Because the bomb has to be found soon. The Shuttle can't stay up forever. Not enough oxygen."

"Then I guess we should find Klaus as soon as we can."

She'd talked herself into it. I felt a little cheap. In half an hour I'd made love to my best friend's girl and gotten her to help me betray him to the law. They kick you out of the Boy Scouts for doing things like that.

"How can you reach him?" I asked.

Ilsa started to say something, but stopped herself midway through the first syllable. She pointed a finger toward her right ear. Evidently she didn't want to talk about it in the presence of listening devices.

"Can you tell me anything?"

"It's just something we arranged a long time ago. A way to get in touch if one of us was in trouble. Maybe he doesn't even remember it, but it's worth trying."

"How soon can you work it?"

"I'll meet you here tomorrow night. I don't know exactly when. But if this works, we might even see Klaus before tomorrow night is over. You just have to promise me that nobody is going to follow me around tomorrow. It won't work unless they can be sure of me."

"Who?"

"The people I need to see. Now stop asking questions. In fact, I should leave right now, before your Mr. Richter finds me here."

"He's out of town. Won't be back till morning."

"What about that monster out in the hallway?"

"He has his television. He's happy."

"Then I can stay?"

"Please do." I reached for her and tried to persuade her that she really was welcome to stay with me. Ilsa was equally ardent in assuring me that she was delighted to accept my invitation. Later, I lit another cigarette and watched the smoke curl up toward the ceiling while I listened to her breathing softly. I told myself that if I wasn't careful, I could find myself in love with her all over again. Falling in love would be an incredibly stupid thing to do. Really dumb. Insane. I promised myself I wouldn't do it. No sir. Not me.

CHAPTER 8

I woke up with a start. It was already light outside. Ilsa was standing next to the bed, getting into her panties. I watched her for a few moments, a big, stupid smile spreading over my face.

"You could be a work of art," I told her. "The way the light from the window hits your hip when you stand like that. Beautiful."

"My fat hip," she said. "And my fat thirty-three-year-old body."

I reached for her and pinched a fingerful of her thirty-three-year-old body. "Still looks pretty good to me."

"I'm five kilos overweight. Look at me."

I did look. I surveyed every centimeter of the rounded curves from her breasts to her belly.

"Three kilos," I said. "Tops."

"Five," she insisted. "I want to lose it when we get to San Vincente. I want to wear a string bikini and be young and sexy and totally mindless. If I don't lose the five kilos, I'll look like one of Gauguin's fat native ladies."

Ilsa pulled her sweater down over her head, then shook like a whinnying horse, setting her hair free. I could still see the outlines of her nipples under the sweater. I grabbed for her again and pulled her down on top of me.

"I know a way you could lose about a half kilo right now."

I smothered her reply in a kiss while I set about peeling back her sweater. That was awkward, so I shifted position and managed to get one hand to the fringe of dark pubic hair protruding from her panties. That was as far as I got. Ilsa rolled away from me, bounced to her feet, and retreated to the opposite side of the room. I wasn't in any condition to follow her. She got into her skirt and smiled demurely.

"I have to leave now, Sam. There are people I have to see."

"Right now?"

"The sooner the better. Then we can find Klaus and straighten out this awful mess and get on a plane to that silly island of yours."

"As simple as that."

"Yes, Sam. As simple as that. Simple is best."

"Then I shouldn't complicate things by falling in love with you again, should I?"

Ilsa looked at me with an odd expression on her face, sort of a blush trying to become a smile. Then she came to me and kissed me on the cheek.

"We'll talk about that tonight."

"When?"

"I'll try to be here by eight. If I'm not, wait for me."

"You be careful. Okay?"

"Don't worry about me. I know what I'm doing. You just make sure that when I get here, you're here, too."

"Wild Clydesdales couldn't keep me away."

She leaned down to kiss me again. That kiss seemed to last most of the morning. Finally, she pulled away, walked quickly to the door, and without looking back she was gone.

I stared at the ceiling for a while and tried to tell myself that the empty feeling in the pit of my stomach was simply hunger.

Suddenly the door opened. Korbach came in, pulling the TV set behind him. He looked rumpled and irritated.

"How'd Little Joe make out?"

Korbach shot me a menacing glare. I couldn't resist needling the ox, but I decided that it wasn't necessarily wise to tease someone the size of an amusement park.

"You should have been up by now," he informed me. "Richter will be waiting."

"Let him. You and I have to eat breakfast, right Korbach?"

Korbach hesitated a few seconds, but I knew my man.

"Okay," he said. "First we eat. Then we see Richter."

I expected Richter to give me a double-barreled dose of Sturm und Drang, but he surprised me. He sat calmly behind his desk and waited for me to sit down and get comfortable. Then he held up some papers and offered them to me.

"Daily surveillance reports," he said. "They make interesting reading."

"I'll bet." I glanced at the papers and skimmed over

some dialogue excerpts, then handed them back to Richter.

"I was misquoted," I said.

"No doubt. And Fräulein Vogel? Was she misquoted as well?"

"Who?"

Richter leaned forward and eyed me very carefully, as if examining a condemned building.

"Let us not play games, Mr. Boggs. Games bore me. You were with Ilsa Vogel last night, all night. We have a record of every word that was said."

"Am I supposed to be impressed? Maybe you get your kicks from bugging bedrooms, but it doesn't mean shit to me, Richter. You've got a complete transcript of two people making love. What are you going to do, print it in *Der Spiegel*?"

"You have me wrong, Mr. Boggs. I couldn't care less what you do in bed, or with whom you do it. I realize you are not subject to that sort of blackmail, nor is Fräulein Vogel. Your cooing endearments interest me not at all. I am, however, exceedingly interested in the parts of your conversation dealing with Klaus Dietrich and the Omega Alliance."

"Then you know what's going to happen tonight. Do us all a favor and don't screw it up. Stay out of it."

"You're not that naïve."

"And you're not that stupid. If the Omegas even smell somebody tailing Ilsa, she won't get within miles of Klaus."

"As you said, we are not stupid. For today, she is on her own."

That seemed unlikely. People like Richter can't stand the thought of anyone slipping out of their control. Still, I trusted Ilsa. She was bright enough to take measures to lose anyone who might be following her.

"What about tonight?" I asked.

"Tonight," said Richter, "you will not be lonely." He said it with a straight face, but the double entendre was not lost.

"One other thing. After it's over, Ilsa leaves the country with me."

"Of course. I'm aware of your plans. I wish you much happiness with Fräulein Vogel. She is an exceptionally attractive and intelligent woman. I'm sure she'll lose those five kilos in no time."

Richter smiled at me. It was an inviting smile, one designed to make me wonder how it would look with my fist in the middle of it. He wanted me to try it. He also wanted to give me a quick course in jujitsu. I decided I would pass.

"You have done remarkably well, Mr. Boggs. Better than I had hoped, frankly. In a single day you have managed to seduce Ilsa Vogel and persuade her to betray Klaus Dietrich. You seem to have a talent for this sort of operation."

It was a compliment I could have done without.

"Concerning Professor Rothenburg," Richter said, "we have no definite leads."

"What about the delivery boy? Emil knew him, so the kid must really have worked for the publisher."

Richter nodded. "Hans Neuhaus. Age twenty. Employed by Rothenburg's publisher for the last four months. No one has seen him since yesterday morning."

"It seems a little strange to me. Why would the Omegas plant somebody with the publisher? Why bother? They couldn't know that Emil was going to talk. Hell, he didn't talk. He just threw riddles at me."

"Yes, I know. Have you figured them out yet?"

"I don't know what the hell he meant."

"He was an old man. Perhaps he didn't know himself."

"He knew. He knew exactly what he meant. I have the feeling he was enjoying himself."

"Well," said Richter, "it appears that the final laugh was at his expense."

Richter had a way of phrasing things that set my teeth on edge. I decided I'd had all of him I could take for this morning.

"I'm going to see McNally," I told him.

"As you wish. Enjoy your day, Mr. Boggs."

I intended to. I was thinking of Ilsa again before I even got out of Richter's office.

"You incredible idiot! Don't you realize what you've done?"

McNally sat up in bed so violently that he winced in pain. He was wearing a neck brace and looked dreadfully uncomfortable.

"No," I said blankly. "What have I done?"

McNally raised a hand to his bandaged forehead and sank back down into the pillows. He took a deep breath. He looked pissed.

"You sent her out to make contact with Klaus Dietrich."

"Yes. So what? That was the whole point, wasn't it? We'll make contact tonight, and by tomorrow we'll be on our way to San Vincente. Mission accomplished. What more do you want?"

"Christ, Boggs, you didn't used to be so stupid. Are you in love or something? Is that why you came in here whistling 'Zip-A-Dee-Doo-Dah'?"

"Was I?"

"My God, you really don't see it, do you?"

"See what, Mac?"

"You are in love, aren't you? Like some sweaty, bubble-brained adolescent. Like the oafs who date my daughter. I wouldn't have believed it."

I was willing to concede the point. "Okay, I'm in love. It happens, you know."

"It's not the sentiment. It's your timing. It stinks."

"The heart does not punch a time clock, Mac."

"Beautiful! Brilliant! 'The heart does not punch a time clock.' Boggs, you jerk, don't you realize what you've done? You've gone so mushy and starry-eyed dreaming about your cozy future that you didn't even think what you were doing when you sent Ilsa out to find Dietrich. That was just a minor detail, wasn't it?"

"Wasn't it?"

McNally sat up again and stared at me, right in the eyes. "Sam," he said, "they tried to kill you and nearly got me instead. They killed Emil Rothenburg and nearly got you as well. What do you think they'll do when Ilsa Vogel starts asking questions?"

It took two or three seconds to penetrate.

"Oh, my God."

"Congratulations. You finally figured it out."

"They could kill her!" My knees felt weak. I sat down on the edge of McNally's bed and tried to think.

"Sam, Richter's men are out looking for her."

"You think that will help? It'll just make them that much more likely to kill her. No, no, this is absurd. If Klaus Dietrich is running the Omega Alliance, they won't do anything to Ilsa. He might refuse to meet her, but he wouldn't . . ."

"They killed Emil Rothenburg."

"But not Ilsa! He wouldn't do that!"

"Dammit, Sam! We don't know what they'll do. We don't know if Dietrich is in charge or only a front. This could still turn out to be a KGB operation. We don't even know if Dietrich's still alive. All we know is that the Omegas have killed or tried to kill anyone who had a decent chance of finding Klaus Dietrich. Ilsa won't be immune."

"I just can't believe that. She said she had a secret way to reach him. It was private, between the two of them. Safe."

"Stop believing what you want to believe. Believe the facts, Sam. If you know where Ilsa is, you'd better find her in one big hurry."

I shook my head. I didn't have any idea where she was. McNally was right. I was an idiot.

"You shouldn't have let her get away. You should have gotten her to tell you whatever she knows about where Dietrich is. Her secret system, or whatever. Once we knew, Richter's men could have handled it. You and Ilsa would already be on that plane."

"Oh, Jesus. I blew it. I really blew it. I really did."

I got up and went to the window. Outside, a cold drizzle was falling from low gray clouds. The stately maze of Bonn blurred and faded in the distance. Ilsa was out there, somewhere, alone. I had blown it.

I spent the rest of the day fretting and kicking myself. I walked past the bookstore, but it was closed and no one was there. I walked past Emil Rothenburg's apartment building. They were still clearing away the charred rubble.

The weather turned even nastier. The clouds spewed out a hard, cold rain driven by an insistent wind that seemed always to be in my face. I took refuge in a bar. Sitting in a dark corner, I applied Scotch to my wounds and thought about things.

I thought about Willie Mays. Like everyone else, I loved to watch Willie play baseball. I could still picture him running, hitting, leaping, sliding. But the image that remained was of forty-year-old Willie Mays falling flat on his face chasing a routine fly ball. Poor old Willie, he didn't hang 'em up in time. Maybe poor old Sam Boggs should have taken the hint.

I was no longer the young, dashing, outlaw scientist. I used to know all the right moves, and be able to execute them often enough to keep in the game. But now, I was falling flat on my face, just like Willie in his alien Mets uniform. I was getting into the habit of being stupid.

Not once since McNally had plucked me out of my unbuilt nest had I really stopped to think things out. I'd just charged into things, albeit reluctantly, without ever getting a handle on the situation. Worse, I hadn't even been bothered by my sloppiness.

Klaus. Emil. Ilsa. I was lulled by the familiarity of it all. I didn't need a scorecard because I already knew all the players. Even Richter was a known quantity. I could deal with it all because I was the great Slammin' Sammy Boggs, the best in the business. A legend in his own time.

"Shit," I said aloud. Another customer a few tables away looked at me curiously.

"*Scheiss,*" I translated. He understood—the word and the sentiment. He went back to tending his own drink.

I assembled the known facts and began to play with them. Better late than never.

The Omega Alliance, a bunch of heavyweight terrorists, had put a bomb on the Space Shuttle—maybe. Klaus Dietrich was their spokesman. Emil Rothenburg knew something about it, but was killed before he could say anything meaningful. And I was nearly killed before I even had a chance to make a mistake.

Klaus had never trafficked in murder, nor had
Emil. Yet the Omegas were not at all squeamish about
offing people—friends and enemies alike. Would Klaus
run such an organization? Not likely. And yet Ilsa remembered him planning the creation of the Omegas.
Could he have been purged by more radical elements? Were they simply using him? Were the Russians involved? Was Klaus even alive? Or was this a
new Klaus Dietrich, so dedicated to his cause that
people no longer mattered to him?

And if he killed Emil, would he kill Ilsa, too?

Something else bothered me. The Omegas hadn't
gone public with their demands, and their time limit
was strangely generous. They'd given NASA enough
time—I hoped—to launch a rescue mission. Surely, the
Omegas knew this. They could apparently blow up
the *Discovery* any time they wanted, or at least prevent its return to earth. The Shuttle itself was a valuable hostage, but their hold would be much stronger if
there were lives at stake. So how would the Omegas
deal with the rescue mission?

And what about the Russians? McNally and Richter
kept mentioning the KGB. I didn't think they were
likely to be involved with a group like the Omegas,
but what did I know? The Omegas were entirely alien
to me, an utterly unknown quantity. What did they
really want? Their demands were oddly pedestrian for
such an elaborate scheme. Empty the jails, they said.
Fine, but you could do that with a simple airline hi-
jack. The U.S. get out of Europe? Interesting, but not
very plausible. The NATO powers would hardly dismantle their defenses for the sake of one spacecraft,
no matter how much it cost. Klaus certainly knew
that.

So what did they want?

I mulled over what Emil had said to me before I left. "You really ought to believe in angels, Sam. Trust them even if you can't see them. They work miracles, you know." I didn't know what to make of it. Emil was old and a little dotty, but I didn't think he was simply flapping his oversize dentures. He had been telling me something. And the other thing he had said was even more puzzling. Round and round, there was my answer. Round and round. It would make me laugh, he said. Okay, Emil, tap my funny bone and spin me some more teasing tautologies, because I'm not laughing.

Ilsa was somewhere out in the streets of Bonn playing hide-and-seek with a band of killers. I sat and waited for her. I was an idiot. For the moment, I was a *live* idiot. If I wanted to stay that way, I was going to have to get smart in a hurry.

I returned to the hotel and did some more fretting in my room. Korbach joined me and turned on the television. Some kind of German sitcom was on, and Korbach seemed to think it was a riot. He laughed frequently, showing off his stainless steel molars. I found it difficult to brood effectively with all that going on.

I finally left Korbach to his joke machine and went down to the hotel restaurant for an early dinner. It was only seven and Ilsa wasn't due for another hour. Scotch was still sloshing around in my empty stomach, so dinner made about as much sense as anything.

No one else was in the dining room at this early hour. The headwaiter seemed to regard me as a thoughtless intruder, disturbing the vacant symmetry of his little empire. But the guy who waited on my table was friendly. He said it was a terrible shame that I was alone. He hinted that he could be induced to remedy the situation. There were plenty of lovely young girls in Bonn, he assured me. He happened to know a few himself. He could arrange an introduction. I told him not to bother, I had a hot date all lined up. I don't think he believed me.

I looked at my wristwatch. Seven-fifteen. My hot date wouldn't arrive for forty-five minutes.

When she did get here, Ilsa would be in for a surprise. My plans for the evening had changed considerably. There would be no midnight rendezvous with Klaus or with anyone else. I'd get Ilsa to tell me how and when the meeting was to take place. Then I'd have Korbach sit on her, if necessary, while I phoned Richter with the details. If anyone was going to stand around on a dark street corner with a carnation in his teeth, it wasn't going to be Ilsa. Or me. If Ilsa wanted to see Klaus, she could see him in the cops' interrogation room. Or at his trial.

She'd hate me for it, of course. This was betrayal, naked and sleazy. She'd hate me, but she'd be alive.

I ate my dinner without paying much attention to what it was. It could have been a Firestone Steel Belt Radial for all I knew. My waiter cleared away the plates and served me coffee. He mentioned that my date still hadn't arrived. Perhaps I had been stood up. If that was the case, he had a close friend who had also been stood up. She was all alone for the evening. She was standing right outside in the lobby.

I looked to where he was pointing. A voluptuous blonde was posing by a potted palm. It was difficult to understand why anyone would stand her up. It was also difficult to understand how she could stand up, period. She seemed a trifle overbalanced.

I told the waiter that I was truly sorry to hear about his friend's plight, but I was certain that she would

not have to spend the night darning socks. I saw three
different men stop and stare at that poor lonely waif.

And one of them, I suddenly realized, was Hans
Neuhaus, delivery boy. I stared at him to make sure.
He felt my eyes on him and stared back. The tousled
black hair, the Army parka—it was Neuhaus, all right.

He bolted for the nearest exit. I shoved my waiter
out of the way and took off after him. I swivel-
hipped, OJ style, past the maze of tables and stiff-
armed the headwaiter. When I hit the lobby, I
stopped for a second and looked for Neuhaus. He
wasn't there, but everyone else was looking toward a
door near the front desk.

The door led to a back stairway, with concrete steps
and steel pipe railings. I listened for a few seconds
and heard a rustling sound from somewhere beneath
me. Down, then.

I took the steps three at a time, hitting the first
landing with a loud thud. I swung around the railing
and sailed down the second flight in two long strides.
I was halfway down the third flight when all the
lights went out. I missed the next step entirely,
twisted my right ankle, and went crashing headfirst
into a brick wall. The rebound threw me back against
the stairs and I cracked my head against them, hard.

In the darkness my labored breathing was the only
sensory landmark. Neuhaus heard it and fired a shot
at the sound. The crack of his gun echoed like a bass
drum in the stairwell.

I flattened out on the landing and tried to hold my
breath. The concrete floor felt cold and clammy
against my cheek. I pressed my ear against it and listened. Neuhaus must have been doing the same thing.
The silence was awesome.

Let him wait, I thought. Sooner or later the cops would arrive. The longer we waited, the less chance he would have.

Neuhaus must have had the same thought. There was a sudden scuffing sound, then the quick rhythm of someone running. I pushed myself up and started after him. I found the next flight of stairs and made my way down cautiously. I stumbled on the last step—the one that wasn't there—and went reeling into another wall. This one made a metallic clang as I hit it with my chest.

It had to be the fuse box. I fumbled with it, making too much noise. I stopped what I as doing for a second and listened again. The running sound had stopped. I ran my fingers over the fuses and switches and realized that I'd never find the one I wanted. With no choice, I started flipping every switch I could feel. With any luck, I probably cut off Korbach's television.

Abruptly, the lights were on again. I shut my eyes against the glare. When I opened them a second later, I was staring at Neuhaus.

We had reached the basement. Neuhaus was standing in front of some heating pipes about forty feet away from me. He raised his pistol and fired.

He was wide, but not by much. I didn't have time to kill the lights before Neuhaus killed me. I hit the floor again, tucking my shoulder under, and rolled to the nearest shelter, a thick concrete stanchion. Another bullet spanged off the floor a foot behind me.

I got up an tried to press myself into the stanchion. Looking around me, I saw that we were in the midst of a jungle of heating, plumbing, and wiring pipes, badly lit by bare bulbs dangling from the ceiling.

There were plenty of places for both of us to hide. But Neuhaus had the gun, not I. If I followed him, he'd probably shoot me; if I hid, he'd get away.

I waited for him to make the next move. Time was on my side. I decided I'd rather have a gun. For two or three minutes there was no noise at all except the thrumming of the pipes. Then Neuhaus made a break for it.

With more optimism than logic, I told myself that he couldn't run and shoot at the same time. I rolled out from behind the stanchion, keeping low, and took up the chase. I caught a glimpse of Neuhaus darting to the left, behind a row of pipes running parallel to the floor. I went left, too, and hid behind some pipes of my own. A bullet ripped into one of them, just over my head, and unleashed a fountain of hot steam. I narrowly missed getting scalded.

I hit the floor again while the air filled up with steam. The pipes were not flush with the floor, I noticed. There was enough room for me to squeeze under them. I decided it was worth a try, although if Neuhaus caught me flat on my back, he could pin me like a butterfly. Inching my way under the pipes, I wondered what would happen if Neuhaus shot one that contained heating oil.

I made it to the next aisle. Neuhaus should be two rows farther on. This was about as close as I wanted to get.

On my hands and knees, I scuttled along like a crab, trying not to make any noise. The steam was still hissing mightily and I hoped it would be enough to cover my movement.

I reached the end of the row of pipes. There was a narrow three-foot corridor running perpendicular to the pipes between me and another wall. If I could sneak down that corridor to the row Neuhaus was hiding behind, I might be able to surprise him.

Nope. Neuhaus was waiting for me. The bastard had the same idea I did. He fired two quick shots from a distance of a dozen feet and missed with both of them. He looked as surprised as I felt. I didn't wait for him to recover. I screamed wildly, faked toward him, then ducked back behind the pipes. A good scream can scare anyone, and mine was world class. Neuhaus took off.

He reached a door at the far wall. I scrambled after him, still screaming. Neuhaus paused, looked back, then rushed through the door without bothering to fire another shot.

I made it to the door and stopped. My throat couldn't take any more screaming, and I doubted if Neuhaus would continue to be scared by it. Besides, I didn't want to go through that door until I knew what was on the other side.

"Neuhaus!" I shouted. I needed something else to keep him occupied. Maybe I could strike up a conversation.

"You sprechen sie English? You understand me, Neuhaus?"

There was a long pause, and then Neuhaus shouted back, "What do you want, Boggs?" His accent was atrocious.

"I want you, Neuhaus! You scummy, motherfucking son of a bitch! I'm gonna rip you to shreds and feed you to the cockroaches, Neuhaus! You hear me?"

Neuhaus stopped to consider the plausibility of my threat.

"You are funny, Boggs! Come and try it!"

That told me all I needed to know about what was on the other side of the door. Neuhaus had it covered.

It occurred to me then that I was probably the whole reason Neuhaus came to the hotel in the first place. I was next on his list. He'd wanted me to chase him down here. I'd managed to unnerve him a little, but he was back in charge now.

I looked around for inspiration. There was nothing small enough to lift that was big enough to throw at him and do any good. Sooner or later he'd come through that door and shoot me. Now was the time to run.

But if I ran, I'd lose Neuhaus. And if we had Neuhaus, we might not even need to make that rendezvous with Klaus Dietrich. Neuhaus was a live Omega, a species never before captured. He could tell us volumes.

I looked heavenward for more inspiration, and suddenly I had my plan.

"Tell me, Neuhaus," I shouted. "Was that bomb meant for me or Emil Rothenburg? Was Emil just in the way, or were you trying to get me no matter what it cost? I thought Emil was on your side."

Neuhaus didn't respond to that. I had to get him talking while I set things up. I tried talking shop.

"That was a pretty sloppy bomb, Neuhaus. I was making better bombs than that when I was in high school."

"It served its purpose," Neuhaus said testily.

"Too big," I said. "Never use more than you need for the job. I'm an expert, you know." I tried to keep my voice conversational while I boosted myself up on the pipes. A light bulb was hanging just above me.

"I have heard them talk of you," said Neuhaus. "They say you used to be very good, before you sold out."

"Good? Hell, boy, I was the best." I got a hand around the cord and pulled it toward me. "You've got possibilities, kid, but you need a little expert tutoring."

"From you?" Neuhaus laughed obnoxiously.

"Why not? I'll give you a little on-the-job training." I grabbed the cord with both hands and jumped. The cord ripped away from it's moorings. I hit the floor with the cord still in my grip.

"What was that?" Neuhaus demanded.

"Mice," I said. "Listen, kid, you've got to be more inventive than just delivering your bombs personally. You'll get caught or blown up that way. What would you have done if Emil had opened that package while you were still there?"

That gave him something to think about while I wedged the bulb and socket between two pipes.

"It was a chance I was prepared to take," said Neuhaus. "I am dedicated to the cause. I don't suppose you understand that."

"Oh, I understand it. I just don't agree with it. I find it much easier to work for a cause if I'm alive. Can't accomplish much when you're dead."

"As you will soon discover, Boggs."

"Brave talk." I wrapped the cord around my fist a couple of times, braced my leg against the pipes, and jerked. The cord pulled free and the bulb smashed against the concrete floor.

"What was that? What are you doing?"

"Come on in and find out. You'll learn something, kid."

"And you will learn what it feels like to die."

"Not from you, Neuhaus, you maggot-ridden little turd."

I wrapped the slack cord around a pipe, leaving just enough to stick out in front of the door. The exposed wire was directly in front of the doorknob. The cord was stiff enough to keep from drooping too much. It ought to stay in place for at least a minute.

"You should be careful what you say, Boggs. I have the gun, remember?"

I remembered. I crouched to the side of the door and waited.

"Boggs?"

I didn't respond. I'd said all I had to say.

"Are you still there, Boggs?" I was, but Neuhaus was beginning to think that I wasn't. Smart kid.

The doorknob began to turn slowly. Neuhaus wasn't sure that I was gone. I might be hiding by the door, waiting to jump him. As a matter of fact, I was.

The door opened an inch. From where he was, Neuhaus couldn't possibly see me. He'd have to open it wider. He did.

The metal knob brushed against the live wires. Suddenly we were in the dark again, except for the brilliant sparks sputtering from the door.

Neuhaus screamed. It was even louder and more scary than mine; his was from the heart.

There wasn't enough juice to fry him, but he'd hang onto that doorknob till his hand was well-done. That was the plan, at least.

I didn't count on his being off balance. He couldn't let go of the doorknob, but gravity slowly pulled him forward. The door swung open, pushing the wires out of the way. The sparks ceased and we were in total darkness.

I dived at the spot where Neuhaus had to be. I hit something soft and started pummeling it with fists, knees, and feet. He pawed back at me, hitting me ineffectually in the shoulder. I grabbed his arm and followed it on back to the rest of him. I was about to smash his nose and loosen his fillings when something whacked me in the side of the head.

I toppled over. I reached out to grab something, but nothing was there. It was all over.

CHAPTER 9

Korbach pulled me to my feet. It was like being lifted out of the hold of a freighter by a giant crane.

"Are you all right?" he asked me.

I didn't know if I was or not. The lights were on again, but everything still seemed dim and blurred. Korbach, towering over me, looked like Mount Rushmore.

"Uh, did . . . did, uh, did he get away?" I couldn't think of the name I wanted.

"Yes," said Korbach. "He was about to shoot you when he saw me. He was too fast for me to follow."

"Neuhaus," I said.

"Yes," Korbach agreed.

I felt the right side of my head. Everything was still there, but several sizes larger. My head felt like a vast, empty airplane hangar.

"Uh, Korbach? Thanks. I guess you saved my life. I'm sorry I threw you out of the room last night."

Korbach muttered something which sounded like the German equivalent of "shucks." He put his arm around me and practically carried me back to the stairs. By the time we got there, my head had cleared a little.

"What time is it?"

"It is nearly eight."

"Jesus, we've got to get back to the room. Ilsa will be here any minute."

"No," said Korbach.

I looked at him. "No? What do you mean, 'No'?"

"You received a telephone call. That is why I came down to look for you."

"A call? From Ilsa?"

"Yes. She insisted on talking to you, but I was able to get her to give me the information."

"What information?"

"The meeting place. She is already there. We must hurry." As if to illustrate the point, Korbach began dragging me up the steps. I shook him off.

"You mean she's already. . . . Oh, Christ! Korbach, did you call Richter?"

"Of course. The area will be sealed off as soon as we arrive."

"We?"

"It is several kilometers north of here. You will need a driver."

Korbach seemed to know what he was doing. I was still wobbly enough to let him run the show for now. We made it up the stairs and emerged into the lobby. I noticed that the lonely blonde was gone. I didn't see the waiter, either. That seemed vitally important for a second, but I didn't know why. I felt as if everything had almost come together for an instant, but then it all slipped away again.

The steady rain was still falling as we drove north on the autobahn. Traffic was minimal and Korbach

drove like Jackie Stewart at Le Mans. Once we skidded on the slick surface, but Korbach scarcely noticed
it.

I opened my window and let the cold air and rain
slap me in the face. I was only wearing a light jacket
over a turtleneck, but I'd rather be cold than coma-
tose. Neuhaus had somehow managed to give me a
damned good poke in the head, and my ears were still
ringing a little. When we got to wherever we were
going, I wanted to be alert.

I didn't know what I'd be walking into, but I didn't
like the feel of it. Why had Ilsa called instead of coming in person? Maybe they wouldn't let her. But then
why would they let her contact me at all? The only
possible answer was Klaus Dietrich himself. Ilsa
wouldn't leave Klaus once she had found him, and
Klaus would probably want to see me even if he knew
I was working for the other side now. That didn't
make a great deal of sense, either, but it was the best
I could come up with.

We turned off the autobahn after a few miles and
headed west. We must have been about midway between Bonn and Cologne, but the night was so dark
that we could easily have been in the middle of a desert. The only illumination in sight came from our own
headlights.

I rolled the window up again. I was as awake as I
was going to be. A sharp, cold ball of tension was
forming in my gut. My number one priority was to get
Ilsa safely away. Number two was to get myself safely
away. There was no number three. Richter could deal
with Klaus and everything else.

We were gradually climbing into some modest hills
as we left the Rhine behind. We passed quickly
through the streets of two small villages, then turned

onto a gravel road. Korbach seemed to know the territory, for he anticipated the sharp curves and potholes.

"Are you sure where we're going?" I asked him.

"The instructions were quite detailed," he said. "It
is about one and a half kilometers from here."

"What is?"

"Our destination. Fräulein Vogel said it was a small
building abandoned by the coal companies."

"Coal companies?"

Korbach pointed to our left. I could make out what
seemed to be a vast pit, barely thirty feet from the
road. Strip mining, apparently.

We made another turn, onto an even narrower road.
This one consisted mainly of mud. We lurched
through puddles like an icebreaker in heavy seas. Finally we reached the top of a hill and Korbach
brought the car to a stop and killed the engine and
the lights.

"It is directly ahead," he told me. "You are to go in
alone."

"Where's Richter?"

"He and the others will be here by the time you
have walked to the building. They will not attempt to
do anything until you and Fräulein Vogel have returned to the car. I will remain here."

"Okay, then. Stay loose, Korbach."

I opened the door and got out. I looked forward,
but couldn't see anything. But anyone who might
have been down there could have seen me with no
trouble, thanks to the interior lights of the Mercedes. I
shut the door quickly and the lights went out.

I started walking. Mud oozed over the tops of my
shoes with each step.

Gradually, the blackness ahead lightened to a vague
gray. There was a small building about a hundred yards

ahead of me. No lights. It looked as if it might have
been a storage shed of some kind. Wooden frame, one
floor, no windows, maybe fifteen feet square.

I was wet and freezing and felt more naked than I
ever did in San Vincente. I wondered if I should have
asked Korbach for a gun. No, that would have been
pointless. I'd be searched when I entered the building,
that much was certain. Anyway, I don't like guns.
They're ugly and they have only one reason for exist-
ing.

Ten feet from the door, I stopped. I waited. Nothing. There was a skinny shaft of light coming through
a crack in the door, but no other sign of life.

"Ilsa?" I waited but heard no response.

My mouth was dry as sandpaper. She was either
here, or she wasn't, and there was nothing I could do
about it now. I wasn't even sure I wanted to find out
the answer. I had to force myself to move.

There was no doorknob, just a latch with a chain
dangling from it. I pulled on the latch and the chain
rattled loudly as the door swung open.

It was a small room. There were large steel drums
lined up along two walls, along with a collection of
industrial junk and tools. A wooden table in the center
of the room was the only visible furniture. A candle
stuck on a tin-can lid flickered uncertainly on the center
of the table.

I stepped inside and saw the rest of the room. In
the corner to the right, two people were wrapped in
an awkward embrace on the floor. They were face-
down, but I knew who they had to be.

I felt light-headed for a moment, and then everything came sharp and clear. It was as if I had stepped
outside myself. I was somehow removed from active
participation in what was about to happen. I wouldn't

have to go to the bodies of my best friend and the woman I loved. Someone else would do it for me, some cold, emotionless drone who was using my body.

The drone walked to the corner, his feet thumping on the wooden floor, while I stayed behind and watched. He knelt down and efficiently pulled Klaus's arm away from Ilsa. Then he took Ilsa by her shoulder and rolled her onto her back.

She looked peaceful. Her eyes were closed and her mouth was at rest in a calm, placid smile. There was a single bullet hole over her heart, an almost surgical wound with a minimum of blood.

The drone turned to Klaus. There was no need to turn over his spindly body. Klaus had been riddled. The back of his head had been blown all over the wall, and enough of his face was visible to tell that somebody had used both barrels of a shotgun on him. His blond hair was matted with blood. Klaus's magnificent brain was dripping out onto the floor.

I watched it all from a safe distance. The drone had gotten blood on his hands. I felt a quick surge of nausea, but it passed. This had nothing to do with me. I was only here as an observer.

The drone backed away from the bodies and stood there in the doorway with me. I felt totally blank, like a clean sheet of paper.

I couldn't go on looking at the bodies, so I cast my eyes around the tiny room. There was no evidence that anyone had lived here. It wasn't Klaus's hideout, just a meeting place, miles from anything. No wonder Ilsa hadn't wanted to come back to meet me in Bonn. It made much more sense to stay here and phone me.

Except that there was no telephone.

I yanked the chain out of the latch and slammed the door shut before I was fully aware of why I was doing it. Everything had fallen into place so suddenly that I didn't have time to think about it. I looped the chain through the door handle, then pulled it taut and wrapped it around one of the big steel drums. There was no lock, but I found a couple of long spikes on the floor. I stuck them through the chain links, then tied a large, clumsy square knot with the remaining length of chain. It was a makeshift arrangement, but it looked as if it would hold. Even Korbach would have a hard time opening that door.

I held my breath and listened. Someone was moving outside. He stopped just outside the door.

"Mr. Boggs," Korbach called. "Are you all right?"

"I'm fine, Korbach. Go away."

"Are you sure you don't need me?"

Korbach didn't give me time to answer. He gave a mighty tug on the door, rattling the chain. The steel drum didn't budge.

"I said go away!"

Korbach tried the door again. The steel drum slid a fraction of an inch toward the door.

"Open the door, Mr. Boggs."

"Can't do that, Korbach."

A bullet splintered the wood of the door and whizzed past my nose, plunking into the other wall. He was aiming at my voice.

I lifted the candle off the table, getting hot wax under my fingernails in the process. Then I turned the table over and squatted behind it. I would have felt safer with the candle out, but I needed some light if I was going to find anything I could use as a weapon.

I had a lot of junk to choose from, but nothing looked immediately useful. Korbach pulled on the door again. I heard him grunting from the effort. The drum moved a couple of inches. I crawled around the

table to the drum and waited. Korbach tried again
and made a little more progress. As soon as the tension relaxed, I pulled the chain taut again and reset
the spikes. I'd eliminated everything he'd gained. He
realized it when he pulled again. He swore in guttural
German.

"We'll be here all night at this rate, Korbach."

"There are quicker methods available," he replied
calmly. "I could burn you out, for example."

"You might have a tough time explaining that to
Richter. It'll be tough enough to explain how I got
shot."

"Not really. Just another Omega execution. The killers escaped before I could reach you."

"Bullshit. There aren't any Omegas. There probably
never were. Isn't that right, Korbach?"

He tugged on the door again, making minimal progress.

"It didn't fit and I couldn't figure out why," I said.
"But I've got it now, Korbach. The execution attempt
on the highway. The delivery boy planted months earlier with the publisher. Even the waiter at the hotel.
He was part of it, too, wasn't he? He made sure I saw
Neuhaus. And Neuhaus made sure I wasn't in the
room when Ilsa's phone call came. But there is no
phone, Korbach, so Ilsa couldn't have called. There
was never any call. How am I doing, Korbach?"

"Very well," he said with a grunt as he made another try at the door. "I suppose you've also figured
out the rest of it."

"Most of it. This whole thing was far too elaborate
for the Omega Alliance, if they even exist. They
couldn't possibly have that much manpower. They'd
need help from someone with more resources. Neuhaus wasn't planted at the publisher just to kill Emil

Rothenburg. And the waiter was there because important people stay at that hotel. He's probably been
there for years. The KGB likes to plan ahead, isn't
that right, Korbach?"

Korbach didn't answer. The silence made me nervous.

"What was the point, Korbach? What were they
after? What do the Russians get out of this? Why the
big charade?"

The entire building shuddered as Korbach crashed
into the door. He hit it again with his full weight. The
wooden slats of the door buckled slightly, but held.

Korbach tried a new tack. He kicked. On the third
try he succeeded in breaking off the bottom six inches
of one slat.

Korbach punted away some more wood. It was only
a matter of time until the Big Bad Wolf kicked my
house down. I needed to find something to use to defend myself before it was too late. I held up the candle and surveyed the dark corners of the shed.

I found a metal hook about eight or nine inches
long, the kind used at the end of a crane's cable. It
looked potentially lethal, if I could only figure out a
way to use it.

Korbach's entire foot bashed through the bottom of
the door, I crawled over to the door and waited. He
kicked again and I came down with the hook.

My aim was bad. Instead of breaking his ankle, all I
did was snare it. Even that was enough to unbalance
Korbach. He yelled something, then hit the ground
with a loud splat. I still had his ankle in the hook, but
I couldn't figure out what to do with it.

Korbach knew where I was. He fired his gun
through the door and just missed hitting me in the

elbow. I scrambled back away from the door and Korbach retrieved his foot. This was getting me nowhere. I could annoy him, but I didn't see any way of stopping him.

I looked around the shed again. There was a wide variety of junk to choose from, and given enough time I might be able to use it to my advantage. But Korbach wasn't going to give me the time I needed. Already he was kicking at the door again.

There was a two-gallon petrol can in the far corner. I crept over to it and shook it. There couldn't have been more than an inch of gas left in it, but that might be enough. Korbach couldn't take a chance of setting fire to the shed, but maybe I could set fire to him.

I carried the gas can back to the door. Korbach heard me and fired another shot, this one safely over my head. He had kicked out a foot-wide hole at the bottom of the door. A few more good boots and the door was going to fall apart.

I raised the gas can over Korback's excavation and waited for his next try. It came, and more wood gave way. Korbach's foot flashed into the room again and I spilled the gasoline on it. His foot was already wet and muddy, so he probably wouldn't notice.

Korbach kicked again, but the door held and I didn't have a chance at his foot. I held the candle out and tried to anticipate where the next jolt would come. With my other hand, I grabbed the chain holding the door and got ready to whip it over the steel drum.

Korbach bashed another hole in the door, and I had him. I jabbed the candle into his foot and jumped back as the gas ignited with a *wumpf!* Korbach

screamed and pulled his flaming foot back through
the shattered door. I yanked the chain over the drum
and came out flying.

The door flew open in Korbach's face. I had a
quick glimpse of him roaring like a bedeviled Gul-
liver, hopping around madly and trying to swat out
the flames curling up his pant leg. I didn't linger to
see how he made out. I was running full speed two
strides from the shed.

My first thought was to make it to the car. Maybe
I'd get lucky and find the keys still in it. I charged up
the sloping road like TR taking San Juan Hill. There
was no way a one-legged Korbach was going to catch
me. All he could do was shoot me in the back.

He tried, but missed. His gun barked again and I
dived headlong into the ditch. I got mud up my nose
and down my pants and everywhere in between.

I looked back, but saw nothing. Korbach had extin-
guished himself, and we were back in darkness. I
crawled out of the ditch and started running again.

I made it to the car before Korbach could fire
again. The driver's side door was open and I felt a
thrilling moment of elation. It died quickly enough.
The keys were gone. I could hear Korback splashing
his way up the road.

The Mercedes was parked at the crest of the hill.
Korbach had set the emergency brake. I released it,
put my shoulder against the door and pushed. The car
rocked forward a few inches and then slowly, slowly
began rolling down the hill. I gave it another shove,
then jumped back out of the way.

I saw Korbach's dark bulk, chugging up the middle
of the road. He stopped suddenly, stood up straight,
and squeezed off a shot that shattered the windshield

of the Mercedes. If I'd been behind the wheel, it would have killed me. But the car kept rolling, straight at Korbach.

He dived into the same ditch I had. The car rumbled past him, picking up more speed, until finally it reached the bottom and slammed into the shed, completing the demolition Korbach had started.

There was nothing to do now but run. I told myself that a man Korbach's size couldn't possibly run fast enough to catch me, not with a scorched foot. I was taking comfort from that thought when I slipped and came down ass first in a huge puddle. I got up and immediately slipped again.

I had to get off the road, that much was obvious. I didn't know what was out there in the blackness, but the going had to be easier than it was on the road. If I didn't get lost, I could run parallel to the road and make my way back to the villages we had come through. They couldn't have been more than a couple of miles.

I went right and found myself lurching across an uneven field that was dotted with thigh-high bushes that were all but invisible until I collided with them. I ran full tilt for two or three minutes, then tripped on something and fell into another puddle.

I lay there and gasped. Too many cigarettes, not enough exercise. I promised myself I'd run a couple of miles on the beach every morning, just as soon as I got back to San Vincente.

San Vincente was too far to comprehend. I'd settle for one of those grubby little towns along the road. Then I realized that I'd lost track of the road. I didn't know where the hell I was. I looked up, but the stars had taken the night off.

If I didn't know where I was going, I also didn't know where I was leaving. Korbach could be anywhere.

But if I couldn't see him, then he couldn't see me. The smartest thing to do might simply be to wait it out. Let Korbach wander all over West Germany while I sat there in my puddle. If I didn't have pneumonia by morning, I could make my way back to civilization when the sun came up.

Then I realized that I wouldn't have to wait that long. Korbach had to have called Richter. He'd blow his cover if he didn't act the part of the loyal, obedient cop. He probably timed it so that Richter would arrive twenty or thirty minutes late, just long enough to dispose of me. Richter would find the three bodies and get a song and dance from Korbach about how he heard some shots after I entered the shed. He got there too late, and the killers had disappeared into the wet night. Very neat, except that I'd already blown Korbach's timetable. Richter's men could arrive at any time.

Fine. I'd wait for them.

I changed my mind about two seconds later. Korbach blundered right into me. He crashed down on top of me, as surprised as I was.

The sheer weight of Korbach pressed me deep into the puddle. I didn't have a chance to take a good breath. I could drown before the stupid oaf even realized what was going on.

I shoved with all the force I could muster. Korbach slid off of me and I raised my head above the water. I rolled to the right, gulping for air. Korbach slammed a massive fist into my ribs and the air rushed out of me again. My whole left side felt numb.

I twisted away from him, dodging his next blow.
Korbach got to his knees and dived at me, flopping
into the mud like a crazed hippo. I tried to kick at
him, but my foot glanced off his back.

Korbach managed to grab my ankle as I tried to
squirm away. We were both extended full length. I
tried to dig in with my free foot and push off, but I
could get no purchase on the mud. Korbach pulled me
toward him, reeling me in like a flounder. I looked
back over my shoulder and he paused to grin at me. I
kicked at the center of that grin and hit it. He rocked
backward and lost his grip on me.

I made it to my feet and staggered forward. I heard
Korbach splashing around behind me, looking for his
gun. There was nothing I could do about that. If he
found it, I was dead. I ran.

I reached the top of another hill and looked back. I
saw Korbach thundering after me, fifty or sixty feet
behind.

A flash of light caught my eye, off to the right. I
zeroed in on it and saw a dim glow in the distance. It
had to be one of those villages. From now on, it was
just a question of who could run faster.

I started for the lights. I couldn't tell what was between me and them. I found out soon enough.

The ground tilted down sharply. My foot skidded
and I lost my balance again. I hit on my back and
started sliding. I flailed around with my feet, trying to
find something to brace myself, but there was nothing
there. I couldn't understand it. Suddenly there was
nothing supporting my ass; my legs and lower torso
overbalanced and I began to fall.

Frantically, I windmilled my arms, as if I could fly
with them, while my spine raked a sharp rock on the

way past. My left arm smacked into something and
halted my plunge before I was completely over the
edge. I felt as if my shoulder would pop out of its
sockets from the impact.

I was still slipping. I flopped around and managed
to get a grip on a rock with my right hand just as I
lost hold with my left. The rock was too slippery to
hold for long. I grabbed at it with both hands and
locked my fingers together around the rock. I came to
a stop, my body swaying back and forth over the
emptiness like the pendulum of a clock.

I'd fallen into the fucking coal mine. I looked down
and saw nothing but an immense blackness. The
damned hole could be three hundred feet deep.

I tried to pull myself up, but the motion nearly
caused my locked hands to slip off of the rock. I held
my breath and waited till I stopped swinging.

I didn't know how much longer I could hold on. My
hands were wet, the rock was wet, everything was
wet. I was supporting my whole weight with nothing
but my knobby knuckles. Gradually, they were being
pulled apart.

A wild, surprised cry rang out above me. I couldn't
see anything but the cliff face in front of me, but I
guessed that Korbach had caught up with me.

I looked up and saw a pair of muddy shoes sliding
over the edge. The calves and knees followed. If he
didn't stop, he'd slide right over my hands, and that
wasn't going to do either one of us much good.

Somehow he managed to halt his slide. He was
stretched out on his stomach, probably clutching at a
rock the same as I was. Korbach struggled to get his
knee over the top. He missed twice, and on the third
try he bashed it right into my hands.

My fingers came apart and I began to slip. I reached for the only thing available, which was Korbach. I wrapped both hands around his meaty thigh and hung on.

"Let go of me!" he screamed. Together, we slid downward another foot.

"Steady, Korbach! I'll take you over with me, you know that!"

"Let go!" He kicked at me with his other leg. I grabbed that one too as we slipped again. Suddenly Korbach went still as a dead tree. His legs were completely over the edge.

"Hold on, dammit!"

He didn't have any choice. I held on tight with my left hand and reached up with my right. I found his belt and hooked my fingers around it.

"Don't move!" I ordered. "I'm gonna climb up over you. It's the only way either one of us can get up."

"No! You'll pull me over!"

"I will if you don't shut up and stop squirming! Just lie there and don't move. When I get up I'll give you a hand."

"I don't trust you."

"I don't blame you. But we need you alive, Korbach. Now shut up!"

I couldn't spare any more breath for shouting. My arms were so tired that I didn't see how in the world I was going to get them to pull me up. But they had to, it was that simple.

I managed to get both hands under Korbach's belt. Now all I had to do was chin myself. I pulled and felt the muscles in Korbach's legs tense. He slipped another inch. I clawed at the back of his coat and got a handful of fabric. I let go of his belt with my right hand and got another hold on his coat. I was halfway up his back now, though my face was still pressed up against his ample gluteus maximus. It was not a pleasant place to stay, but I had to rest again.

The sound of ripping fabric changed my mind. Korbach cried out and I lunged for the back of his collar. I got it, and Korbach made a gurgling, strangled noise. I wouldn't mind strangling him, but this was not the right time for it. I adjusted my hold on his collar and gave him a chance to breathe while I groped around for his shoulder.

One last heave, and suddenly I was on top. I saw that Korbach was hanging on to nothing more substantial than a big clump of weeds.

I found a solid place to put my foot and managed to stand up. Korbach immediately let go of the weeds and clutched my ankle. I dived forward, gaining the top of the slope with my arms and elbows. Korbach grunted as he grabbed for my knees. We had suddenly reversed positions.

But I had a better hold than he did. I kicked at him and inched forward before he could use his full weight on me. There was a fist-sized rock just in front of me, if I could only reach it. At full extension, I could just tickle it with my fingertips. I managed to dislodge it and it rolled toward me a few inches. I had it.

Korbach was still grabbing at my legs. I turned my upper body, took aim, and drilled Korbach in the head with the rock.

Korbach lost his grip entirely and started sliding again. He checked his fall after a couple of feet and immediately started clawing his way back up. In the meantime, I was free. I wasted two seconds trying to decide whether I should stomp on him or run. But one

more look at the yawning blackness beneath Korbach
made up my mind. I got to my feet and ran.

And a few seconds later Korbach was running after
me.

I made my way around the edge of the pit, still
trying to reach the lights. They never seemed to get
any closer.

I ran as far as I could, then subsided to a stumbling
trot until Korbach got too close. He didn't have as
much speed as I did, but his endurance was incredible. He kept a steady pace and gradually gained
ground on me as I alternated between sprints and
gasps. I knew I was reaching my limit. I couldn't seem
to get enough air into my lungs.

Korbach kept coming. He wasn't human. He just
kept coming. I slipped and fell for the hundredth
time. I got up. I ran.

A dark mound loomed in front of me. It was a thick
place in the darkness and rain, towering fifty feet into
the air. I couldn't possibly climb it.

I looked behind and saw Korbach coming at me, no
more than ten yards away. There was no time to look
for a way around the mound. I threw myself at it.

It was a gravel pile. For every foot I gained, I
slipped back another foot. I felt like Sisyphus. But he
had it easy; no one was chasing him.

Korbach plowed into the gravel just behind me. He
dived for my foot but fell short by inches. I dug in
and climbed, showering loose gravel down on him.

I was gaining. Every time I stepped into the gravel,
part of the pile gave way and made Korbach's climb
steeper than mine. With hands and feet pumping furiously, I reached the top a full twenty feet ahead of
Korbach. I looked back and saw lights.

I couldn't believe it. I blinked and wiped mud out

of my face. The lights were still there, a half dozen of them. They cast cone-shaped fields of illumination ahead of them, and they were coming toward me.

"Help!" I screamed. "I'm here, I'm here!"

It had to be Richter's men. Korbach saw them, too.

"Korbach's after me! He's KGB!" I wanted to make sure they shot at the right man, but I didn't even know if they could hear me. Korbach did, though. He cut through the gravel like a bulldozer and was almost on me.

I couldn't wait any longer for help. I got to my feet and stumbled down the other side of the gravel pile, hitting the bottom at a full run. Ahead, there was a dark, open area, and beyond that the lights I'd been trying to reach for what felt like years. One last sprint and I'd be safe. My legs were wooden, but I forced them to move. I couldn't have more than a couple hundred yards to go. Just thirty more seconds.

At the last possible second I saw what was ahead of me and stopped myself. The open area wasn't a field. It was a canal.

I felt like crying. No more. I just couldn't take any more.

I heard Korbach's heavy steps behind me. He'd have me in another second.

I jumped. I hit the water, pushed off the bottom, and bobbed to the surface. The water was so cold that I didn't even feel it for a moment. I splashed away from the embankment and tried to organize myself into some sort of recognizable swimming stroke. But my arms and legs refused to move the way I wanted them to. It was then that I realized that my limbs were numb with cold. I could freeze to death in minutes.

Korbach appeared on the edge of the bank. He looked at me, then turned to look back at the way we had come. I heard voices.

He might have bluffed it out and blamed it all on me. He could have concocted some kind of story. It wouldn't even have to be very good for Richter to believe it.

Instead, Korbach ran. After a few seconds he stopped short, seeing that he had nowhere to go. His only choice was the same as mine. He stripped off his sodden overcoat and dived into the canal. He hit the water with a sound like a depth charge going off.

I waited for him to come up.

He didn't.

The rippling water smoothed out and erased the last traces of Korbach. A man his size, after a desperate chase, simply couldn't take the shock. His heart must have given out.

My own heart couldn't take much more. I tried to paddle toward the near shore, but didn't accomplish very much. I couldn't even tread water anymore. I slipped below the surface. I got my mouth back into the air and managed one breath, but I knew it had to be the last one. I didn't have anything left to fight with. I drifted down into the freezing blackness and didn't even struggle. It was almost pleasant down there.

Somebody roughly jerked me back into the world. I surfaced, choking and coughing weakly. Two of Richter's men were in the water with me. They pulled me back to the edge of the canal, where I could stand without their help.

I looked up the embankment and saw Richter. He stared at me with a face as cold as the water. Behind him stood McNally. Mac, clad in topcoat and neck brace, raised his hand to me in a little salute.

"Get me out of here, Mac," I pleaded. "Get me the hell out of here."

"No problem," he said airily. "We're sending you to Florida."

CHAPTER 10

Over the Atlantic again, this time courtesy of the United States Air Force. McNally and I were high-priority passengers, veritable VIPs. I wasn't overly impressed.

I wasn't feeling much of anything, in fact. Maybe the cold water of the canal had numbed me all the way through. If it had, I was grateful.

McNally compensated by being unusually cheerful and chipper. He spent most of the flight up in the cockpit, chatting with the crew, leaving me alone in the passenger's lounge of the giant C-141. I stared out the window and contemplated the clouds.

Somewhere over the western part of the ocean, McNally reappeared. He sat down beside me and grinned. The grin, on top of his neck brace, made him look like some odd circus act.

"Notice anything unusual the last hour?" he asked eagerly.

"I haven't seen any flying saucers, if that's what you

mean. No sea monsters, no Atlantis. The Bermuda Trapezoid is quiet today."

"What about the plane? Feel any bumps or swerves?"

"None to speak of."

"I didn't think so," McNally beamed. "That's because I was flying the plane. Smooth as silk."

"They let *you* drive a fifty-million-dollar airplane? Jesus, no wonder taxes are so high."

"What do you care? You haven't paid any in years."

"It's the principle of the thing. Mac, what happens when we get to Florida?"

"I told you. You'll spend the next three days training the mission specialist in bomb disposal. He's already gone through a quick course from the FBI, but you can give him the bomb maker's perspective."

"And then what?"

"Then we launch the Shuttle and you and I go to Houston. You'll watch on television and give advice when needed. When the mission is completed, you can go back to your island and relax in the sun. I'll go back to Washington and shovel snow. As usual, you get the best of it."

"Yeah."

McNally looked at me and realized that his little joke had fallen flat. His grin quickly disappeared.

"I'm sorry, Sam," he said. "I know you had a rough time of it. I'm truly sorry about Ilsa."

I looked out the window and watched the wispy clouds for a few moments. I didn't want to look at McNally or anyone else. I was heartily sick of the entire human race.

"Do me a favor, Mac," I said, still gazing at the clouds. "Never mention Ilsa again. She'd still be alive if you hadn't dragged me into this. I don't blame you, but just don't mention her again, okay?"

McNally didn't say anything for a while. Maybe he was assessing guilt factors. Forty percent here, twenty percent there; he could write a departmental memo.

"Okay, Sam," he said at last. "If that's the way you want it. But first I'm going to tell you something you already know. Ilsa would have been killed anyway. She knew how to reach Dietrich, and that was all that mattered. Sam, it was never just some clever little scam put together by a bunch of Lefties from the good old days. It was a KGB operation. They play for keeps, and no one's immune. Emil Rothenburg wasn't. He was killed because he knew how to reach Dietrich. And Ilsa Vogel was killed for the same reason. You didn't cause it, and you couldn't have prevented it."

"It must be nice to be so certain of things."

"It helps," he said.

"So tell me this. Why did they kill Klaus? Have you got that one figured out yet?"

"Not definitely," he admitted. "But if you look at the whole picture, it begins to make sense. From what Ilsa told you, we know that at least six months ago, Dietrich had in mind the creation of the Omega Alliance. Obviously he made some progress toward that goal. The bomb on the Shuttle may have been his idea from the beginning. But at some point the KGB co-opted the operation. Dietrich didn't like it, so they sat on him. Used his name but kept him out of the way. But when we got too close to Dietrich, they decided they didn't need him anymore, and he was more useful to them dead. With Dietrich gone, it's impossible to pin down the Omega Alliance. We still don't know if they're real, or just a KGB fiction. We don't know where we stand regarding the Shuttle, or the

Omegas' demands. Maybe that's all the Russians wanted. We're confused, which gives them an advantage."

"An advantage in what? Tennis?"

McNally shrugged. "Hard to say, precisely. They've thrown a monkey wrench in the Shuttle program, but beyond that, it's impossible to say what they have in mind. The Soviets have a lot of orbital operations that they don't want us interfering with. Their killer-satellite program, .for example. Or maybe their goal really is just to free all the terrorists and put the West in chaos. As far as you're concerned, it doesn't even matter. If there is a bomb on the Shuttle, no matter who put it there or why, you've got to make sure it doesn't go off. You can leave the rest of it to the pros at Langley."

"Who are infallible."

"We try. By the way, Richter told me to tell you that he's grateful for your help in exposing Korbach. Seems Korbach spent some time in East Germany as an agent for our side. Somewhere along the line, the Reds got him and turned him into a double agent. Richter knew there was something badly wrong after the ambush on the highway, but he didn't suspect Korbach. With Korbach dead, we can't find out who else might have been involved, but Richter did pick up the waiter at the hotel."

"And Neuhaus?"

"Still at large. They're working on it. Anyway, Richter wanted me to thank you and express his regrets over the way things turned out."

"The guy's all heart."

"He also told me to tell you that if you ever again set foot in West Germany, he'll throw you into the blackest dungeon he can find."

"I imagine he knows of a few. It doesn't matter. I've had my fill of Germany. But let me tell you something, Mac. You think you're on top of the situation now, but you're not. You can construct all the scenarios you want, but it still doesn't make sense. There's still something missing."

McNally sighed and sank a little deeper into his seat. He stuck a finger inside his neck brace and massaged his Adam's apple.

"Yeah," he said wearily, "I know. It's all a little weird still. But we're getting there. And from now on, it's my headache, not yours."

"I wish I could be sure of that."

"What's to worry about? You teach a few tricks of your trade to some astronaut, then relax in Houston while he does all the work. From here on out, you've got it easy."

I didn't say anything. I was already certain that McNally was wrong. There was nothing to do but wait and see who would try to kill me next.

McNally tried to kill me next. They let him take the controls again and the incompetent cretin flew us into a thunderstorm. Maybe he didn't put that storm in our way, but if he was flying, then he was responsible. The crew took over again and banished McNally from their bailiwick, but the damage was done. We bounced and shuddered all the way to Florida. If man was meant to fly, why did they invent airsick bags?

We landed in the rain at the Kennedy Space Center on Cape Canaveral. In the interest of efficiency, McNally told me, we had come in directly on the Shuttle runway, which was one of the longest in the world—fifteen thousand feet. With the weather as bad as it was, I was glad for every foot of it.

It was late afternoon, Florida time, and late evening, my time. Since NASA runs on Florida time and not mine, they gave us a quick dinner and put us to work immediately. McNally went into conference with some FBI guys, while I was taken to meet the astronauts.

I was driven across the base to a large office-complex. My driver was a NASA functionary named Wheeler, a drab, monotone man who looked as if he hadn't slept in several months. When I asked about the status of the *Discovery*, he gave me a terse assurance that everything was fine. If everything truly was fine, then I'd have hated to see Wheeler on a bad day.

Wheeler led me into the building and down a long, gleaming corridor, to a small auditorium with about fifty seats and a movie screen. Five men were there waiting for us. Two of them were from the FBI, Hoskins and Lang, and the remaining three were the men who would fly the rescue mission.

Bill Braxton was the Spacecraft Commander. He looked the part; steel-gray eyes, steel-gray crew cut, and a Steve Canyon jaw. He was in his early forties and somehow reminded me of Johnny Unitas. The Pilot was Ted Anderson, who was shorter and younger than Braxton, but had the same squint-eyed, hard-assed look about him. The third crew member was Chuck Bigelow, the mission specialist. Bigelow was in his early thirties, but looked considerably younger. Unlike his crewmates, his sandy hair was long enough to comb. His eyes were sky blue and he looked as wholesome as the cover of *Boy's Life*.

Wheeler introduced me as "Dr. Boggs," which gave me a momentary shock. After I got over the unfamiliarity of it, I kind of liked it. I felt legitimate again.

"Dr. Boggs is the bomb specialist we told you

about," Wheeler said. "For the next two days he'll give you an intensive course on how to disarm any explosive device you're likely to find up there. Pay attention to him, he knows what he's talking about."

I saw Lang, one of the FBI agents, give me a distasteful look. He obviously knew who I was. Apparently the astronauts didn't know, which was fine with me.

"We thought we'd start you off with a quick orientation session to familiarize you with the Orbiter," said Wheeler. "If you'll take a seat, we'll run some slides for you and you can ask questions as we go."

I didn't have many questions. I was already generally familiar with the Shuttle, and the slides simply fleshed out my earlier impressions.

The entire Orbiter was about 120 feet long, but the crew module was considerably smaller. It consisted of a three-level section in the nose of the spacecraft. The flight deck was located immediately above the middeck, which was where the crew would spend most of its time. Facilities were there for eating, sleeping, and hygiene. The lower deck was really only a crawlspace where the environmental-control system was located. It all looked incredibly cramped for a crew of seven, but Wheeler reminded me that in zero gravity all of the 2,500 cubic feet could be utilized.

Aft of the crew module was the payload section, which was unpressurized. For this mission, however, the *Discovery* was carrying the European Spacelab, a self-contained tin can crammed with an array of electronic equipment and connected with the crew module by a short tunnel. Here, the mission specialists and scientists conducted most of their experiments.

The bomb was almost certainly located in either the crew module or the Spacelab. If it wasn't, we were in big trouble. A bomb hidden in the honeycomb structure of the aft fuselage or in the reaction-control subsystem—the collection of fuel tanks and small engines for orbital maneuvers and deorbit—would be all but impossible to find and disarm.

"Can you get at the aft fuselage?"

"You'd have to go outside for that," said Braxton.

"So you'd be in a space suit. How much dexterity would you have?"

"Not much," Anderson answered. "You can handle tools well enough, but for really fine work, it's best to take whatever it is you're working on inside, if you can."

"Well, you can forget about that. If you find the bomb, rule number one is to leave it where it is. Which one of you is going to have the honor of working on it?"

"That's me," said Bigelow. He sounded enthusiastic about it.

"Have you ever done anything like this before?"

"Disarming a bomb? I'm afraid not. But I have a degree in electronics and I'm used to finicky work. My hands are steady, if that's what you mean."

I nodded. "That's what I mean."

Wheeler stood up and motioned for the projectionist to turn on the lights. He glanced at his wristwatch.

"Dr. Boggs," he said, "I just realized that it's well after midnight by your time. You'll probably want to get some sleep."

"I wouldn't mind it." I'd managed a little shut-eye on the plane, but not much. And I'd spent the night before running for my life from Korbach.

I shook hands with the astronauts again and told them I'd see them tomorrow. Wheeler escorted me back to the car.

"You've got a motel room over in Cocoa Beach," he told me as he started the car. "McNally will be there, too."

We drove across the vast spaceport toward the mainland. In the distance, I saw an immense floodlit structure. It was about the size of a mountain.

"The VAB," said Wheeler. "Vertical Assembly Building. That's where they put together the Saturn boosters for the Apollo missions. Right now, they're mating the *Columbia* to its boosters. We're actually a couple of hours ahead of schedule."

"Sounds pretty hectic around here."

Wheeler shook his head wearily. "Hectic doesn't begin to cover it. Controlled panic is more like it. This place hasn't been so shook up since the fire."

I was about to ask which fire he meant, but I caught myself in time. He could only have been talking about the *Apollo 1* fire back in 1967, the one that incinerated Grissom, White, and Chaffee as they sat in their command module. That was still the only American fatality directly related to the space program. The Russians had lost three men on reentry, but so far no one had ever died in outer space itself. As time went by, the odds got shorter.

"Tell me about your astronauts."

"Well, you've probably heard of Braxton. Orbited the moon on one of the Apollo missions. This will be his third Shuttle flight. Anderson's been up twice, both times on the Shuttle."

"And Bigelow?"

"Chuck's a good kid," said Wheeler. "He's one of the thirty-five mission specialists recruited for the Shuttle program. He's got a level head and good instincts."

"Has he been up before?"

"This'll be his first trip."

"How was he chosen?"

"They all volunteered."

"Any trouble getting volunteers?"

Wheeler turned and looked at me. "We've all got friends on the *Discovery*," he said flatly.

"That doesn't answer my question."

"Who the hell are you, Boggs?" Wheeler exploded. "Just who the fucking hell are you? Washington shoves you down our throats without a word of explanation, and then you barge in and start asking smartass questions about our crews. We were doing just fine without you, Boggs. We can handle this."

I waited for him to calm down. Wheeler was entitled to blow off steam. I could imagine the pressure he was under. He was a competent engineer and he and his men had done everything that anyone could expect of them. They routinely put people into outer space, and then brought them safely home. No one had ever done anything like it in the history of the world. Building pyramids and canals and bridges was child's play compared with the exploration of space. Yet now Wheeler was at the mercy of the irrational forces of politics and hate, and there was nothing he could do about it.

"Sorry," he mumbled after a few moments.

"Forget it."

"We had plenty of volunteers," Wheeler said. "For spacecraft commander and pilot. Braxton and Anderson are the very best."

"And the mission specialist slot?"

Wheeler was slow to answer. He drummed his fingers on the steering wheel.

"Look," I said, trying to make it a little easier for him, "I know about bombs. Nobody in his right mind wants to fool around with one."

"Do you know what Bigelow will have to do?"
Wheeler asked. "I mean, exactly? The *Columbia* will
match orbits with the *Discovery* and park about one
kilometer away. We don't dare get any closer because
if the bomb goes off, we don't want to lose both
spacecraft. So Bigelow will have to fly over to the
Discovery without an umbilical, using just the jet
pack. Then everyone on the *Discovery* will go over to
the *Columbia* the same way. Some people will have to
make three or four trips. Bigelow will stay behind, all
alone, and hunt for the bomb. It could take days.
Then, when he finds it, he'll have to disarm it."

"A lousy job."

"The worst you can imagine. Our astronauts are
brave and talented people, but they're not fools. It's
not a job a sane person would be eager to accept. We
had a few reluctant volunteers. Bigelow was the best
of the lot."

"Why did he ask for it?"

"At the moment," said Wheeler, "we have a corps of
sixty-two astronauts. Only twenty-four of them have
ever been in space. Some of them will have to wait
years for a mission. Some of them never will make it
up."

"So Bigelow saw this as a shortcut?"

"Don't sell him short. He's as concerned about saving the *Discovery* as anyone. More so. If he didn't
want to wait three or four years for a mission, can you
blame him? He knows he might not come back, but
he's going anyway. What more can you ask of a man?"

I didn't know the answer to that. I was just glad
that Bigelow was going, and not me.

The FBI boys had rigged up some fake bombs for
Bigelow to practice on. We spent the morning going

over procedures and techniques, and in the afternoon Bigelow got his first crack at disarming a bomb. If it had been real, he wouldn't have gotten a second try.

"You lost track of your wires," I told him. "You had the one you wanted to cut, but then you got them confused and cut the wrong one."

"Yeah," said Bigelow sheepishly, "I see that now."

"Now is too late."

"Well, let me try another one."

We were in the middle of a large, roped-off hangar, standing over a workbench. Lang, the FBI man, opened up a box and placed a device on the center of the workbench. It was a cube about six inches on a side, with screws stuck into three of the sides.

"Well?" I asked Bigelow.

He picked up the cube and examined it closely. I took it out of his hand and put it back on the bench.

"You're already dead," I told him. "What was rule number one?"

"Not to move the bomb. But this is just—"

"This is just for fun, right? Look, Chuck, if you're going to get anything out of this, you've got to assume that whatever Lang gives you is packed with gelignite. Now try again."

Bigelow stared at the little metal box for a few seconds, then rummaged around in his toolbox for an electronic listening device. He ran it over the cube and looked at his readings.

"Nothing," he said in bafflement.

"They don't all tick and hum. Now what do you do?"

"Uh, I guess I just have to pick one of the screws and go to work."

"How do you choose which one?"

"There's nothing to go by. All I can do is guess."

I shook my head. "Look again, Chuck. There are some faint scratches around one of the screws. Tool marks. What does that tell you?"

"Well, I guess it means that it's been opened. That must be the right screw, because the other screws have been left alone."

"Not necessarily. Those tool marks could have been put there purposely to get you to go for the wrong screw."

That seemed to trouble Bigelow. He scratched his chin thoughtfully.

"I didn't think of that. I mean, I'm not used to . . . to deception, you know what I mean? Electronic circuits are confusing, but that's just their nature. No one is trying to confuse you. It just happens. But with this . . ."

"Which one, Chuck? Which screw?"

"Uh, I guess I'll go for the one with the tool marks."

"Okay. Why?"

"Why not? One is just as likely as another."

"No, dammit, you can't approach it with that attitude! *Never* guess, unless there is absolutely nothing else to go by. In this case, you know something about one of the screws and nothing at all about the other two. What you know is that this screw has possibly been unscrewed in the past. Either that, or it has been tampered with intentionally. You've got maybe a fifty-fifty chance that this is the right screw. With the other two screws, your odds are down to one in three. So you go with this one, even with the chance that it's been tampered with. It's not much of an edge, but it's the only one you've got. Never do anything without knowing why you're doing it. Unless you've got ESP, don't guess."

Bigelow swallowed hard, then nodded. He picked

up the screwdriver he needed and went to work. Sweat was dripping down his forehead. It took him nearly five minutes to remove the screw.

"Now what?" I asked him.

"Remove the plate?" he asked hopefully.

I shook my head. "Again, you've got a new bit of information that you haven't used yet. Look into the hole. See what there is to see."

He did, shining a pencil flashlight into the hole recently occupied by the screw.

"Anything connected to the plate?"

"Not that I can see."

"Then go ahead."

Gingerly, Bigelow stuck the tip of his screwdriver into the hole and pried up the plate. It came away freely, exposing a tangled mass of wires inside the cube. Bigelow grinned triumphantly.

"Good," I told him. "Now you've got to examine each wire, see where they go, and get a feel for how it's all put together. Then you can decide what you have to do next."

I walked away from him, to the hangar door. Across the open expanse of concrete I could see the VAB in the distance. It looked like a strange outhouse, but the distance made the scale deceptive. The VAB was one of the largest buildings ever constructed.

"What do you think, Boggs?"

Lang had snuck up on me. FBI training, no doubt.

"Of what? Bigelow?"

Lang nodded.

"Two days isn't much time," I said.

"Two months wouldn't be enough. The kid hasn't got it. These are just toys we're giving him, and he's oh-for-two. What would he do with one of your bombs, Boggs?"

I looked at Lang. He was about my size, my age. He and Richter would have hit it off great.

"Look, G-man," I said, "shove it. We're on the same side now."

"For how long, Boggs? I know your kind."

"Spend your off-hours studying old Wanted posters, do you? That's real dedication, Lang."

"I don't know why you're here, instead of Leavenworth," he said coldly, "but I'm keeping my eyes on you, Boggs. I'm watching every move you make."

"Really? I'm flattered."

"You've got quite a mouth, Boggs."

I was going to prove it with another snappy comeback, but decided the hell with it. Lang wasn't worth the effort. I was resigned to the fact that wherever I went, there would always be a Richter or a Lang to remind me that I was the scum of the earth. My past was as persistent as ring-around-the-collar.

I strolled back over to the workbench and watched. Bigelow had sorted things out and was ready to cut the wires he wanted. I lit up a cigarette and leaned close to Bigelow.

He looked up at me, annoyed. "Hey, could you smoke that someplace else?"

I calmly blew a mouthful of smoke in his face.

"Work," I told him.

"But—"

"Do it! Now, dammit! You gutless prima donna flyboy, do your work!"

Bigelow stared at me. He didn't know how to react. I blew some more smoke at him.

"Look at that sweat. You're sweating like a pig, Bigelow. Are you nervous? Scared? Worried? Is that why your hands are shaking?"

"Hey, cut it out!"

I reached over to him and tapped the cigarette ash down the front of his shirt. He yelped, jumped, and dropped his wire cutters into the center of the cube.

"Boom," I said. I dropped the cigarette and stepped on it.

Bigelow was dancing around, his shirttails hanging out, as he tried to brush away the ash. He got it at last, then turned to me with a murderous look on his Boy Scout face.

"Pressure," I said. "If that were a real bomb, Chuck, you wouldn't dare stop to notice me, even if I put that ash down your Jockey shorts. Pressure, Chuck. It's different when it's real. When you get up there, remember that."

Bigelow was still pissed off. "I think I can learn without your little demonstrations," he said petulantly.

"I hope so," I said. "That was the third time today you've been killed. And it's not even two o'clock yet. You could die a dozen more times today. When it's real, though, once is enough."

"I know that," he said.

"If you don't now," I promised him, "you will."

That evening I met with McNally, Wheeler, and the FBI boys. It was thirty-five hours before lift-off.

"Postpone it," I said.

Wheeler had been resting his chin on his fists, elbows propped up on the conference table. His head snapped up, he blinked a couple of times, then turned to look at me. His forehead looked like a plowed field, with neat, parallel rows of furrows.

"Say that again."

"Postpone the launch," I repeated. "Bigelow isn't going to be ready in time."

"Are you sure?"

"Ask Lang."

Wheeler turned to Lang, who nodded. "No way you can send him up on Monday," he said. "I don't think you should send him at all. Bigelow can't hack it."

Wheeler chewed on his lower lip. He didn't look happy.

"Look," I said, "go ahead and launch, but forget about bomb disposal for now. Get the people off and then go back for the bomb when you're ready."

"No dice," put in McNally.

"Oh?" asked Wheeler. This was news to him.

"I talked with Washington today," McNally explained. "They don't want the *Discovery* left alone up there."

"Why not?" asked Lang.

"You know what happened in Germany," said McNally. "We turned up a KGB operation connected with the Shuttle. We don't know how extensive it is, or if they have any direct involvement with the bomb on the *Discovery*. Until we do know, we can't take a chance on leaving the ship unattended."

"I still don't get it," said Hoskins, the other FBI man.

"Salvage," said McNally. "You find a ship, a seagoing ship, that's stuck on a reef, unmanned, and you can claim it for salvage. The Russians could do the same thing with the *Discovery*."

"Nonsense!" Wheeler said hotly. "There are treaties."

"None of which cover a situation quite like this. There's a big gray area in the legalities. The Russians could grab the *Discovery* and argue about it later. Do you think they would hesitate for two seconds if they found an aircraft carrier abandoned on the high seas?"

"This is ridiculous," said Wheeler. "We don't even know if the Russians really are involved."

"They are," McNally said flatly. "We don't know the extent of their involvement, but we know they're up to something. The operation in Germany was too elaborate for a group like the Omega Alliance. At the very least, they're getting Soviet help. At worst, it's Russians top to bottom."

"But we don't *know* that," Wheeler insisted. "I mean, the only people we've heard from are the Omegas."

"Yes," said McNally. "And we've just heard from them again. A bomb went off at the headquarters of the European Space Agency this morning. One man was killed and two were critically injured. Another letter from Spartacus was delivered an hour later. He says they mean business. The European governments involved are getting jumpy. They're considering releasing some of the terrorists."

"And what is Washington doing?" I asked.

"The President is talking with the other heads of state, trying to keep everyone calm. We don't want anyone to do anything until we've taken our shot with the rescue mission."

"Which brings us back to Bigelow. Can't you delay the launch a day?"

Wheeler shook his head. "That would only give Bigelow a few hours on Tuesday to find and disarm the bomb. He'll need that extra day up there."

"He needs it down here even more. It doesn't matter how much time he has on the *Discovery* if he doesn't know how to do the job."

"It's a moot point," said Wheeler. "Meteorology says there's a seventy percent probability of heavy rain at the Cape beginning Monday evening and lasting through Wednesday morning. If we don't launch Monday, we don't launch at all."

"Then it looks like you're stuck with Bigelow," McNally said.

Wheeler looked at me and then at Lang, hoping we'd change our minds about Bigelow. I busied myself lighting a cigarette. I felt sorry for Wheeler.

"It can't be done," said Lang. "You can't take an astronaut and turn him into a bomb expert in thirty-five hours."

"What about the other way around?" McNally asked.

The cigarette lighter slipped out of my hand and thumped on the table. I looked at McNally, but his eyes shifted away from mine.

"You mean take a bomb expert and send him up in place of Bigelow?" asked Wheeler.

"Why not?" McNally kept his eyes on Wheeler and refused to look at me.

Wheeler scratched his left eyebrow and thought about it for a few seconds. "It would be almost as bad as sending Bigelow," he said. "Your expert wouldn't have any training for work in space. He'd have to be able to function in zero gravity—and anyone who thinks that's easy hasn't tried it."

"Bigelow hasn't tried it," McNally pointed out. "This would be his first time up."

"But he's had two years of intensive training."

"Not for this. It doesn't matter how well he can handle himself in zero-G if he can't disarm the bomb. I say it's better to go with someone who knows bombs, and let him deal with zero-G as well as he can."

"Well," said Wheeler, "it might be possible. One of the ideas behind the Shuttle program was that it would make space accessible to people other than astronauts. There are two European scientists on the *Discovery* right now, and neither one of them is technically an astronaut."

Lang and I looked at each other. It was obvious where this was leading.

"You'd have a problem with security," Hoskins noted. "The press is already getting suspicious of this mission. If you pulled Bigelow and sent up a replacement, you'd have a lot of explaining to do."

"No problem," said McNally. "Just keep Bigelow on ice until after the mission and tell everyone that he's in orbit."

"Bigelow wouldn't like it," said Wheeler.

"Bigelow's happiness is not our prime concern here. My question is, can you send up someone else, yes or no?"

"I'm against it," said Wheeler, "but I suppose the answer is yes, if that's the only option. Now all you have to do is find someone to volunteer."

Wheeler, McNally, and Hoskins turned to look at Lang and me. No one said anything.

I started cataloging excuses. I knew I'd need a big arsenal against McNally. For one, I was just an outside consultant; Lang was already on the payroll. And my physical condition was suspect. I might have caught something during my moonlight dip in the canal. And I get airsick—no telling what zero-G would do to my sensitive stomach.

I suddenly realized something that scared me as much as anything ever has: *I wanted to go!*

I didn't want to find a good excuse. I didn't want to duck out of it. I really wanted to go!

Outer space! All my life I'd watched it unfold, from the first beeping satellites to the first seven-iron shot on the moon. When Armstrong stepped out onto the Sea of Tranquillity, I paused between bombings and marveled at it all. I sweated out *Apollo 13*'s long, wounded trip homeward from the moon. I stared in wonder at the first Viking photos from the surface of Mars. I watched it all and felt lucky to be alive to see it. But never once did I think I could ever be a part of it. Space was for heroes and supermen, the Glenns and Gagarins, not for the skulking Sam Boggses. But now . . .

I was so shocked by my revelation that I couldn't say anything.

"I'll go," said Lang. Instead of relief, I felt anger. No miserable Fed was going to beat me out of the chance of a lifetime.

"No," I said. "It has to be me."

McNally gave me an odd look. He was used to thinking of me as a reasonably intelligent mule, useful only if one had a plentiful supply of carrots and sticks.

"You can't send Boggs," Lang insisted. "You can't send up a wanted criminal!"

"I was pardoned, Lang, and you know it. I'm not wanted for anything." Not in this country, at least.

"Are you sure about this, Sam?" McNally asked. "I dragged you into this thing in the first place, but I honestly didn't think. . . . Let me get this straight. You actually *want* to go?"

"You got it. Look, it's got to be either Lang or me, right? Then it might as well be me. If Klaus Dietrich had anything to do with that bomb, then I'm the logical choice. Whatever Klaus knew about bombs, he learned from me. It would be like disarming one of my own bombs. It would be tough for Lang, but a snap for me."

Lang saw that he was losing, so he made a counter-offer. "Send us both," he said. "That would cut the search time in half."

Wheeler shook his head. "Can't," he said. "There are seven people on the *Discovery*, and our maximum load is ten. We can only send up three on the *Columbia*—Braxton, Anderson, and. . . . Look, do you guys know what you're letting yourselves in for?"

"Wouldn't you go?" I asked him. "If you could?"

Wheeler smiled. "In a minute," he said.

"I'll flip you for it," Lang suggested.

"No," said McNally. "Boggs is right. If he really wants to do this, then he's the man. You sure about this, Sam?"

"Start your countdown," I told him.

CHAPTER 11

So there I was, sitting in my spaceship waiting to blast off. You can have a lot of second thoughts in thirty-five hours. And even more in thirty-five seconds.

I spent the day before launch getting a crash course on how to survive in free fall. I realized how Bigelow must have felt the day before. Braxton, Anderson, and three other astronauts pumped me full of space wisdom, giving me detailed instructions on everything from eating and sleeping to the recommended method of eliminating one's bodily wastes. In zero gravity, if you weren't extremely careful, the shit would hit the fan, literally.

A team of NASA physicians put me through a battery of tests to make sure that I could be counted on to survive the rigors of lift-off and reentry. In the old days, when men were men, astronauts had to endure G loads of nine or ten times their normal weight; this can be tough on the heart. The Shuttle subjects its

passengers to a piddling three-G peak, but even that
is too much if you've got a bum ticker.

My heart was fine, if increasingly faint, but I was
more worried about my stomach. Braxton warned me
that if I were to be careless enough to puke while
suited up, I could easily drown in my own vomit. Up-
chucking inside the Shuttle was not as dangerous, but
it would not make me popular with my fellow astronauts.

It seems that just about everyone who goes into
space gets at least a little sick. About one in three get
very sick. In zero-G your bodily fluids tend to collect
in the upper part of the body. That makes you feel
puffy and stuffed up, but it also screws up the fluid
in your semicircular canals. Your body literally doesn't
know which way is up. After a few hours—or a few
days, in some cases—the body and mind finally get
accustomed to the weightless environment, and you
stop feeling sick.

I just knew I was going to be the one in three who
gets very sick. I didn't want to duck out of the mission
on account of an upset tummy, but I decided it would
be foolish not to mention my susceptibility to motion
sickness. The doctors told me not to worry about it.
Based on results obtained from the Apollo and Skylab
programs, they had come up with a generally effective antinausea medicine. It would minimize space-
sickness if I felt it, although nothing could completely
eliminate it.

After the doctors got through with me, I spent the
rest of the day studying schematic diagrams of the
Discovery and the Spacelab. Three NASA engineers
went over the plans with me and explained everything
in more detail than I could handle. Together, we
blocked out a search schedule, concentrating on the

Spacelab. The consensus of opinion was that it would be easier to get a bomb into the lab than the crew module, simply because no one crewman was likely to be familiar with every piece of equipment in the lab.

On this mission the Spacelab carried thirty-seven different experiments, and each one would have to be checked out. Part of the problem was that many of the experiments belonged to corporations and universities all over the world. They paid anywhere from three thousand to half a million dollars to get their experiments into orbit. Some of them were totally automated, and some had to be conducted by the mission specialist. In addition, there were ongoing investigations being conducted by the four scientists on board.

I was going to make those scientists extremely unhappy. I'd have to disassemble every piece of their equipment, ruining their experiments, some of which were still in progress, bomb or no bomb. The *Discovery* crew, against orders from Houston, had already begun a preliminary search, but they'd turned up nothing.

By evening I felt familiar with every nook and cranny on the Shuttle. But Braxton told me that when I actually got up there, I'd probably find that I was badly disoriented. In zero-G you see things from strange angles and can fail to recognize familiar objects. If I did get confused, I could always broadcast TV pictures back to Houston and get help from the ground.

My final instruction session was the most important, from my point of view. I was shown the self-contained maneuvering unit I'd have to use to get from the *Columbia* to the *Discovery*. It looked like a portable dentist's chair, or a backpack with armrests. The backpack was about a foot thick and three feet wide and extended from neck to buttocks, with a fuel tank below that, reaching down to the knees. The armrests stuck out like the tines of a forklift and housed the controls. There were six separate thrusters arrayed on the unit. Each one would spurt out jets of nitrogen gas that would propel me in the direction I wanted to go—or in directions I didn't want to go, if I wasn't careful.

The entire contraption weighed several hundred pounds on the ground, so it was impossible for me to get in any flight time. I played with the thruster controls and tried to imagine my motions in free fall, but complete freedom of movement in three dimensions is difficult to visualize when you've spent your entire life in what is basically a two-dimensional environment. Braxton told me I'd get the hang of it quickly enough in orbit. It was much easier, he said, than flying a helicopter.

Lift-off was set for 7:33 A.M. Monday morning. By nine o'clock on Sunday night my schooling was completed. It was a little like trying to get a Harvard education by reading the course catalog. In the morning I'd merely felt uninformed; now, I felt truly ignorant. I'd learned just enough to realize how much I hadn't learned.

The instruction sessions had at least kept my mind off the central issue. Tomorrow morning I was going to be launched into outer space. Details about thruster controls and zero-gravity defecation seemed insignificant beside that one overwhelming fact.

Wheeler took me to the astronauts' sleeping quarters and told me to relax and not worry about anything. His team was the best in the world, and they'd get me up and back without a hitch. I thanked him and said I'd sleep like a baby.

I'm not sure if I slept at all. I kept having weird, dreamy fantasies about flying and floating aimlessly through an endless dark. Perhaps that *is* how babies sleep, dreaming of the only thing they remember, the womb.

Once, I got up and stumbled through the darkness to a window. Miles away, I saw the brilliance of the floodlights fixed on pad 39A, where the *Columbia* was poised for flight, strapped piggyback on the immense bullet of the booster rocket. I stared at it for a long time before going back to bed.

They came in to wake me at four-thirty. The lights went on, and the floating fantasies receded but didn't quite vanish. They hovered around me, not quite real, like something you think you see out of the corner of your eye.

Doctors and technicians fussed over me solicitously, filling the gray pre-dawn with an artificial cheer, a kind of emotional "Tang." When they served me a steaming hot breakfast of bacon, scrambled eggs, coffee, and juice, I realized that the whole scene reminded me of morning on Death Row. Astronauts and condemned killers are the only people who ever have an entire squad of people assigned to make sure they enjoy breakfast.

The technicians taped biomedical sensors to my chest and back while the doctors tapped my knees and looked into my orifices to make sure I hadn't contracted bubonic plague overnight. I took an antinausea injection in the left cheek and smiled grimly at the jokes about this job being a big pain in the ass. Then I got into my quilted astronaut underwear and my golden-brown coveralls and waited to be told what to do next.

McNally and Wheeler arrived, and everyone else

left. McNally looked as if he had been up all night, and Wheeler looked as if he had been up all year.

"Any last-minute instructions?" I asked them.

"Not exactly," said McNally. "But wheels have been turning."

"And?"

"Washington has decided to lay all the cards on the table, face up. Last night the President got on the Hot Line and talked with some folks in the Kremlin. He let them know that we are aware of the KGB's interest in the Shuttle, and that we don't appreciate it. He told them that any interference with our operations would be considered a hostile act, and that we would take appropriate measures."

"As opposed to inappropriate measures?"

"Boggs, this is a high-stakes game. As soon as *Columbia* reaches orbit, SAC will go to a modified yellow alert. We want the Soviets to know that we're ready to deal with any situation that might develop."

I shook my head in wonder. "You mean you guys are prepared to blow up the planet in order to save the Shuttle?"

"I wouldn't put it quite that way. But we have to show some backbone here, for the sake of the European powers as well. Some of the governments over there have begun to waffle after that bomb went off at ESA. The Italians say they may release their prisoners on schedule. The British haven't made up their minds yet. They're all pretty nervous about Spartacus and the Omegas."

"Well, so am I. I mean, why did they give us enough time to launch a rescue mission? My guess is that they are mighty damn confident that the bomb on *Discovery* can't be disarmed. I think they want us to find that out for ourselves. Then we might be more willing to give them what they want."

"Forget that, Boggs. A few terrorists may end up on the street if the Europeans get scared, but there's no way we're going to pull our troops off the Continent. The Omegas certainly can't make us do it. Neither can the Soviets."

"You think they'll try anything?"

"They could," said Wheeler. "Four hours ago, they launched their own shuttle."

"What? I didn't even know they had one."

"It's called Kosmolyot. They haven't publicized it yet because it still has some bugs. We think they lost one last year. Premature booster cutoff combined with a failure of separation. It crashed in Siberia. But if the Kosmolyot is fully operational, it's the equal of the Shuttle. In any case, they've got one in orbit right now."

"How close to the *Discovery*?"

"Close enough to make us suspicious. With a two-degree plane change, it could match orbits."

I didn't like the sound of it. There were still too many loose ends in this mess. How many of them led to the Russians?

"What do you think, Mac? Are they going to try anything?"

"Washington doubts it. They probably just want to observe."

"Probably? You mean they don't really know."

"Not for certain," McNally admitted. "But the prevailing theory now is that Dietrich was running his own operation and needed help from the KGB. They provided it, but when we got too close to Dietrich, they decided to close shop. They already had what they wanted—a bomb on the *Discovery*—and they didn't care whether the Omegas got what they were after or not."

"Great. I love prevailing theories. But tell me, what do we do if you're wrong? What if this Kosmolyot matches orbits, turns on its siren, and tells us to pull over to the curb? What then?"

"You don't need to worry about that," said McNally. "Your one and only job is to find that bomb and disarm it. Braxton and Anderson will handle everything else."

"Is that supposed to comfort me?"

"What you don't know, you can't worry about."

"Wrong, Mac. I'm worrying plenty right now."

"Don't. We'll handle it. Trust me."

Wheeler clapped me on the shoulder. "Cheer up," he said. "You're about to make history. The first common man ever to go into space."

"All I want," I told him, "is to be the first common man ever to *come back* from space."

I don't remember much about how I got from my quarters to the flight deck of the *Columbia*. I do recall feeling light-headed and weak-kneed and worrying about the queasy sensation in the pit of my stomach. The antinausea potion they'd given me didn't seem to be doing much good; I wasn't even in motion yet.

What I needed was an antifear injection. I remember Braxton and Anderson making idle, joking small talk in the van that took us to the launching pad. They were so cool, I wanted to scream.

I'd known fear and fright before, too many times, perhaps. But this was something new to me. I didn't understand why I felt the way I did, and because I didn't understand it, the apprehension grew worse. It wasn't the controlled fear I always experienced when I was working with a bomb, and it wasn't the blind panic I felt when Korbach was pursuing me through that nightmare landscape. This was a brand-new shade of fear, a color never before seen on my emotional spectrum.

The van delivered us to the gantry elevator. Woodenly, I followed the others into the elevator. We went up, and even that tiny acceleration was enough to make my stomach climb halfway up my throat. I swallowed hard and kept on swallowing, trying to keep all the demons inside me. If I let them out, I knew I'd never be able to get into the spacecraft. Fear was all I had now, and if I let it go, there wouldn't be anything left of me.

Braxton moved next to me. He looked at me for a moment. I couldn't even focus on him.

"Boggs," he said quietly, "let me tell you something. From the moment you get into that ship, you're part of my crew. You understand? It doesn't matter what you're doing here, or how you got here, or what you did before. You're part of my crew. I take care of my crews, Boggs. That's my job. You do yours, and I'll do mine. Got it?"

I nodded. Braxton looked at me for a few seconds more. Then the elevator lurched to a stop, the doors opened, and we trooped out.

We were in a large room, enclosing most of the nose of the *Columbia*. From a distance the Shuttle looked just a little comical, with its fat fuselage, stubby wings, and blunt nose. Up close it didn't even look like a vehicle. The surface of the nose section was coated in a reusable insulated tile which would serve as a heat shield on reentry. The tiles were laid out exactly like a brick wall, with row after row of rectangular slabs. They gave the inescapable impression that the entire spacecraft was constructed of bricks.

A brick spaceship. A Jules Verne vehicle·if ever there was one. Inside, there would be plush carpets and graceful Victorian furniture, perhaps a bottle or two of brandy. And cigars, of course. Polished brass knobs on all the controls, and a crystal chandelier to let us read the *Times* in gaslit splendor.

It would have been a pleasant way to travel. I played with those thoughts while the ground crew led me in through the hatch. I was in the mid-deck of the Shuttle, and the Victorian fantasies vanished as I surveyed the antiseptic fixtures. The place looked like the inside of a computer cabinet.

To get to the flight deck, I had to crawl up a wall, past an utterly useless ladder. Sitting on its tail, the Shuttle was ill-adapted for normal movement. I crawled through another hatch ("Primary Interdeck Access"), clambered over and around the Spacecraft Commander's seat, then down to my own seat. The ground crew strapped me in, then got out of the way while Anderson and Braxton climbed into position with practiced ease.

I was wearing my bulky space suit during all of these maneuvers, and I found myself feeling relieved just to be sitting in one place without having to move. Space suits should not be worn anywhere but in space; on the ground, they are hot and awkward, and as completely useless as a Hart, Schaffner & Marx three-piece suit would be in orbit. It was a bad interface, as they say in the space biz.

The cabin was pressurized, but during lift-off I'd have to wear my helmet anyway. If something went badly wrong early in the flight, I wouldn't have to worry about sudden decompression. The last of the ground crew made sure I had my helmet sealed properly, then plugged my suit into the cabin oxygen supply. He tapped me on the visor, gave me a thumbs up, then climbed back up between Braxton and Anderson. A moment later he was gone. They closed the hatch and left us alone in there.

Now that there was nothing for me to do except listen to the incessant chatter of the radio, I closed my eyes, took deep measured breaths, and tried to relax. There was no point in worrying now. I was part of Braxton's crew. He'd take care of me.

My faith in Braxton was not unlimited. I managed to find a hundred things to fret about during the long drone of the countdown. I worried about the health of things like differential-pressure transducers and the flash-evaporator system. It occurred to me that all of the marvelous gizmos surrounding me had been built by the low bidder.

My palms were sweaty. Presently, the rest of me was sweaty. The oxygen flowing into my suit was supposed to keep me cool, but it was not up to the task. I began to itch. You can't scratch in a space suit.

They finally called off "Mission Specialist," and I responded with a firm "Go." I suspected that if I'd screamed "No!" they would have gone right ahead with the countdown.

The last minute blinked away on the digital display above my head. One glowing red number magically became another, smaller number each second. Soon, there would be no numbers left.

At fifteen seconds I heard Braxton's voice in my earphone.

"Boggs."

"What?"

"Just remember this," he said. "If my ass gets there, your ass gets there. And my ass is gonna get there."

Before I could reply, I felt a deep, sonorous vibration, a rumbling chord from the left hand of the piano. Bassoons, bass fiddles, trombones, and sousaphones joined in, shaking my gut with Wagnerian power. It was a music for behemoths, for creatures who dwelt in caverns, belching fire and farting earthquakes, an unearthly rock and roll for teen-age titans. And the lyrics to this awful song crackled in twangy country-western counterpoint:

"We have lift-off."

Ah, God, such a song!

CHAPTER 12

If you like amusement parks, if you're a roller coaster, loop-the-loop, fifty-cents-a-ride-let's-do-it-again freak; if you used to hang around the merry-go-round and the whirligig; or if you drive like Joie Chitwood, downshift at sixty and take the turns on two wheels, if you stand on the brakes and tromp on the gas; or if you skydive, skin dive, or swan dive; or even if you sit in dark, reefer-scented rooms with headphones clamped to your cranium and bass, treble, and volume set on "Stun," then it's possible that you may enjoy space flight.

It was too late to be afraid, so I wasn't. Perhaps the G forces squeezed the fear right out of me, like an apple in a cider press. The vibrations subsided as we took our leave of the earth, but they were soon replaced by a steady, insistent pressure that made breathing a chore and everything else impossible. Braxton and Anderson didn't seem to mind, but I felt as if I had been dipped in bronze. My head felt like a bowling ball balanced on a pipe cleaner; my chin dug into my chest and my eyeballs sank back into my skull. I had become a puny, five-hundred-pound weakling.

I was aware of staccato conversations between Braxton and people back on the ground. They recited numbers and sounded downright cheerful. I looked forward and saw Anderson reaching over his head to flick a couple of switches. I was suitably impressed by his feat of strength.

I was even more impressed when I looked out the forward viewpoint. The blue Florida sky had turned the color of india ink. And Florida, I reminded myself, was already a hundred miles behind us.

"How you doin', Boggs?" Braxton asked.

"Fine," I croaked.

"Coming up on separation," said someone on the ground.

I felt a brief shudder run through the spacecraft, then a sudden lessening of the pressure that was pushing me into my padded seat. Before I could enjoy it, the vibrations began again and the pressure resumed, stronger than before.

"We have separation," said Braxton calmly, "OMP operation nominal."

That meant that we had shed the two solid-fuel boosters, and were now using the orbiter main propulsion system. The fuel from the huge tank under our belly—a million and a half pounds of it—was pumped into the *Columbia* and transformed to a searing fire in the Shuttle's main engines.

I had lost my time sense entirely. We could have been on the OMP for hours. In fact, it was less than eight minutes. Braxton warned me what was coming next.

"We'll dump the tank in about forty seconds," he

said, with all the professional boredom of an airline captain pointing out downtown Zanesville beneath our left wing. "Then we'll go on OMP for a couple of minutes. I suggest you get out of your helmet now."

I didn't need a diagram to see what he meant. I hauled my leaden arms up to my head and gave my helmet a twist. I lifted it up over my head, then quickly brought it down to my lap. I was finally able to scratch my nose if I wanted, but I didn't think it would be worth the effort required.

There was a loud thump from somewhere within the ship, and then an unexpected moment of weight-lessness, as brief as you'd feel in an express elevator. Then more pressure, as the engines switched over to internal fuel. The empty tank was left behind us and was destined to splash down somewhere in the Indian Ocean. Meanwhile, we were headed for orbit.

"OMP cutoff in ten seconds," someone announced. I closed my eyes, sucked in my stomach muscles, and waited.

It wasn't a dramatic event, like lift-off. It was al-most pleasant. Everything simply came to a stop. The rumbling, the vibration, the lead-weight pressure, even the crackling in my headset, all just stopped.

I was astonished to see my helmet drifting upward from my lap, rotating lazily, till it tapped me gently on the tip of my nose. I grabbed it and pulled it back down.

Zero-G, by God. The only thing I could compare it to was scuba diving off San Vincente, when you're perfectly weighted and exquisitely balanced. My arms had a tendency to float up from the rest of my body. I felt giddy and curiously energetic. I wanted to do handsprings or some damn fool thing.

Anderson looked back and grinned at me. I grinned

back. He pointed to the viewport, slightly ahead of
me on the right. I looked.

There was something huge and blue out there. The
light reflecting from it was dazzling.

"The Indian Ocean," Anderson informed me. "Just
south of Sri Lanka."

"Jesus," I said. The window was too small to grasp
the size of it all, so there was no sense of scale, no
ant-size people or matchbox cars to wonder at. There
was no instinctive way to calculate relationships and
distances. I was suddenly outside every frame of reference I'd ever known. Yet the immensity of that tur-
quoise gumball was unmistakable. That was the earth
out there, and I was no longer a part of it.

"You can unstrap if you want," said Anderson. "Go
over to the port and enjoy. Just be careful and try not
to kick anything important."

I undid the buckle of my seat belt and watched in
fascination as the straps wiggled back and forth like
sea plants waving in the current. I shoved off with the
tips of my fingers and found myself floating toward
the ceiling. I felt like giggling.

You can't swim in air. Flailing your arms and legs
will not change your direction. You can't stop and you
can't speed up. You just keep going. I kept going until
I rapped the top of my head on the cockpit ceiling. I
pushed off again and drifted back down toward the
floor. I pulled my knees into my chest and wrapped
my hands around my ankles. That was enough to start
me rotating, and I managed a full revolution around
my own center of mass before I bumped into my seat
again.

I righted myself in relation to Anderson and Braxton, then shoved off of the seat's armrest and sailed

toward the starboard viewport, to the right of Anderson. I hit the wall a little hard and bounced off. Anderson grabbed me as I went by and pulled me back over to the window.

"Steady," he said. "Hang on to the back of my chair and don't do any more aerobatics. Not enough room for that in here."

I hardly heard him. I had my nose pressed up against the window and was staring at the earth below us. It was hypnotic. The globe was so huge that its curvature was obvious only on the horizon, which was a hazy band of light blue that trailed off into utter blackness. Directly below us I could glimpse what must have been the southern coastline of Sri Lanka, all green and brown and flecked with white clouds. Farther south, the intense blue of the ocean was blotted out by a huge cloud-bank that extended all the way to the horizon.

I focused on the horizon and gradually became aware of our motion toward it. Brown dots got bigger and closer, and then a long green coastline crawled into view. Malaysia, I calculated. Somewhere down there, they were sipping Singapore slings before dinner at the Raffles.

Braxton and Anderson did their jobs while I gawked like the tourist I was. We were heading southeast, I knew, at an inclination of thirty-five degrees to the equator; when we reached 35 degrees south latitude, we'd head north again, relative to the earth. Australia's west coast came into view on the horizon, as did the terminator line and night. We left the sun behind us, rising over Florida, as we plunged into an Asian sunset.

I saw lights, twinkling like stars. But up here the

stars did not twinkle, and the lights were below us.
Perth, Australia. Half a million people, indistinguish-
able from a lightning bug.

"God *damn!*" I exulted. "In-fucking-credible!"

I realized something even more incredible: I was
having so much fun, I had completely forgotten to be
sick.

But I remembered in a hurry.

Anderson helped me chase down and bag the last of
my scrambled eggs. I was embarrassed, but Anderson
was remarkably cool about the whole thing, despite
the trouble I'd caused him. Braxton seemed mildly annoyed.

"Okay, Boggs," he said. "That's it. One to a customer."

"Sorry," I said meekly.

"Don't sweat it. Happened to me my first time up.
You'll be okay if you relax and let your body adjust."

"How could anyone ever adjust to this?"

"They do, and you will, too. For now, though, you
should get yourself strapped in again. We'll be maneuvering in a few minutes, soon as we reacquire Houston."

Unlike the Apollo missions, which were in almost
constant communication with the mission controllers
at Houston, the Shuttles were on their own a large
percentage of the time. A globe-girdling ground network was too costly to maintain, and there was no real
need for it. We had been in touch via a station in Australia while I was busy being sick, but we wouldn't
reacquire Houston for another few minutes, when Hawaii hove into view.

I strapped into my seat again and tried to keep my

mind on the coming maneuvers. My stomach felt like a large, empty volleyball, embedded just south of my esophagus.

Somewhere over the Pacific, we reacquired Houston. The communicator on this shift was another good old boy with a grits-and-hush-puppies accent.

"Got your orbit numbers, Brax," he said cheerfully.

"Read 'em off," said Braxton.

"Apogee is one ninety-four point three miles, perigee is one eighty-seven point eight miles. You're a couple of miles too high, *Columbia*. We'll be doing a short burn in a few minutes. Stand by for some more numbers."

"Roger, Houston."

The computers in Houston had already calculated exactly what we'd have to do to rendezvous with the *Discovery*. All Braxton had to do was feed the correct numbers into our own computer.

I busied myself with some calculations of my own. I had been surprised by the immensity of the earth when I looked out the window. I'd somehow imagined it as small and far below us. But we were only two hundred miles over the surface of a sphere that was eight thousand miles in diameter. If the earth were the size of a baseball, we'd be skimming along barely a tenth of an inch above it; if the earth were a peach, we'd be hedgehopping the fuzz.

"Here we go," Braxton announced.

I heard a muted roar from within the ship, then felt a slight tug on my body. I was settling deeper into my seat as gravity again brushed over us. The sensation was actually a trifle annoying. I wanted to get back to zero-G again.

We did, soon enough. The engine burn lasted less

than a minute. Braxton confirmed cutoff, and Houston told us that we were on the money.

The *Discovery* was somewhere ahead of us, slightly below our altitude. During the course of the next orbit, we would gradually overtake her. When visual contact was established, Braxton would jockey our reaction-control subsystem system—a collection of small thrusters in the nose and the tail—to stabilize us relative to the *Discovery*. The *Discovery* itself would be passive throughout, since they didn't dare take a chance of applying even momentary gravity to the bomb.

The bomb. Damn, I hadn't even thought about it. In a couple of hours I was going to have to start earning my flight pay.

And that brought another thought: I wasn't even on the payroll! Here I was, risking my neck and other vital spots on behalf of Uncle Sam, and they weren't even going to pay me.

That was okay, though. If I'd known what it was going be like up here, I'd have paid *them*. Gladly.

"There she is," said Anderson. He pointed to a gleaming dot visible through the viewport in front of Braxton. It looked more like a distant streetlight than a spaceship to me, but I was willing to take Anderson's word for it.

"*Discovery*, *Columbia* here," Braxton said into his radio mike. "We have visual contact."

"*Columbia*," came the reply, crackling over my headset, "we see you coming. You look awful pretty, Brax."

The *Discovery* didn't look bad, either. It was growing noticeably larger each second. We were oriented so that the earth was "up," over our heads. The *Discovery* was a delta-shaped trinket that seemed to be rising out of the Gulf of Mexico. As we got closer, I noticed red and green acquisition lights blinking on the ship's wing tips.

"You guys just sit tight," said Braxton, "and we'll be sittin' on your doorstep in a few minutes."

"Roger, *Columbia*. We'll have the welcome mat out."

"*Discovery*, Houston," said a new voice on the loop. "We copy visual contact. At my mark, thirty seconds to burn. And . . . mark."

"Houston, we copy. We're looking for a delta V of thirteen mps."

"That's it, Brax."

I strapped myself in again and waited. Anderson and Braxton flipped a few switches. Braxton gripped the stubby joystick on the panel in front of him, then nervously flexed his fingers a couple of times. He'd done this before, but a maneuver like this wasn't exactly duck soup.

Braxton fired the nose thrusters, producing a quick surge of G forces, about the equivalent of braking your car suddenly. I pressed forward against my safety strap. The burn ended after only a few seconds, and I rebounded back into my seat.

The burn didn't seem to have had much effect. We were still falling toward the *Discovery* at what seemed to be an undiminished rate. She was near enough now that I could read the "USA" painted on her tail fin.

"Closing at three mps," said Anderson.

"Close enough for government work. Range?"

"Sixteen forty meters."

"Check," said Braxton. "Boggs, you still with us?"

"Where else would I be?"

"Don't know. But that's where you're going. We'll

close to about a kilometer and then park 'er. You'll have to go the rest of the way on foot."

Distances are difficult to judge in space, but the *Discovery* still looked a long way off for pedestrian traffic.

"You couldn't maybe nudge her a little closer, could you?"

"Houston would shit. Look, Boggs, I'd like to drop you off on their starboard wing, but we just can't risk it. You're looking at our entire operational fleet of Orbiters. We can't afford to lose one, let alone two. If the *Discovery* blows, we don't want to lose this baby, too. Don't sweat it. Anderson'll hold your hand the whole way. Range?"

"Eleven-eighty."

"Two thirds of a mile, Boggs," Braxton assured me. "You couldn't get lost if you tried."

"You make it sound like a walk in the park. Just a casual jaunt in outer space with no umbilical. Tell me, Cap'n, how'd you make out the first time you tried it?"

"I haven't," he said.

"Oh? Well, what about you, Anderson?"

"Uh, I haven't tried it yet, either. Just short hops outside our own ship."

I didn't like the sound of this. "You mean to tell me that neither one of you guys has ever done this before?"

"Well," said Braxton, "the fact is, nobody has."

"*What?*"

"We never had two ships up at the same time before. For satellite retrieval or placement, we get close and use the payload handling arm. There's never been an opportunity to try this before."

I hit the ceiling, literally. You can't pound your fist

on an armrest in zero gravity, not without running into Dr. Newton and his famous third law. I bounced back to my seat and restrapped myself.

"I don't believe this," I said. "You mean *nobody* has ever done a ship-to-ship transfer? And you didn't even bother to tell me?"

"Hell, Boggs, the first man to jump with a parachute was scared, too. But he made it."

"Fine. Give me a parachute."

"Won't help you a bit up here. You just relax and leave the driving to us. Range?"

"Ten-twenty," said Anderson.

"Good, good. You know, this reminds me of when I was back at the Air Force Academy. We had to go on this survival hike. They dropped us off up in the mountains with nothing but three matches and a knife, and we had to figure out how to stay alive for three days. We'd never done it before, but—"

"Mark," said Anderson.

"Whoops. Sorry 'bout that." Braxton squeezed the thruster control, giving it a couple of gentle squirts.

"Rate of closure is point three mps," said Anderson.

Braxton nudged the controls again. I was amazed by his delicate touch. Hell, I couldn't even parallel-park.

"Bingo," said Anderson.

"Range?"

"Eight-eighty," said Anderson.

"Damn. Overshot. Got so wrapped up in that story, I missed the mark. Well, there's no point in trying it all over again. Sorry, Boggs, but we're about a hundred twenty meters closer than we're supposed to be."

"Thanks," I said, grinning at him. "You don't have any more stories, do you?"

"Fresh out. Eight-eighty's okay, though. I used to run the eight-eighty in track."

"Really? What was your time?"

"Phenomenal. Really phenomenal."

Anderson tapped me on the helmet. "All set, Boggs. How do you feel?"

"Increasingly stupid. Whose idea was this, anyway?"

Anderson, also suited up, slung my tool pack over my head so I could carry it like a purse. Not exactly like one, though, since the pack would tend to swing free in the absence of gravity. To prevent this, the pack was stuck to a Velcro tab on my right hip.

Even without gravity I felt bulky and constricted in my suit. We were standing on the mid-deck, next to the side hatch, which was only forty inches in diameter. In space suit and backpack, we could just fit through. We'd have to get into our Buck Rogers maneuvering units outside.

"All ready down here, boss," Anderson announced.

"Okay, kids. We're venting."

Normally, to get outside the Shuttle, astronauts used the air lock on the aft wall of the mid-deck, which led to a tunnel connected with the payload bay. That eliminated the need to purge the cabin air during egress. Unfortunately, the maneuvering units were too much of a problem to get through the tunnel, so we were taking the most direct exit. I couldn't hear it, but all of our air was hissing away into space. Braxton wouldn't repressurize until everyone got back from the *Discovery*.

"Zero pressure," said Braxton. "Have a nice trip."

Anderson floated down to hatch level, hovering calmly a few inches off the floor. He grabbed the hatch lever and pulled it back, then gave the door a gentle push. The hatch swung downward and open. It was absolutely black outside; this was going to be like crawling into a sewer.

Anderson held the sides of the hatchway with both hands and carefully pulled himself through. The top of his backpack snagged for a second, but he was able to free himself without my help. Anderson disappeared outside momentarily. Then I saw his face at the hatchway. Our helmets were polarized, and outside in the sun our heads would look like large golden balloons. Here, illuminated only by the cabin lights, I could make out Anderson's face inside his fishbowl.

I pushed the first of our two maneuvering units toward him. The unit was about four feet long, with two armrests sticking out nearly three feet. It wouldn't quite fit directly through the opening, so we had to jockey it around, as if we were trying to move a big desk or table through a doorway. With no weight, you'd think it would be easy, but it wasn't. There was no weight, but everything still had mass, which forced us to contend with Dr. Newton's first and second laws. I was glad old Isaac stopped at three.

The second unit went through more smoothly than the first. Anderson guided it through and moved it out of the way.

"You're next," he said. "Come on in, the water's fine."

I decided I'd rather take it feet first. I held onto the hatchway and swung my feet through. I felt Anderson grab me by the ankles. He pulled while I pushed, and abruptly, I was outside.

I forced myself to keep my eyes planted on the brick-tiled fuselage of the *Columbia*. I was only too aware of the yawning nothingness on all sides of me; the Shuttle was my only reference point.

"Hold still," Anderson told me. I did, and Anderson moved a maneuvering unit in behind me. He moved it a little too quickly, and the resultant bump sent me sailing into the side of the Shuttle. I bounced back and Anderson steadied me. I felt the control arms of the maneuvering unit slide in under my elbows. I found the shoulder straps and slid my arms through them. I was now a miniature spaceship in my own right.

I floated a few feet away from the *Columbia* to give Anderson room to operate. He handed me the remaining maneuvering unit, then turned his back to me. I carefully positioned the unit and gave it a gentle shove toward him. He clutched at the control arms, steadied himself, then slipped into the shoulder harness.

"Okay, Boggs. Good work. You know how all the controls work, right?"

I nodded. Then I remembered that Anderson wouldn't be able to see a nod in a space suit. The same thing went for winks, raised eyebrows, smiles and frowns.

"I'm ready," I said.

"Okay, then. Try a quick squirt to rotate a hundred eighty degrees. Turn right. When you see the *Discovery* give another squirt with the left."

I rotated a handle on the right, like gunning a motorcycle. I couldn't actually hear the nitrogen jet, but I felt it as a vibration in the maneuvering unit. Anderson quickly disappeared on the left of my faceplate. I saw the rest of the *Columbia*'s fuselage and the stubby wings as I spun to the right.

For a split second there was absolutely nothing in sight. My view of eternal limbo gave me a deep fright, but it disappeared as quickly as it had come. Ahead of me now was the earth, so overwhelmingly beautiful that it was impossible to think of anything else. It seemed so close, as if I had my nose pressed up against a window of a store, and there, in the display case, was the whole of Arabia, on sale. Curving above me, I saw the blue of the Mediterranean and the rocky isles of Greece, as they must have appeared to Zeus himself.

The *Discovery* swung into view. From my vantage point it appeared to be floating in the Persian Gulf, like some sort of ultimate supertanker. It was oriented so that we would be coming in from "above" it. The doors of its payload bay were wide open, exposing the tin can shape of the Spacelab. Aft of the lab there was a collection of scientific paraphernalia, with aerials and booms sticking out at odd angles. Our target was the air lock at the aft end of the Spacelab.

I realized that I should already have hit my thruster. It was too late now. "Missed it," I said to Anderson. "I'll get it the next time around."

"Take your time," he said, "and get it right."

I completed my first rotation and noticed that in the process, I'd moved ten or twelve feet farther away from the *Columbia*. Apparently I hadn't been oriented correctly when I began my spin. Space is exacting and unforgiving; there's no gravity around to cancel out random motions. If I didn't hit my thrusters again, I'd probably just continue to corkscrew away from the ship.

I tried to ignore the earth this time around, but that was not easily done. I wondered if I could see the Suez Canal, and while I was looking for it, I damn near missed the *Discovery* again. Just in time, I hit the controls and spurted out some nitrogen in the opposite direction from my spin. My rotation slowed, then stopped, and finally reversed itself. I gave another short spritz on the right and managed to bring myself to a complete stop.

"Not bad," said Anderson. "Just remember to have a delicate touch. It's like squeezing a virgin's tits."

That cracked me up. Clean-cut All-American astronauts weren't supposed to have dirty minds.

"Okay now," he said, "we're ready to boogie."

"Tits? Boogie? What the hell's gotten into you?"

"Am I getting strange?" he asked in complete seriousness.

"You do sound a little different."

"Oh, hell. Gotta watch myself. Some folks tend to get a little giddy out here. Guess I'm one of them. We've got pure oxy in our tanks, and that can get a little heady after the air in the cabin. Can make you feel drunk. Also, there's a kind of . . . sort of a . . . hell, I can't describe it. Just watch yourself, okay? Don't get too happy. Keep your mind on your work."

Braxton's voice cut into our circuit. "You be careful, too, Ted. Don't go drifting off."

"What are you guys talking about?" I demanded. I had the feeling that there was something they still hadn't told me.

"Don't get excited," said Braxton. "It's nothing to worry about much. You ever been scuba diving, Boggs?"

"Some."

"You know about rapture of the deep? Nitrogen narcosis?"

"You're kidding! We're not even breathing any nitrogen."

"That doesn't really matter. It's mostly a psychological thing. We've had some hints of it in the program, but nothing serious so far. Just keep your mind on your business. Don't get caught up in the mystery and grandeur of it all, okay? That goes for you too, Ted."

"Roger. We'll be fine, Brax. What about it, Boggs? You ready?"

"To boogie? Why not?"

"Okay," Anderson said, "it'll be just the way we planned it. Get yourself lined up with the air lock of the *Discovery*. That's just about mid-ship, so even if you miss, you'll still probably hit something. Remember we want accuracy, not speed. When you think you're about halfway there, turn yourself around, get lined up with the *Columbia*, and hit the jets again. Try to stay even with me, and keep your head pointed north. If you start spinning or wobbling, don't touch anything. Just hang loose till I reach you. Are you lined up?"

I was facing the center of the *Discovery*, and my head was north, in relation to the earth. I didn't feel as if I was perfectly oriented, but I could probably spend hours jiggling the controls without getting it right.

"Let's do it," I said.

"On my mark. We'll burn for five seconds, my count. Here we go. Three . . . two . . . one . . . *mark!*"

I pushed my thruster control forward and immediately felt a tickle of acceleration. I tried to keep my head steady, with the *Discovery* in the center of my faceplate, but I had to fight a tendency to tip forward and to the right. Either my thrusters weren't operating evenly, or my mass was distributed badly. It had to be the damned tool bag.

Anderson was counting. "Three . . . four . . . *five!*"

I let go of the control. The *Discovery* didn't seem much closer than it had been, but I knew I was moving toward it at several feet per second. I turned my head to the left and saw Anderson floating serenely about twenty feet away from me.

"One of us is off line a little," he said, "and I think it's you."

"I think you're right. What should I do?"

"Nothing, for now. We'll try to correct it with the second burn. You're doing fine."

I was doing great, as a matter of fact. For the first time since lift-off I had a sensation of speed. It was exhilarating. We were all—ships and men—whizzing around the earth at eighteen thousand miles per hour, but it seemed as if we had been standing still while the earth whirled beneath us. Now, though, I was definitely moving at a good clip. The *Discovery* was appreciably larger, and that was almost annoying. It blotted out my view of southern Iran. If I could just get it out of my way, I'd be able to see all the way to Pakistan.

The sun was above and behind me, over my left shoulder. Noontime in the States, but late afternoon here. There would be a sunset before long. Sunsets in space were supposed to be unbelievable.

I looked down and saw stars burning steadily between my feet. I hadn't noticed the stars before. God, what would it be like to go to them? To sail the infinite deep, to drift across the unimaginable gulfs of the galaxy. . . .

"Boggs!"

"Hmmm?"

"Snap out of it! You're drifting!"

"No, I'm not. I'm just strolling. Sam Skywalker here. Beam me up, Scotty!"

"Dammit! Boggs, this is Braxton! Get your ass in gear!"

"This rig has gears? How do I get into second?"

"Don't touch anything!" Braxton fairly screamed. It was so loud my eardrums hurt.

"Boggs, you hear me? This is Anderson. We're almost at the halfway point. You've got to get yourself turned around. You understand? You've got to point yourself at the *Columbia.*"

"Hell yes, I understand! Stop shouting at me. I can handle this. Watch me."

Flying this maneuvering unit was the easiest thing in the world—or off it. I twisted my right hand control and immediately started spinning. The sun hit my face, and even with the polarizer, it was brighter than I'd ever seen it. Dazzling. Unbelievable. There it was again.

"Boggs, cut your jet! You're spinning!"

I sure as hell was. It seemed like the sun had become a fantastic cosmic strobe light, flashing once a second. But I was going too fast to see anything else. I raised my hand and tried to shield my eyes.

"That's it! Now hit your left!"

"My left what?"

"The control. The thruster control. With your left hand!"

"I'm getting a little dizzy."

"Use your thruster control and it'll stop."

"Really?" I tried it. Things slowed down considerably. My stomach felt better.

"Now cut it!"

"Like this?" I held both hands up.

"Perfect! Now when I say go, hit your forward thruster. You know which one it is? Right, you got it. Now, three, two, one, *go!*"

I pushed forward on the control and felt the now familiar vibration from the maneuvering unit. This was remarkably easy, once you got the hang of it.

"Cut it!"

"Roger Wilco! A-okay! I copy, Houston. Or Dallas."

"You're doing fine, Boggs. Don't touch anything. I'm right behind you. I'll get you turned around."

I felt something push me, starting me spinning again. I made a half revolution and slammed into Anderson. At least, I figured it must have been Anderson. Didn't look much like him, with that golden bowling ball perched on his shoulders.

"Are you okay?"

"Fine 'n' dandy."

"You see the *Discovery*? I want you to look at it and nothing else, you understand? Just keep looking at the ship and don't look at anything else."

"If you say so." It seemed like a silly thing to do, but I figured that if I did it, Anderson would stop bothering me.

The *Discovery* was close now, no more than a hundred yards away. We were drifting toward it at a very leisurely pace, no more than a foot or two a second. The payload bay doors were wide open, ready to devour us. Someone was standing there watching us. I waved to him. He waved back.

It dawned on me that he was there to catch us if we needed help. Hell, I didn't need help, I was doing fine. Of course, that little spin might have been foolish, but still . . .

"How do you feel?" Anderson asked.

"Okay, I guess. Jesus, this is really something, isn't it."

"You bet. Now keep your mind on business. I can't hold onto you and grab the *Discovery* at the same time. I'm going to let go now. If you need any help, there's a man down there who'll be able to reach you. We're right on target."

"Bull's-eye, eh?"

"Just about. Now get ready."

The *Discovery* was only a few feet away. I was just above the collection of junk in the aft bay. I knew I had to stop soon, or I'd hit and bounce off—or break something. I didn't want to do that. There was something that looked like an empty trash barrel, and I was headed right for it. I figured I could fit inside it. Maybe that was the air lock.

I was just about to sail into the trash barrel head-first, when someone clutched my backpack and jerked me away. I tried to stop, but there was nothing to hold on to. I kept going until I banged into something soft. I started to rebound, but a gloved hand suddenly grabbed my by the chest, and I came to a stop.

The third astronaut and I were face to face against each other, wedged into a narrow gap between the trash barrel and what looked like another hatch. It occured to me then that what I thought was a trash barrel was very likely something else. It was, in fact, a twenty-million-dollar telescope, and I had nearly walked all over its delicate mirror.

"You okay, Boggs?" asked Anderson. I managed to get turned around and saw Anderson and yet another spacesuited figure, standing on their heads near the air lock.

"I'm fine. Hey, you guys, thanks, whoever you are."

"All part of the service," said one of them. "Welcome to the *Discovery*. It's mighty good to see you."

I couldn't tell which one of them was talking, since both of their helmets were completely polarized. I turned to the man who had snared me and smiled at him, thinking he might be able to see my face in the shadow, even if I couldn't see his. He clapped me lightly on the left shoulder.

"Okay, Boggs, you can get inside now. Get out of that maneuvering unit and crawl into the air lock. Stay there till the door opens. You'll be okay."

"What about you, Anderson?"

"These gentlemen and I have to get back to the *Columbia*. They've got one unit, and we've got two. They'll be enough to ferry everyone across while you do your work."

I managed to get out of the shoulder harness with the help of my anonymous astronaut friend. For a moment I felt naked and unhinged, but someone gave me a shove toward the open air-lock door.

I sailed right into the tiny air lock and the door swung shut behind me. The sight of walls all around me was unnerving for a few moments. In seconds I had gone from a limitless limbo to a coffin-size container. And I still didn't know which way was up.

I found out a moment later. The inner hatch swung open, and I stared into the Spacelab. Staring back at me, upside down, was a beautiful woman.

CHAPTER 13

They pulled me inside. Someone unscrewed my helmet and yanked it off my head. There were people all around me, upside down, sideways, floating, and spinning. They all wanted to shake my hands and slap me on the shoulders.

I was still confused and disoriented. Coming in from outer space was like waking up from some strange, surreal nightmare. I realized that I had been behaving oddly, and that I must have succumbed to a dose of space rapture, or whatever it was called. Understanding it didn't make it any easier to deal with.

"Dr. Boggs," someone said, "welcome aboard!"

"Uh, yeah, thank you."

The speaker had been hanging from the ceiling as he spoke; I didn't know whether to look at his eyes or his Adam's apple. He must have realized I was having problems, so he pushed off the ceiling and did a half gainer that turned him right side up, from my point of view.

"I'm Hollings," he said. "Spacecraft Commander.

You already met Gibbons, the pilot, and Dr. Crespi outside. These folks here are Drs. Stanszak, Nichols, and Morley, and Mission Specialist Powers."

I hadn't been hallucinating after all. Mission Specialist Powers turned out to be the beautiful woman I'd seen through the hatch. Right side up, she looked even better. I knew NASA had several female astronauts, but it hadn't occurred to me that I'd find one on the *Discovery*. I'd expected more or less what I'd gotten in the four men—grubby, red-eyed, unshaven, puffy-faced men of science.

Everyone said hello. Nichols had a deplorable cockney accent, which made him the Britisher. Crespi, the Italian, was already on his way to the *Columbia*. Morley looked wild-eyed and dangerous, like Eli Wallach in an Italian western. Stanszak was the youngest of the lot, a blond All-American kid with broad shoulders and a bald spot. Hollings looked like the runt of the astronaut litter, not at all the square-jawed Braxton type. He was gap-toothed and scrawny and looked like the kid who gets picked last in a softball game and has to play right field. But I knew that Hollings had been to the moon with Braxton.

Mission Specialist Powers was in her early thirties and had a no-nonsense look about her. Thin lips, blue-gray eyes, and close-cropped brown hair that wasn't very flattering—although I could see where long, flowing locks would be no end of trouble in zero-G. I couldn't tell much about the rest of her, since she was clothed, like the others, in the shapeless golden-brown coveralls that NASA was so fond of. But she had a nice smile.

"I guess you'll want to get out of that space suit," said Hollings. "Why don't you follow me into the cabin?"

"Fine." Hollings turned, pushed off, and glided the length of the Spacelab. It looked like fun, but I was in no mood for more gravityless acrobatics. I held on to the instrument cabinets along the right-hand wall and half walked, half bounced toward the forward bulkhead. Hollings helped me get into the connecting tunnel, then gave me a slight shove. The tunnel was about ten feet long and led to the air lock on the middeck of the cabin. The doors were open, so there was no need for cycling.

I bobbed out into the cabin, a twin of the one aboard the *Columbia*, except that this one had a lived-in look. Little bits of trash, a pocket calculator, and a pen were floating around randomly on the air currents.

Hollings floated out behind me. He turned and closed the air-lock hatch.

"How do you feel?" he asked.

"Not too bad," I replied. In fact, I didn't know how I felt. The whole experience was a little like getting off a plane in a strange city and being greeted by a flock of people I'd never seen before. Not unlike my arrival in Bonn.

"We heard you out there," said Hollings. "Sounded like you got a little happy."

"I'm okay now. Just takes a little adjustment."

Hollings began unzipping the umpteen zippers on my space suit while I held on to a table and tried not to get in his way.

"I don't know how much they told you about the situation here," Hollings said as he worked, "but the truth is that you guys got here just in time. We're worn to a thin edge. Houston's been giving us a lot of chin-up bullshit, but nobody's been buying it. I've already had to break up two fights."

"Pretty rough, huh?"

"You put seven people into a glorified subway car, tell them there's a bomb aboard, then leave them there for a week, and yes, it's pretty damn rough. The worst part was not being able to do anything about it. Houston refused to let us hunt for the bomb."

"They were right," I said.

"Maybe. But they were down there and we were up here. We damn near had a mutiny. And let me tell you, I would have led it."

I could easily picture Hollings with an eye patch and a cutlass clenched in his teeth. I had a vague memory of his leading a sit-down strike on one of the Skylab missions. Houston wanted more work from the astronauts, and after nearly six weeks in space, the astronauts told them to fuck off.

"Lift your feet," he said. Instinctively, I lifted my right foot so he could get at my boots. Then I remembered how things were up here; I lifted my left one, too.

"There," he said. "Help me get this stuff stowed." I grabbed my helmet and one boot out of midair and followed Hollings to one of the storage lockers in the forward part of the cabin. When he opened it, a half dozen pieces of space junk popped out. That, I had been told, was the notorious "jack-in-the-box" effect, one of the many small oddities that made life in space tedious. We gathered up the flotsam and stowed it along with my suit.

"Okay," said Hollings, "you can begin work as soon as we get everyone to the *Columbia*. Gibbons'll come back with two extra maneuvering units, and the next two people will leave with him. Then one more trip for the last two."

"That still leaves one," I pointed out.

"That's right." he said. "I'm staying here with you. You're going to need someone to show you around and help you find things."

"I won't object," I said, "but I hope you realize the chance you'll be taking. Disarming a bomb isn't easy anywhere, and up here it may be impossible."

"She's my ship," Hollings said flatly. He was a refreshing man to discover in the technobureaucratic web of NASA. Put him on a four-masted schooner bound for the Horn, and he'd fit right in.

"It may be your ship, Captain Hollings, but it's *my* job!"

We spun around and saw Mission Specialist Powers emerging from the air lock. She looked angry. Behind her was Morley, who also looked angry, but I suspected that wasn't unusual in his case.

"I told you, there's nothing more to discuss!" Hollings said sharply.

"The hell there isn't," Morley objected. "I'm not blowing four years of work just because you want to play Captains Courageous. This is the only shot we'll get, and you're not going to tell me—"

"I already told you! If you don't like it, you can write a memo to NASA when we get back. Now get suited up, you're going in the next shift."

"Not until this is resolved."

"It is resolved. The only question left is whether you'll arrive on the *Columbia* with all your teeth still in your head."

"I'm fed up with you throwing your weight around, Hollings!"

Throwing one's weight around in orbit was a dubious concept, at best, but Morley clearly wasn't going to be bothered by logic. He was hanging onto a bulkhead, feet off the floor, his nostrils flaring. For the first time, I noticed a purplish welt below his left cheekbone. Apparently they'd had a jolly cruise on the good ship *Discovery*.

"There's no need for anyone to get angry again," Powers put in. "Our functions are clearly defined here. Houston will tell you the same thing I told you."

"Houston can go shit in its hat," Hollings told her. "I'm in command here."

"Look," I said gently, "I don't know what's going on, but I think someone ought to tell me before we go any further."

"It's not your worry," said Hollings.

"You'd be surprised how much I can worry about. Now somebody please tell what the hell this is all about."

"It's about four years of important work," said Morley. "It can be accomplished with no additional risk to anyone, but Hollings is too stiff-necked to see that."

"Hold it!" I put in quickly. "Anything that has to do with the bomb is my decision. Not Hollings's, not yours, Morley, and not NASA's. Mine. Now somebody fill me in, and kindly keep the crap to a minimum."

Hollings gave me a nasty look but didn't say anything. Morley still had his gaze fixed on Hollings. I turned to Mission Specialist Powers.

"There's an experiment," she said. "It's Dr. Morley's, and he's right, it is important. We have an opportunity to observe the occultation of a quasar by the planet Mars. An occultation occurs when a planet passes between a distant object and—"

"My doctorate isn't in tiddlywinks. I know what an occultation is."

Powers looked at me. Our eyes locked for a second or two and I found myself wondering what she'd look like back on earth, with the wind in her hair. She

pursed her lips, then continued. "Anyway, the occultation will occur tomorrow. The entire mission schedule
was built around it. We'll be in orbit above the central
Pacific, in perfect position to observe it, in conjunction
with observatories in Europe and the States. Our ob-
servation is critical because it will give us the longest
possible base line. We could get the first good measure-
ments of a quasar. The observational equipment is
mainly external, so the experiment can be run with a
minimum of disruption to your work. There's no good
reason why we shouldn't proceed with the investigation."

"Thank you. What about it, Captain Hollings? Is she
right?"

"Hell no, she's not right. We don't know where that
bomb is or what it would take to set it off. I'm not
about to risk this ship just to satisfy Morley and his
MIT Mafia."

"That is so typical of NASA and this whole fucking
program," Morley agonized. "Science always takes a
backseat while the engineers and flyboys play with
their expensive toys."

"Crap!" Hollings shot back. "You damned eggheads
think that the whole program is there for your conven-
ience. We've got more important things to worry
about than the size of your miserable quasar."

"Knock if off, both of you!" I stomped my foot on
the floor for emphasis and immediately started floating toward the ceiling. There was nothing I could do
about it but wait for a handhold on something.

Hollings turned his attention to me. He looked like
a man poised right on the breaking point. I could
imagine the pressures he had been under, but I was
getting a little sick of refereeing this orbital donny-
brook.

"Boggs," Hollings said tersely, "don't tell me what to do. This is my ship, I make the decisions."

"You're wrong, Hollings. I've been in command since the minute I came through the air lock. If you don't believe me, you can get on the horn and ask Houston. They'll tell you the same thing."

"What is this shit?" Hollings looked angry but wary.

"I'm the bomb expert," I said, "and right now the bomb is the only thing that matters. Dr. Morley, Ms. Powers, I understand your point of view on this. And Hollings, I see your point, too. But in the end, it'll be my decision that counts. Now somebody please tell me, can the quasar experiment be run without maneuvering the ship?"

"Yes," said Powers. "The optical and X-ray telescopes are steerable. No maneuvers will be necessary."

"And how extensive is the equipment?"

"It's complex, but there's not much of it, if that's what you mean," said Morley. "Most of it is outside."

"The bomb could be outside, too," Hollings reminded me.

"Or there might not even be a bomb," said Morley. "We don't have any proof that there is one."

"If it goes off, you'll have all the proof you need," said Hollings.

I could see that Hollings and Morley were getting cranked up for another go-around. I hadn't been on board for a half an hour, but already I was getting sick of it.

"Okay, okay," I said. "I won't make any promises to anyone. But it might be possible to search all the equipment involved in this experiment first and make sure it's clean. Then, if I'm convinced it's safe, I might let you run your experiment. But I'm taking no chances, is that clear?"

"I think you're taking one hell of a chance," said Hollings.

"We're all taking a chance just by being here. What about it, Hollings? Will you run the experiment if I say it's safe?"

"Hollings?" moaned Morley. "You've got to be kidding!"

"Well?"

"Me? I'm just an ignorant bus driver. All that complex science is beyond my pea-brain. I've flown a ship to the moon, but don't ask me to do anything complicated, Boggs. Morley would have an anxiety attack if I even touched his precious equipment."

Hollings didn't look well, and he sounded even worse. His voice was getting high-pitched and whiney. His bloodshot eyes were surrounded by dark, shadowy coronas. It was obvious that his nerves were shot. I no longer wanted him around while I was working with the bomb.

"I can do it," said Powers. "That's my job. I know every piece of equipment in the lab. I could run the experiment and help you search in the meantime."

It was the obvious solution, but for some reason I resisted it. Hollings might crack at any moment, and Morley was a hothead who would be useless for anything but his damned experiment. It had to be Powers, but . . .

"I know what you're thinking, Doctor," she said.

"Oh?"

"I'm a woman and this is a job for a big strong he-man. Isn't that right?"

"I never said—"

"Nobody *says* it! They don't have to. It's in their

eyes, their attitudes, every breath they take. But whether you like it or not, the right man for this job is a woman. Me. If you try to push me out of this, I promise you I'll make a stink like NASA has never seen."

"Uh—"

"I mean it."

"I can see that. What about it, Hollings? Can she do it?"

Hollings looked at the floor. "Why ask me? I'm only the bus driver?"

"I am asking you. I want an answer."

"Hell, yes, she can do it. If she's crazy enough. If you're crazy enough to let her. You want to run things, go ahead and run them. You make the decisions, Boggs, because I'm sick of it. Do what you want. Tell Houston I've retired. Tell them anything you want."

Hollings pivoted, then abruptly sailed out of sight, up into the flight deck. I felt sorry for him, but I was glad he was out of the way. He was trained as a test pilot, not a group encounter therapist. There are times when it's just not enough to be brave and competent.

"Morley? Will you be satisfied if Powers stays here to run the experiment?"

"That's all I wanted in the first place."

"Fine. Now get suited up, I want you off this ship."

"With pleasure." Morley paused long enough to give me a brief, venomous stare, then he disappeared into the tunnel.

That left me alone with Powers. She relaxed and a faint smile appeared. "Dr. Morley," she said, "is known and hated on three continents."

"And over them. How long has Hollings been like this?"

"The last two or three days, he's been . . . well,

difficult. He gave Morley that shiner yesterday. He's a good man, but he couldn't stand not being able to do anything. He wanted to ignore Houston and hunt for the bomb ourselves. We managed to talk him out of it. I feel badly for him. I don't think they'll give him another mission after this."

"He'd be crazy to want one."

She smiled again. "I can see you don't know much about astronauts," she said.

I watched Gibbons, the last of our shipmates, as he disappeared into the forward hatch of the *Columbia*, half a mile away. Gibbons and Anderson had alternated on the ferry run between the two ships. The whole operation was reminiscent of the classic mathematical puzzle about a group of people who want to get to the other side of a river and have only one boat which holds just three people How do you get everyone over with a minimum number of trips? In our case, we also had to end up with two maneuvering units for us on the *Discovery* and one for the *Columbia*. After everyone was gone, Gibbons had to make an extra trip to tow the maneuvering units back to us, and then return alone.

Before Hollings left, I asked him to do a search of the external equipment connected with Morley's experiment. He was sullen about it, but I think he was glad to have a chance to do something constructive. There was a television camera mounted aft of the Spacelab, so I was able to watch him as he worked. He hovered around the antennas and detectors like a gourmet hummingbird in search of the perfect nectar. His mastery of the maneuvering unit was impressive, and his performance was flawless; he didn't look like a man on the brink of a nervous breakdown. On the other hand, the pressure was off Hollings. He was out of it now, and the ball was in my court.

"Time to go to work," I said to Powers after the *Columbia*'s hatch closed. We had been watching Gibbons through the window in our hatch.

"Just tell me what to do," she said.

"What you have to do is stay out of the way. That's your primary responsibility."

"I thought we'd overcome that male chauvinist nonsense."

"We have, we have. Rest assured, you'll hear not a single oink from me. I'm telling you exactly what I'd have told Hollings. Disarming bombs is not a spectator sport. I don't want you peering over my shoulder and joggling my elbow. You can help me hunt and tell me what I need to know about the equipment. Beyond that, just stay out of my way."

"I certainly shall," she said huffily. She floated away from me, then dived into the tunnel headfirst. I shook my head, wondering if my social etiquette was everything it should be.

A moment later Powers reemerged from the tunnel. She floated toward me slowly, an embarrassed half-smile on her face.

"Dr. Boggs? I think I owe you an apology. You've come a long way to help us, and all you've gotten for your trouble so far is a lot of static from everyone. Including me."

"Well, shucks, ma'am, I weren't expectin' no medals."

She laughed softly, and I gave her a big shit-eating grin. I decided I'd done a pretty good job of choosing my shipmate.

"Dr. Boggs," she began.

"It's Sam," I told her. I extended my hand. She took it, and we shook hands. She had soft skin.

"I'm Victoria," she said. "But they call me Vic."

"*They* can call you whatever they want. I'll call you Victoria. We need a little more class around here."

"We need a hell of a lot more than that," she said, releasing her grip on my hand. She spun around and floated back into the tunnel.

I followed her into the Spacelab. The lab was only about twenty-five feet long and barely a dozen feet in diameter, and it was crammed full of equipment. Still, it seemed much roomier than the crew module. There was a row of computer cabinets along the center line of the lab, dividing the floor into two aisles. More electronics lined the walls and ceiling.

The lab was not designed with zero gravity in mind. It looked pretty much like a normal, if small, laboratory on earth. On the earlier Skylab missions one section of the lab had been designed to take complete advantage of zero-G, with instruments and consoles projecting every which way from the walls. Most of the astronauts had hated it. Without gravity, each person seeks his own local vertical, so any direction can be "up" at any given moment. But as soon as you move around, so does "up," with the predictable result of confusion and disorientation. Some of the Skylab astronauts actually became momentarily lost inside their lab. To prevent this, the smaller Spacelab was designed to keep "up" constant.

Even in a rationally designed environment it can still be inconvenient to go floating around all the time. For my work, particularly, I'd have to be firmly anchored. Fortunately, the floor of the Spacelab consisted of a metal latticework with thousands of small triangular holes. Special mushroom-shaped cleats could be attached to our shoes, and the cleats fit neatly into the gridwork. The system worked well as an anchor, but if you tried to move too quickly, you could sprain your ankle.

Consulting with Houston, Powers and I had already developed a search procedure. The ground controllers were ambivalent about the decision to go ahead with the quasar experiment, but they agreed to let me make the final determination. They wanted Powers to keep a TV camera trained on me as much of the time as possible. I didn't especially like that, but I gave in when Powers told me that it would only amount to about thirty-five minutes out of each ninety-minute orbit. The rest of the time we wouldn't be in communication anyway.

We got to work with a minimum of conversation. With Powers's help I removed the outside panels from Morley's equipment. I needed her help just to keep track of all the nuts and bolts. They had a tendency to float away as soon as I let go of them. I became fairly proficient at leaving big objects such as screwdrivers hanging almost motionless in midair, but it was almost impossible to do that with all the tiny widgets. Inevitably, as you release a small object, your fingers impart a little spin or motion to it, and that's all it takes. The trick is to release an object evenly, like pitching a knuckle ball. Most of the time I threw curves and sliders, forcing Powers to chase after everything. Some of the stuff got away and we never did find it.

After I removed the panels, Powers aimed the camera at the equipment to give Houston a good look. They didn't see anything amiss and neither did Powers. I hadn't expected that they would. Our bomber was too clever to leave anything obvious, like, say, a stick of dynamite taped to a wiring terminal.

I studied circuitry diagrams, comparing them to

what I saw inside the instrument cabinet. That was more difficult than it sounds, because reality is seldom as tidy as an engineer's drafting table. It was necessary to check the circuitry because the "bomb" might not be a bomb at all. Switching a few key wires could be just as effective and deadly as planting a keg of blasting powder. A short circuit in the wrong place could start a fire that would gut the entire Spacelab.

It was tedious. It was boring. It was scary. Imagine a CPA at tax time whose adding machine is rigged to explode in his face if he makes an incorrect entry. If the FBI ever wants to recruit a team of bomb specialists, they should concentrate on the people who build ships in bottles and engrave the Old Testament on the heads of pins. They have the right mentality for the job.

I completely lost track of time. So did Powers, apparently, for she was as surprised as I was when a brand-new set of voices came on the Houston loop. The midnight shift had just come on duty.

"Midnight?" I looked up from the third of Morley's four instrument cabinets and tried to find a window. There were none, not that it mattered.

"Roger," said somebody in Houston. "You folks have been at it for quite a while."

Powers floated over to the squawk box on the wall, as if to get closer to the voice in Houston. "Why didn't somebody tell us?" she demanded. "We haven't even eaten today!"

"Sorry, *Discovery*," came the embarrassed reply from Houston. "Everyone was pretty wrapped up in the work. How are you doing?"

"We're about three quarters finished with Morley's equipment. We haven't found anything yet. We'd have told you if we did."

"We know that, honey," the controller said sooth-ingly.

"I'm not your honey, Houston!"

"Uh, roger, Powers. You have our apologies. How is Boggs?"

"Boggs is pooped," I said. "Boggs wants to know if he can have dinner, a stiff drink, and a hot shower."

There was a pause while they discussed it in Texas. Maybe they had to go upstairs for a decision.

"We can give you a Go on dinner, *Discovery.* Sorry, no booze on economy flights. Our recommendation here is that you knock off work for the night and get some sleep. We'll give you a wake-up call around six. That will leave you time to finish what you're doing before the quasar occultation, if you still plan to go ahead with the experiment."

"We do," I said.

"We'll go along with that for now, *Discovery,* but we may change our minds overnight. Remember, the deadline is just under twenty-four hours from now. You need to get some sleep, but we may not have time to spend on the experiment."

"Any word from the Omegas?" I asked.

There was a pause, then a new voice took over. With a start, I realized it was McNally.

"Another calling card from Spartacus. This one was planted at NASA headquarters. We got lucky, though. A janitor found it in a waste can, and they got rid of it before it went off."

"Was there a letter?"

"There was. Spartacus expressed the hope that we'd be able to rescue our people before the bomb goes off on *Discovery.*"

"Thoughtful of him. Anything else?"

"Negative," said McNally. "Nothing from the Russians, either. Kosmolyot is behind and above you, but it's not maneuvering. We'll keep you informed."

"Thanks, Mac."

"Boggs?"

"What?"

"What's it like up there?" I thought I could detect a note of envy in McNally's voice.

I realized that I couldn't answer his question. There was no way to describe it.

"You'll have to come up and see for yourself sometime, Mac."

"No thank you." A blurt of static interrupted the link. When the static subsided, McNally was gone and the controller was back.

"We're about to lose you, *Discovery*. Have a good night's sleep, and don't you kids do anything we wouldn't do. Houston, out."

"Half of those clowns think they're talking on a CB rig in their pickup truck," Powers said with disgust.

I rubbed my eyes and tried to think of what I had to do next. With my eyes closed, I still saw circuitry diagrams.

"I'll heat up some dinner," said Powers. "Do you have any preferences?"

"Anything but scrambled eggs," I answered, remembering the last sight I'd had of my breakfast. "Let me finish getting this panel back on, then I'll join you. Uh, by the way, Victoria, I don't draw any chauvinist inferences from the fact that you'll be cooking dinner. I just wanted you to know that."

She granted me a smile "I must sound like a harpy at times. I'm sorry. It's been a lousy week."

"You do good work," I told her. It was the only compliment I could think of that she'd be likely to respond to. She did, saying a quick, "Thank you," as she floated toward the tunnel.

I wrestled with the panel for a few more minutes. I'd kept all the screws in a plastic bag, but whenever I reached in for one, five more floated out. I finally finished the job and found that I still had three screws left and no place to put them. That was the kind of thing that could keep me awake all night. The hell with it, I decided.

We had chicken stew for dinner. Space food is not quite as dreary as some of those early predictions about "nutrition bars" and dehydrated glop. Our dinners, packaged in plastic bags, were not much worse than what one would get at an automat, which our galley mightily resembled.

It took me a while to get the hang of it, though. Since everything doesn't automatically fly off in eighteen different directions in zero-G, it is perfectly possible to eat with knife, fork, and spoon. The gravy adhered to the chicken and biscuits, so there was no undue mess. The problem is that once you start your spoon toward your mouth, you are committed. If you stop to say something, the food sails out of the spoon, continuing on its predetermined trajectory. Twice, I had to mop chicken stew out of my eyes.

We ate standing up at a chest-level table on the mid-deck. Sitting down is difficult to do, anyway, since you get no help from gravity; the stomach muscles have to do all the work.

We didn't say much during dinner, partly because of the difficulties involved with eating and talking at the same time. But more than that, the break from work had given us time to think about our predica-

ment. We were sharing our little home in orbit with a
bomb that would go off in less than a day. Somehow,
we had to find it. And then, I'd have to disarm it.
Thinking about it didn't improve my appetite, and I
certainly didn't want to talk about it.

Aside from that, there didn't seem to be much to
say. Two hundred miles above North Africa, zipping
along at eighteen thousand miles an hour, I couldn't
think of anything worth conversing about.

Powers seemed to have the same problem. I noticed
her looking at me strangely a couple of times, but she
quickly looked away when my eyes met hers. She
seemed to have something weighty on her mind. God
knows, there was enough for us to think about.

I finished my dessert of strawberry shortcake, then
helped Powers dump the trash in a galley bin. On
Skylab they'd simply ejected the garbage out into
space, but the Shuttle astronauts were expected to be
more tidy.

I could have used a good, strong gin and tonic, and
maybe a couple of cigarettes. I was dead tired, but
too keyed up to sleep immediately. My bed consisted
of a sleeping bag, slung vertically on the other side of
the cabin from the galley. It didn't look very inviting.

Powers also looked at loose ends. She floated aimlessly, a foot off the floor, her back against the air
lock. I had the feeling she wanted something, but I
was so tired that I couldn't imagine what it might be.

"Sam?"

"What?"

"Something has occurred to me. I don't quite know
how to say it."

"What? Something about the bomb?"

She shook her head. An odd smile played around

---

the corners of her mouth. "It's not about the bomb," she said. "It's . . . well, I suppose you could say it's about science."

"The quasar experiment?"

She smiled again. "I had a different discipline in mind. Not physics. Biology."

"Biology?" Foggily, I tried to remember the various experiments. I knew there was one that had to do with silkworm larvae, but I didn't think that could be it. Powers bit her lower lip, as if trying not to laugh.

"You can be pretty dense at times, you know that?"

"I'm sorry," I said helplessly. "I just don't know what you're talking about."

She grinned openly and floated toward me. "It occurred to me," she said, "that you and I have a unique opportunity to perform an experiment that could prove highly interesting." She arrested her flight by reaching out and holding my shoulder. "You don't see it?"

"See what?" I was honestly baffled.

"You've had your mind on other things, so possibly it escaped your notice that you and I are alone here. You, a man, and I, a woman. In zero gravity."

She waited for me to figure it out. It took me a while.

"Wait a minute. You mean that you . . . and I . . ."

"Exactly."

Now that I understood what she was talking about, she didn't need to draw any circuit diagrams. Zero gravity! I hadn't even thought about anything like this, not since Ilsa—no, it wouldn't do to start thinking about that. I hadn't even felt the urge—but zero gravity!

"Uh, it sounds like a worthwhile experiment. I don't know where we'd publish the results, but . . ."

"How about in the letters column of *Penthouse*? That seems like an appropriate forum to announce the details of the experiment."

"Undoubtedly. In the interest of pure science."

I started to kiss her, but she pushed off and drifted a few feet away.

"Before we start," she said, "I want you to realize that I don't normally do things like this. Jumping into bed with strange men."

"I realize that. Although, jumping into bed hardly describes the circumstances. Where should we . . . ?"

"Here, I think. There's more room, and we don't want to bump into anything important."

"Definitely not." I floated toward her. We collided gently, and she wrapped her arms around my shoulders to keep from rebounding. We kissed softly . . . experimentally, you might say.

"Not bad," she observed. "For a scientist." She pulled down on the long zipper of her coveralls, opening them to the waist. Underneath, she wore the same quilted long johns that I had on. I busied myself with my own clothes. I had to stoop to untie my shoes, and the motion set me spinning. By the time I was finished, I was upside down in relation to her. I shucked my coveralls while she did the same, letting them float languidly through the cabin.

I pulled off my top and threw that away. Victoria seemed to hesitate, so I helped her. I pushed the underwear upward and prayed silently that there would be no bra. I couldn't begin to imagine the engineering nightmare that a zero gravity brassiere would be. Fortunately, I didn't have to contend with that.

"You have good hands," she said. "Does that come from working with bombs?"

"Blond ones."

"I might have known. You obviously need more practice with brown-haired ladies."

A kiss *is* still a kiss, even in zero-G. We proved out that theorem for a while.

"I think it would be more a valuable experiment if we were to perform it without touching anything," she said.

"In midair, you mean?"

"I think we should try it that way." Together, we pushed off the wall and started on a lazy trajectory toward the forward bulkhead. Almost immediately we started spinning, doing perhaps five or six rpm. Not enough to get dizzy, but definitely an interesting sensation.

We shed the rest of our clothes and began the experiment in earnest. I was interested to observe the motions of her breasts in zero gravity. They described parabolic arcs and seemed to be in sympathetic vibration. I checked the responses of the rest of her body.

"Stop squirming," I said. "You're making us spin faster."

"Is that better?"

"Uh huh."

"I think the response would be more pronounced if you applied the stimulus more, uh, more, uh, uh, *uh*, directly."

"Like this?"

"Yes. Oh, *yes!* Like that, yes. I generally respond better to that sort of stimulus, yes, just that sort. Here, let me . . ."

"What?"

"Do you want—"

"Jesus! That's just, uh, that's really, uh, nominal."

"We're getting too close to the floor," she said. "Can you . . . ?"

"How's that?"

"Fine. That's fine. Oh, God, yes, that's fine!"

Someone's coveralls floated in my face. I brushed them away.

"I think I'm ready to . . . to pro*ceed!*" she announced.

"How . . ."

"No, I think . . ."

"Like that?"

"Can you . . . uh?"

"Is that . . . ?"

"Just a lit— *Oh yes!*" she screamed as we banged headfirst into a bulkhead. We bounced off and caromed toward the far wall. We seemed to be picking up speed.

"Oh, God!" she cried. "*I love science!*"

The next morning, bruised and still tired, we got back to work. Powers didn't mention our experiment, so neither did I. There wasn't much that could have been said about it anyway. But I did catch her smiling to herself during breakfast.

We finished up the fourth of Morley's instrument modules with half an hour to spare. I relaxed and told Powers to go ahead with the experiment. Morley, kibitzing from the *Columbia*, interrupted her with a constant stream of questions and suggestions. Powers finally told Morley to shut up. To ensure that he did, I turned off the squawk box.

Powers rotated the instruments toward the appointed spot in the heavens where Mars would pass in front of the quasar. Ever since they'd been discovered, the quasi-stellar objects had been nothing but trouble for astronomers and cosmologists. They spit out more energy than entire galaxies, moved at nearly the speed of light, and were aparently quite small. This experiment would give some indication of their actual size, as the radio signals from the quasar disappeared and then reappeared from behind the bulk of the planet Mars.

The entire occulatation lasted three minutes and forty-two seconds. Powers fiddled with her instruments to keep everything lined up properly, then allowed herself another self-satisfied smile when it was finished. I guess she really did love science.

With Morley placated and science served, it was time to get back to work. I savaged someone's infrared cameras, then dismembered someone else's laser ranging-device. This time I didn't worry about putting it all back together, since the equipment would not be needed for any further experiments on this mission. I'd let the people on the ground salvage the mess.

I was probing around in the guts of Dr. Crespi's quark detector when I saw something that shouldn't have been there. I didn't need to check the circuit diagrams.

I'd found the bomb.

CHAPTER 14

Powers aimed the television camera at the device, nestled deep inside the clutter of Dr. Crespi's instruments. It was a little larger than a book and roughly the same shape. A dozen colored wires connected it with surrounding gadgets, none of which could I identify.

The device itself was something new in my experience. The metal face of the box included a readout window and a keyboard, exactly like that of a cheap pocket calculator: a digital bomb. The power was on, and a ghostly red zero registered on the readout.

"Thank you, *Discovery*," said a voice in Houston. "We've got the picture on tape now. You can turn off your camera."

Powers lowered the camera and began reeling in the cord. I made my way around some computer cabinets and stopped next to the squawk box.

"What do you think, Houston?" I asked.

The reply came a few moments later. "We're working on it. But it doesn't look like any bomb I've ever seen before. Are you sure that's it?"

"Whatever it is, it doesn't appear on any of Crespi's circuit diagrams. It doesn't look like it belongs there."

"It's pretty small, isn't it?"

"Small in comparison with what, Houston? The thing is obviously well designed. We have to assume that it's big enough to do the job they had in mind." And that job, it was needless to say, was to blow the *Discovery* to flinders.

I went back to the quark detector and stared at the device while Houston mulled things over. The keyboard was an open invitation to try to find the correct sequence to disarm the bomb. With eight digits available, there were only 99,999,999 possible combinations to choose from. More than that, really, since the keyboard included a decimal point and the four standard mathematical functions. I guessed that the thing was designed to make it simple to disarm if you had the right code. Probably Klaus had intended to provide the necessary numbers as soon as the Omega demands were met.

That was if Klaus really had anything to do with it. There were enough loose ends in this fiasco to make me wonder if we were even close to the truth. But it seemed likely now that Klaus had been killed because he did know the code. If that was the case, then he had probably designed the device.

Well, he'd done a good job of it. The little box was wedged in between two other devices that seemed to be legitimate pieces of Crespi's experiment. There was no way to tell precisely how it was attached, not without ripping out the entire cabinet and everything in it. And I couldn't do that until I knew everything there was to know about those twelve colored wires snaking out of the tiny box.

"*Discovery*, Houston," said the squawk box. "We're about to lose communications for eleven minutes. You are not to attempt anything until we have reacquired signal."

"Don't worry about that, Houston. I'm going to have to think about this for a while."

"That's fine, *Discovery*. By the way, we have some news for you. Tracking indicates that the Soviet Kosmolyot has altered its orbit. We believe they intend to match your orbit."

I didn't like the sound of that. The fucking Russians again.

"Any idea what they're up to, Houston?"

"Best guess here is that they want a close look at whatever happens. Washington is trying to get an explanation from the Soviet Embassy."

"How about the Omegas?" I asked.

There was a pause. When the controller came back on, he sounded almost apologetic.

"Uh, regarding the Omegas, I'm afraid we have a little bad news for you, *Discovery*. We've discovered two more bombs. One was at the tracking station outside of Madrid and the other one was at the Canberra station in Australia."

I didn't like the sound of it. "What happened?"

"They got to the one in Madrid in time."

"And the one at Canberra?"

"*Discovery*, Canberra has gone off-line."

"Off-line! You mean they blew it up?"

"There was damage," the controller admitted—reluctantly, I thought. "But repairs are already under way. We hope to have it back on-line in eight or ten hours."

"We've only got fourteen hours till the bomb goes off."

"We know that, *Discovery*. We're sorry. I'm afraid this means we'll have a bit of a hole in our tracking."

His no-sweat attitude was beginning to get to me. "A bit of a hole!" I shouted. "Dammit, we'll be blacked out all the way from Madrid to Hawaii!"

"We . . . that, *Dis* . . . best we can down here. Beginning to lose you right . . . again at Goldstone . . . minutes . . ."

The signal broke up and disappeared entirely a couple of seconds later. I didn't like the idea of that gap, but I was just as glad to be rid of Houston for the moment. I like to be alone with bombs. Well, I don't *like* it, but things seem to work out better that way. But I wasn't alone yet.

"Victoria," I said, "you've done all you can here. It's time for you to go over to the *Columbia*."

"I can still—"

"There's not a thing you can do now. You'd just be in the way, and there's no point in your staying and taking a chance on getting blown up. Anyway, you have to take the tapes from Morley's experiment. After all that work, I don't want them left here. I don't think Morley does, either."

"Well," she said, "I won't argue. But I still think I could be helpful."

"You have been. Very. I'm kind of sorry we found the bomb so soon. I'd like to have continued our experiments."

I thought I detected a slight blush from Mission Specialist Powers, but she covered it quickly. "I suppose I should get into my suit," she said.

"Need any help?"

"I can manage," she said as she disappeared into the

connecting tunnel. I allowed myself a single sigh, then got back to work.

I called the *Columbia* and told them that Powers would soon be on her way over. Braxton said they'd be waiting for her.

"What do you think about the Russians?" I asked him.

"I don't like it," he said, "but I doubt if there's anything we can do about it. We'll keep our eyes on them. You just tend to the bomb. Is there anything we can do to help?"

"Yes. Let me talk to Dr. Crespi. I've got some questions for him."

"I am right here, Dr. Boggs," said an Italian-accented voice. "How can I assist you?"

"You know the bomb is in your instrument?"

"I was told," he said sadly. "I cannot think how it could have been put there. This is very embarrassing."

"It's not your fault, Dr. Crespi. But I'm afraid I'm going to have to dismantle your experiment."

I could almost see him shrug. "These things happen," he said. "In my country they happen all too frequently. I am sorry that we have brought the problem with us into outer space."

I was properly impressed with Crespi's sorrow and chagrin, but that was no help to me. "Braxton, is there any way we can send our TV picture to the *Columbia*? I'd like Dr. Crespi to get a look at this thing."

"No way," said Braxton. "I suppose it could be done, but we'd have to rig the right kind of transmitter on the *Discovery* and a receiver over here. It would take too long."

"Wouldn't it be simpler," asked Crespi, "if I returned to the *Discovery* to see it for myself?"

It was a tempting offer. I was more than a little

intimidated by the complexity of Crespi's instruments.
But if Crespi came over, he'd be risking his life simply
because of bad luck. If the bomb had been in Morley's experiment, I might not have minded having him
risk his obnoxious ass. It wasn't Crespi's job to fiddle
with explosives. That was my job, and I didn't want
anyone else to get killed if I blew it.

"Dr. Crespi, I appreciate the offer. But for now, I
think I should handle this solo. If I need your help, I
can describe the situation to you on radio."

"I still think I should come over. I feel responsible."

"You're not. Look, if I get stuck, you can always
come over later on. In the meantime, just stand by
and answer any questions I come up with. For starters, just what the hell is a quark detector?"

"It is to detect quarks," said Crespi. "It is that simple. On earth we use giant accelerators to produce the
energy needed to split apart subatomic particles and
release the quarks. But I believe that the process can
be done much more simply here in space. The bom-
bardment of cosmic rays and particles from the sun
should provide all the energy that is necessary. There
is a collector mounted outside, and the collisions of
incoming particles with the atoms in the collector
should result in the creation of free quarks. The in-
strumentation is necessary to detect the quarks. This
is done by measuring any changes in the mass of the
collector. Once we have the data back on the ground,
we can feed it to a computer and sort out all the other
particle interactions."

"Ingenious," I said. It seemed a shame to have to
tear all that sophisticated equipment apart. I appreciated good scientific technique, and Crespi sounded
like he knew what he was doing. I'd never heard of
him before, but then, I'd been out of touch.

"If there is anything specific I can tell you . . ."

"Not right now, Dr. Crespi. I want to study the circuitry for a while. I'll be in touch. Thanks."

I cut the conversation short because Powers had just emerged from the tunnel. She was big and bulky in her space suit, floating along like something out of the Macy's Thanksgiving Day parade.

"All set?"

"If you'll give me a hand with the helmet."

"Glad to." I took the helmet from her and started to lower it over her head. She looked me in the eye for a split second and I stopped. Leaving the helmet in midair, I leaned over and gave her a kiss.

"I hope we can work together again sometime, Dr. Boggs."

"Anytime. You're an interesting lady, Mission Specialist Powers. It's been a pleasure serving with you."

I retrieved her helmet and started to put it on her, but she stopped me.

"Sam?"

"What?"

"I want to see you on the *Columbia*. Don't hang around here too long, okay?"

I smiled at her, then lowered the helmet into position. She checked it, then headed for the air lock. I've had a lot of women walk out on me, but I never had one float out on me. The air-lock door closed, and I missed her already.

Powers made it to the *Columbia* without incident. She was too damn serious about everything to succumb to the space rapture that had hit me. Of the others, only young Dr. Stanszak had experienced any similar problems. That annoyed me a little; nobody likes to be the only one to get sick on a roller coaster ride.

With Powers gone, I had nothing to distract me from my work except for occasional radio checks with Houston. I dug into the manuals and tried to make sense of Dr. Crespi's marvelous quark detector.

It was slow going. Crespi must have been a brilliant man. Things that were obvious to him were pure Sanskrit to me. I puzzled over his diagrams and kept checking the design against the real thing, and gradually some semblance of order began to emerge. I determined—or thought I had—that the red and white candy-striped wire coming out of the bomb was connected to some sort of counting device which kept track of the total number of particle collisions with the collector grid. There might be current running through that wire. Or there might not.

That left me with only eleven more wires to figure out, and about twelve hours to do it. I let go of the manual—I was getting used to releasing large objects and letting them hover instead of instinctively setting them down—rubbed my eyes, and wondered what I should tackle next. I looked around the Spacelab for inspiration and found none. The damn place had never seemed so big and empty.

And I had never felt so utterly alone, I realized. I wondered if the first Mercury astronauts had felt the same way. Probably not, since their capsules were about the size of the backseat of a Volkswagen. No room to get lonely.

I left the lab and floated up to the flight deck of the crew module. The earth was still out there, below our left wing. I had been so busy, I hadn't bothered to look at it since I arrived on the *Discovery*. We were over the States. I could see the great, twisted groove of the Grand Canyon, and the geometrical patterns of

the irrigated farmland of California and Arizona. If I
didn't look directly at it, I could even see what must
have been Interstate 10, straight and thin as a needle,
stretching across the desert. New Mexico, coming toward me, was covered by storm clouds. I watched the
freakish play of lightning bolts inside the clouds, an
awesomely beautiful sight.

A man could spend his whole life watching this
magic. Perhaps that is why all the astronauts have
been practical, unimaginative, nuts-and-bolts guys.
They'd write no poems while gazing at the rotating
splendor below, but they'd get the job done. But even
the most stolid of them had to have been affected by
it. Most of the early astronauts were out of the program now, busy with industry or politics, indistin-
guishable from a million other executives. But for a
few of them, things had never quite returned to normal. Several of them, I knew, had turned to religion
and become space age evangelists. One was research-
ing ESP. One of them had a breakdown. And the first
man on the moon, at last report, was teaching engineering in Ohio and living in a house with a moat
around it.

I wondered if I would be the same when I got back.
Then I realized that it wasn't just a question of a few
people who had gone into space and returned. None
of us were the same. Ever since that first picture of
the cloud-draped earth floating alone in space like
some prized blue marble, none of us was the same.
We had all been changed by it, permanently and forever. Some of us just didn't know it yet.

A man could also go completely crazy up here,
alone and vacuum-sealed. I flicked the radio switch
on the spacecraft commander's console.

"Hello, *Columbia*. Anybody there?"

"Right here, Boggs. What can we do for you?"

"Ask Dr. Crespi if he still wants to come over. I could use some help." But mainly, I realized, I could use some company.

I waited for Crespi in the Spacelab. I asked if he wanted me to suit up and go outside to catch him, but he said it wouldn't be necessary. That boggling, never-before-attempted half mile walk through space had already become routine.

I turned on the TV camera mounted outside and played with the controls until I had Crespi in view on the flickering ten-inch black and white screen. He ran into problems as soon as he left the forward hatch of the *Columbia*. Instead of coming directly toward the *Discovery*, he spun around in circles for a few seconds. Over the squawk box, I heard him complaining about one of his thruster controls. He floated around the nose of the ship for a minute or so and apparently fixed whatever was wrong.

Once he finally got moving, he looked quite graceful out there. He was a tall, thin man, a fact not completely disguised by the space suit he wore. I was anxious to meet him. His experiment was the product of genius, and it's always interesting to meet a genius.

Crespi slowed himself with a last blast of nitrogen, then reached out and grabbed hold of a projecting antenna. He steadied himself, got out of the maneuvering unit, and left it hanging on the antenna, moored by its shoulder straps.

I turned off the television and waited for him to come through the air lock. A red light above the door told me that he was cycling. At last the red light turned to green and the air-lock hatch swung open. Crespi floated into the lab. I grabbed his gloved hand

and shook it, then began undoing his helmet so we could talk. The truth was, I'd be mighty damned glad not to be alone anymore.

His helmet came free and I lifted it up over his head. Dr. Crespi turned and smiled at me.

"It's good to see you again, Sam," said Dr. Crespi.

Except that it wasn't Dr. Crespi.

It was Klaus Dietrich.

CHAPTER 15

It is difficult to think of something to say to a dead man. A thousand different reactions flashed across my mind, but none of them lingered long enough for me to have something to latch onto. I tried to say something—anything—but nothing came out.

Klaus watched me, an amused smile on his face, clearly enjoying the moment. His hair, once blond, was now dark, and he sported a bushy moustache, but this man was unquestionably Klaus Dietrich and no one else.

"One moment," he said. He pushed off the floor and sailed across the lab to the squawk box.

"*Columbia*, Crespi here." He spoke with a completely convincing Italian accent.

"Yes, Dr. Crespi," answered Braxton.

"I am safely aboard *Discovery*," Klaus reported. "Dr. Boggs and I have much to discuss. We would be grateful if there were no interruptions."

"Roger," said Braxton. "We'll pass the word along to

Houston. In a few minutes we'll be out of touch with them, anyway. Canberra's still out. Let us know if you need anything."

"Thank you, *Columbia*," Klaus said politely. He switched off the squawk box and turned to me.

"Now we can talk," he said in his normal voice, which contained only a hint of his German accent. "Sam, when they told us a Dr. Boggs was coming up, I couldn't believe it. I didn't think it could possibly be you. But when I caught you outside, when you came across, and I looked into your helmet, well, I was astounded."

"I know the feeling," I said, weakly.

"Yes, I can imagine. You should have seen your face when I came through the air lock. You looked—"

"Like I'd seen a ghost?"

"That describes it, yes."

"Maybe it was because I thought you were dead."

"Is Klaus Dietrich dead?" Klaus Dietrich asked me. "Pity. He was a fine fellow. I shall miss him. Did they say how it happened?"

"Shotgun in the face," I answered.

"Yes, that would make sense. I suppose they made positive identification through his fingerprints."

I thought of that pulpy, mutilated face on the floor of the shed. It didn't look like Klaus, it didn't look like anyone. But it had to have been Klaus.

"Who *is* dead?" I asked him.

He smiled. "Klaus Dietrich, of course. The fingerprints proved that beyond any doubt, did they not?"

"They changed the dead man's fingerprints?"

"That would have been possible, I suppose. But it was much easier to change the data in the computers. When the police attempted to match the dead man's fingerprints, they would have found a perfect congruence with the prints of Klaus Dietrich. No one ever thinks to doubt anything a computer tells them."

"So who did die?"

Klaus shrugged, a motion which sent him bobbing up into the air. "It doesn't really matter," he said.

"It probably mattered to the man they killed."

"Possibly. But it doesn't matter to us. One man out of the hundred million the Soviets had to choose from. Just someone who had the bad luck to be my doppelganger, or near enough. If he had been run over by a trolley in Minsk, we would not even have noticed."

"I noticed," I said. "I found the body."

Klaus couldn't hide his surprise. "*You?* Sam, what the devil are you doing in this thing? I thought you were basking on some tropical isle."

"I was drafted," I told him. "They sent me to Germany to find you. I saw some of our old friends. Emil Rothenburg. Ilsa Vogel."

"And how are they?"

"Dead."

Klaus's eyes went wide. His mouth opened and closed soundlessly. He seemed to be taking this a little more seriously than he took the news of his own death.

"Emil was blown to bits," I said. "Ilsa was shot. I found her next to the late Klaus Dietrich."

"My God, Sam! I didn't know."

"Didn't you?"

"How could I? I've been up here—"

"That's not what I meant."

Klaus raised his right hand, as if to swear, but instead used it to arrest his glide toward the ceiling. "Who did it?" he asked.

"I thought you could tell me."

"Sam, this wasn't part of . . . this wasn't supposed to happen. I don't understand it."

"You just don't want to understand it."

"Sam, you don't think I would—"

"No, no, of course not. Some poor slob who looked like you, that was okay, wasn't it? Necessary to the plan. But Emil and Ilsa, that's a big shock, isn't it? That wasn't in your little scenario."

"No," he said. "It wasn't." He sank slowly toward the floor.

The shock was wearing off. The numbness was flaking away, leaving a hard, hot ball of anger. I gripped the edge of a computer cabinet, pressing it hard enough to hurt.

"You goddamn fool! Did you think the KGB would stop with a dead Dietrich? They had to kill anyone who could ever identify the real Klaus Dietrich. They tried to kill me. They killed Emil. And they killed Ilsa."

"My God," he said softly.

I looked at him, hanging limply in midair, like a balloon with a slow leak. My old buddy. I wanted to puke.

"It's funny," he said. "My knees feel weak. On earth, I'd sit down. But here, what can I do? There is no gravity, yet my knees feel weak. How did she die, Sam?"

"They shot her."

"Then it was quick."

"That part of it was. But there must have been time for her to realize what was going to happen."

"I suppose so. God, Sam, I swear to you, I didn't know this was going to happen. I didn't think they would do that. I didn't think—"

"Bullshit! Thinking is what you do best, Klaus. Kill-

ing Emil and Ilsa was part of the plan from the beginning. Maybe it was just one of the details you didn't
concern yourself with. But it was part of the plan."

Klaus made no response. His new moustache
drooped at the ends, and he looked like a man who
had discovered remorse for the first time and didn't
know what to make of it.

"They shouldn't have done it," he said quietly. "It
wasn't necessary."

"Evidently they thought it was. Your new playmates don't seem to have your finely drawn sensibili-
ties."

Klaus looked up at me. "My new playmates!" he
said with scorn. "You have a unique way of phrasing
things, Sam. You always did. Let us talk, then, about
our new playmates. Mine and yours. You will tell me
about the hundreds of millions enslaved by the Soviet
tyrants. And then I will remind you of the hundreds of
millions enslaved by the capitalist overlords. You will
say 'Czechoslovakia,' and I will answer 'Vietnam.' I
will trump your 'Jewish dissidents' with the blacks
and Hispanics and Indians. You will play your Ana-
tole Shcharansky card and I will play my Wilmington
Ten card. You will say 'KGB,' and I will say 'CIA.'
Yes, by all means, let us talk about our new playmates."

I didn't feel like engaging in polemics. There was
no position I wanted to espouse. I just wanted him to
answer one question.

"Was it worth it?"

"Yes," he said flatly. "I didn't want it to happen this
way, but yes, it was worth it. The plan is complete,
and nothing can stop it now. It will change history,
Sam. It will do nothing less than assure the survival of
the human race. For such a result, yes, it was worth

the lives that were lost. Even the lives of those I loved. It wasn't my intention, but if I thought it necessary to the success of the plan, I would kill Emil and Ilsa with my own bare hands. Or you, Sam. I would kill you, too. I will, if you make it necessary."

There was suddenly a short, flat-bladed knife in his hand. It was no bigger than a butter knife, but it looked sharp and lethal. It must have been concealed in one of the countless zippered pouches of his space suit.

Klaus suddenly smiled. "This is very embarrassing," he said. "I've always felt that physical confrontations are crude. They should be avoided when possible."

"Or left to the pros."

"The KGB again. And the CIA as well. Yes, we should leave this sort of thing to them. Maybe someday they will all kill each other and leave the rest of us in peace. In the meantime, however, have no doubt that I will use this knife, Sam. There is far too much at stake."

"Yes, yes, I know. The survival of the human race, I believe you said. Lofty goal, Klaus. Very lofty."

"You are still cynical. And rightly so. But I will explain it to you, Sam. While I do, I want you to stay aft of that cabinet. And keep your hands where I can see them. If you try anything, I will have to kill you. And then you will die without knowing how I got here and what my plan is."

"If you kill me, I don't imagine I'll care very much one way or the other."

"Undoubtedly true. So try to stay alive, Sam. For the next few minutes, at least. Listen to what I have to tell you."

"I'm all ears." I was still holding the computer cabinet, keeping my feet planted on the floor. I didn't

want to let myself get adrift. Klaus continued to hover
a few inches above the floor.

"First of all," he said, "I suppose I ought to intro-
duce myself. Dr. Angelo Crespi, at your service."

"Angelo? *Angel?*"

"Yes. Why?"

"Nothing. I just figured out the punch line of Emil's
last joke. He said I should believe in angels."

Klaus smiled. "He was right."

"He also said that he didn't know where you were
within ten thousand kilometers."

"Again, he was correct."

" 'Round and round,' he said. That was the answer.
He was telling me you were in orbit. He told me I'd
laugh when I had the answer."

"But now that you have it, you don't feel like laughing."

"Not much," I admitted. "So Emil did know. He
was part of it."

"Emil was not simply part of it . . . Emil was
Spartacus."

"*What?*"

"The original idea was his. The plan was his. He
first suggested it to me three years ago. We refined it,
of course, but Emil was the first to see it clearly. He
knew what had to be done."

"And what is that?"

"In a moment. First let me tell you about Angelo
Crespi. Three years ago, I realized that I needed to
establish a new identity. Klaus Dietrich was spending
too much of his time on the run. He wasn't accom-
plishing anything. All his old comrades were dead or
in jail, and the Revolution had degenerated to mindless violence and anarchy. A new approach was
needed. I invented Angelo Crespi to implement it.

"I established myself at Milan as Dr. Crespi. I had letters of recommendation from no less a scholar than Emil Rothenburg. No one questioned my identity, for I claimed to be a scientist and that is exactly what I was. Within a year I was actually publishing papers under my new name; Crespi became one of the top men in his field."

"Which was what? Quarks?"

Klaus nodded modestly. He pointed the knife toward the uncovered guts of his instruments. "The Crespi quark detector. I think it might actually work, although that is unimportant at the moment. What was important was that the people at ESA and NASA believed that it would work. Really, it was surprisingly easy to get them to accept it and me. I went through a year of training for this mission, and ESA put up five million dollars to build the instrument."

"All that, just to put a bomb on board? That can't be the point of this."

"Obviously not. Sam, tell me, why did you turn your back on the revolution?"

It was not a question I could answer easily under any circumstances. Maybe the Revolution was never real to begin with. Maybe I simply grew up.

"I don't really know," I said.

"Then I'll tell you. Sam, you gave it up because it was pointless. You knew there would be no revolution except the kind that ends with the likes of you and I facing a firing squad. You knew that one generation was not going to change the direction of ten thousand years of history."

"That sounds like a pretty good answer," I said.

"It is. I arrived at the same conclusion. The question of capitalism versus communism was irrelevant. The farmer in Asia, the factory worker in Detroit, the

bureaucrat in Moscow—none of them will ever be liberated by ideology. In fact, none of them will ever be
truly liberated by anything. They and their descen-
dants are doomed to be slaves throughout eternity.
And when I speak of eternity, by the way, I am only
talking of the next fifty or a hundred years. That is all
the time remaining for what we know as civilization.
Too many people, too few resources, too many ways
to blow up the world. It can't last much longer, Sam."

"The end is near, huh?"

"It is and you know it."

Perhaps I did know it. Klaus wasn't saying anything new. Everyone from the Club of Rome to the
Seventh-Day Adventists was predicting the Apoca-
lypse. War, economic collapse, famine, ecological catas-
trophe, a new ice age—you could take your pick.
Maybe, down deep, I thought of San Vincente as my
fallout shelter. Whatever happened, it wouldn't be as
bad on my tropical retreat. I could face Judgment
Day with the sun at my back and a gin and tonic in
my hand.

"Civilization," said Klaus, "is groaning under the
weight of a hundred centuries of greed and stupidity.
And it is tied to a small and dying planet. It must
collapse."

"And you plan to prevent it?"

"No, I plan to make it irrelevant. Sam, what do you
know about the concept of space colonies?"

"I read O'Neill's book," I said. "That's about it."

"And what do you think of it?"

"I think it's a grand idea whose time is never going
to come." It *was* a grand idea, and reading about the
space colonies, it was easy to get swept up in the romance of it all. I knew there were entire societies and

clubs devoted to the concept of space colonies. Mine the moon, they said, capture a couple of asteroids, and you'll have all the raw materials you'll ever need. Build great cylindrical habitats in orbit around the earth, and send people to live in them. Twenty thousand or more in each habitat. They'd have gravity (provided by spin), unlimited energy from the sun, and endless room to grow. Each habitat could have a climate of its own choosing, and an environment to go with it. There would be mountains and rivers inside the habitats, with small towns and modest cities scattered around the curving interior. Farming could be taken care of on specially designed agricultural satellites, where the growing season never ended. Heavy industry would take place outside in the vacuum, and the colonists would commute to work on solar scooters or futuristic cable cars. There would be no pollution, no population pressure, no shortages. Pie in the sky, for ever and ever.

"You think it is impractical?" Klaus asked me.

"Technically, probably not. I suppose it could be done. But it won't be."

"And why not?"

"You already said it. Too many things are falling apart here on earth. They'd never get it started. Nobody is going to appropriate a hundred billion dollars just to let a few thousand people live in space. I know they say it would pay for itself by converting solar power to microwave and beaming it down to earth. They may be right. In the long run, it may make sense. But in the short run, it would be a tremendous investment of resources, energy, and manpower. I don't see anyone around who is going to be willing to foot the bill. When the oil wells start to go dry in the next fifteen or twenty years, people will want immediate solutions for themselves, not science fiction for their grandchildren."

Klaus was beaming. "I knew you would see it," he said. "But there is something else you haven't considered. In these habitats there will be populations composed exclusively of relatively young, adventurous, intelligent people. How long do you think they will be content to let their lives be controlled by the bureaucrats on earth? Sam, they will be the most revolutionary population in history! They will have true self-determination, because they will be completely independent of history. Think of it! One habitat will be run like a New England town meeting. A hundred kilometers away, there will be a collective habitat. A habitat for fascists, a habitat for communists, one for every possible shade of opinion. People will be able to choose the way they want to live for the first time in history. They will control their own destinies, independent of geography and climate and culture and politics. They will be *free*, Sam! Free in a way no one has ever been free before. There will be no revolution on earth. But here, in space, the Revolution will succeed. It will be endless!"

"Sure," I said. "Why not?"

"You don't believe it."

"Nope."

"Sam, here you are, in orbit around the earth, your feet off the floor, and yet you tell me you don't believe it."

"Like you said, I'm cynical. Maybe the space colonies would be everything you claim. And maybe not. I don't think it matters, because I don't think they'll ever be built."

Klaus pushed himself away from the floor, as if levitating. His eyes were intense and unblinking, shiny with the emotion of his vision.

"Sam, that is why I am here. That is what the plan is all about. You are right, the habitats would never be built if events continue on their present course. But I've changed it, Sam. I've changed history. I've ensured that the colonies *will* be built!"

I pointed at the bomb, hidden in the bowels of his quark detector. "One bomb is going to do all that?"

"Precisely. Sam, why did you Americans decide to go to the moon? Was it in pursuit of knowledge? Was it a noble quest to expand the frontiers of humanity?"

"Hardly."

"Of course not. You went because if you didn't, the Russians would have. Sputnik had the same effect on you as Pearl Harbor. It awoke the sleeping giant, as the cliché would have it. And what happened? Fifteen years after Sputnik was launched, our friend Braxton was prancing about on the Ocean of Storms. You Americans are truly phenomenal about getting things done once you have been properly aroused."

"And that's the point of this? Blow up the *Discovery* and get people angry enough to worry about space again?"

"In a nutshell, yes."

"I don't get it. The Russians are in this up to their necks, but where's the advantage for them? the last thing they want is to get us riled up again."

"Ah, yes, my new playmates. The Russians. At this moment, there is a Russian spacecraft less than ten kilometers away from us. It will make rendezvous within the hour."

Now we were getting down to it. Klaus's vision of that great golden city way up in the middle of the air was entertaining, but I was far more concerned about

the bomb on the *Discovery* and the knife in his hand.
I wanted to know what was going to happen next; I
was willing to postpone my worries about the next
century.

"What happens then?" I asked.

"To an extent," he said, "that will depend on you.
Your presence here expands our options. Really, it is
an incredible stroke of luck to find you here, Sam. I
couldn't be more pleased."

"Is that why you pulled that knife on me?"

Klaus glanced at the blade in his hand and grinned
self-consciously. "I am sorry about this," he said. "But
until I know where you stand, I'm afraid I'll need the
knife. You know how it is."

"Of course."

"You were asking about the Russians a moment ago.
You obviously don't like them, and if the truth be
known, neither do I. But one must make do with what
is available. The Soviets are involved in this because
they believe it suits their own purposes. In the short
run, they are correct. In the long run, I don't believe it
will help them very much."

"What do they want?"

"They would like to put the Americans out of business for a year or two, as far as space is concerned. I
suppose you are aware of the Soviets' killer-satellite
program?"

I nodded. People had been sounding the alarm
about the killersats for years, but no one ever seemed
to get very upset about it. The Russians were develop-
ing a high-energy particle beam—a genuine Buck Rogers disintegrator ray—that was capable of destroying
missiles launched from the earth. Theoretically, with a
well-placed armada of killersats, the Russians could
neutralize any American nuclear strike, thereby tip-

ping the balance of power. The Soviets could black-mail the Western powers, or simply obliterate them, without having to worry about a massive retaliation.

"The Russians are quite enthusiastic about their killer satellites," Klaus continued. "They like to believe that their particle beam will be as decisive as gunpowder was when it was first introduced. For the first time, they will have an exploitable strategic advantage. There is only one problem from their point of view."

"The Shuttles."

"Precisely. As you know, not all the Shuttle missions have been devoted to observing quasars and finding quarks. Every fourth or fifth mission is conducted by the military. In the past year the Americans have destroyed sixteen killer satellites and captured at least three of them intact. In essence, as fast as the Russians put them up, the Americans knock them down."

"So now they're fighting back, huh?"

"They believe that if they can eliminate the Shuttles for nine months, they will have the time they need to get their satellites in position. The two Shuttles under construction will not be operational for at least a year. That leaves the Americans with only the *Discovery* and the *Columbia* to contend with. As far as the Russians are concerned, the whole purpose of this plan was to get both Shuttles aloft at the same time. This, you will have noted, has already been achieved."

"That's fine for the Russians. But I don't see how it helps your grand design for the conquest of the galaxy."

"Oh, it does, believe me. Obviously, the Americans are not going to take this passively. Production will be stepped up on the other two Shuttles; I would guess they'll be operational within six months, rather than a year. Additional Shuttles will be built. More and more attention will be paid to the situation in outer space. Eventually, the overall investment of both nations will be so great that it will be impossible for them to turn their backs on space exploration. Each, out of fear of the other, will allocate ever increasing amounts of money and resources. Orbital power stations will be built. Inevitably, the first space colonies will be established—and the Revolution will begin."

Klaus seemed pleased with his predictions. He was a certified genius, so maybe he was right. I wasn't quite as certain, but then, I'm not a genius.

"You've got it all figured out, don't you?"

"In considerable detail," Klaus replied.

"Too bad you weren't so meticulous about some of the other details. Emil and Ilsa might still be alive."

"No one can predict everything," Klaus insisted. "We're talking about *history*, not the lives of individuals. Yes, some people are going to die. No one can prevent that."

"You could," I pointed out.

"You mean the bomb, of course."

"That's what I mean. You still haven't explained exactly what you intend to do, but that bomb has to be part of it."

Klaus floated closer to his quark detector. He looked at me to make sure I was keeping my distance, then poked his head into the instrument cabinet for a couple of seconds. I might have been able to make a move at that moment, but I didn't. There were still things I needed to know.

Klaus backed away from the quark detector and turned to me with a smile on his face. "Figured it out yet?" he asked.

"I can see how it works," I said.

"But can you disarm it?"

"Probably not," I admitted. "With twelve different wires tied into all that sophisticated electronic gear, it would be pretty damn difficult to figure out what to cut. I'd say the only way to disarm it would be to have the code. There is a code, isn't there?"

"Of course there is. A digital bomb is a great concept, don't you think? The whole thing is built from a programmable pocket caculator. To disarm it, all you need to do is to punch in the proper code. But first you have to know it."

"What is it?"

Klaus allowed himself a brief, unfunny laugh. "You expect me to tell you? Very well, I'll give you a few hints. The correct code consists of two eight-digit numbers linked by one of the four standard mathematical functions. And remember the movable decimal point. There you are, Sam. Does that help?"

"You know it doesn't."

"No, I suppose not. There are about ten to the eighteenth possible combinations involved. If you were able to try one combination every second, it would only take you about five hundred million years to cover them all."

"I don't think I can spare that much time. Why don't you save me the trouble and just tell me the right sequence?"

"I'll do even better than that, Sam. Watch."

Klaus reached into the cabinet, keeping his eyes on me. He fumbled around for a few seconds, then tugged at something. Smiling again, he withdrew his arm from the cabinet. He was holding the bomb.

"A fake," he said. "I never intended to blow up the *Discovery*."

"You mean there never was a real bomb?" I was so surprised, I didn't even feel relieved.

"Oh, there's a bomb all right," Klaus told me. "It just doesn't happen to be on the *Discovery*."

"Then where is it?"

"On the *Columbia*, of course. It will explode in about twenty minutes. No one can stop it."

CHAPTER 16

"I told you, Sam, some people must die if the plan is to succeed."

"Braxton, Hollings, Powers—all eight of them. They get to be the sacrificial lambs?"

Klaus pursed his lips and tried to look regretful about the whole thing. "I truly wish it weren't necessary. I've known some of them for more than a year, and I will be sad to see them die. But it must be done."

Clearly, Klaus had made up his mind. He had rationalized everything and dispensed with antiquated notions about the morality of deliberate murder. He was going to save the human race, and that entitled him to kill as many people as he thought necessary in the process.

He'd said twenty minutes. That didn't leave me any time to argue matters of conscience. I had to disarm him and get on the horn to the *Columbia* to warn them. They'd never find the bomb in the time remaining, but at least they could abandon ship and make it to the *Discovery*. And with Canberra out, we couldn't even contact Houston. This was neatly planned.

"What happens after the explosion?" I asked. If I could keep him talking, he might let his attention stray for a second or two. That might be enough; or it might not.

"There are several options," said Klaus. "We knew the Americans would send somebody up to defuse the bomb. If you had been someone else, the situation would be essentially the same, Sam, except that I wouldn't need this knife. The explosion would be a tragic surprise to both of us."

"Undoubtedly."

"The Russians will then offer their help. They will send two crew members over to pilot the *Discovery* back to earth. It's an offer Houston will be unable to reject for the simple reason that they have no way of getting up here themselves for at least the next six months. Alas, it will turn out that there was yet another bomb concealed aboard the *Discovery*. When the Russians attempt to deorbit the *Discovery*, their two brave cosmonauts will die tragically, along with the American bomb expert and Dr. Angelo Crespi. I'll miss Crespi."

"I'll miss the American bomb expert."

Klaus was enjoying himself. I could see where it might be a certain amount of fun to manipulate history. And people.

"Of course," he continued, "there will be no one aboard the *Discovery* when it explodes. But the Americans will have no way of knowing that. I'll return to earth aboard the Kosmolyot and assume a new identity. The cosmonauts who die will naturally be fictitious."

"And what about me?"

"A good question. Indeed, what about you, Sam? If you were an ordinary, run-of-the-mill bomb expert working for NASA, you would probably be killed and left in orbit along with the wreckage of the two Shuttles. But there is another option."

"I land in the Kosmolyot and sign up with the KGB."

Klaus nodded. "What difference would it make?" he asked. "You work for the Americans now. Why not work for the Russians? I've been promised an important position in the Soviet space program, Sam. If I ask them to, they'll make you my assistant."

"Would I get Blue Cross?"

"I'm serious, Sam. Your only alternative is to die here with your former shipmates. You must decide now, Sam. After the explosion, we will reacquire Houston. If you aren't willing to go along with the story, I can't let you speak to the people on the ground. I'd have to kill you now. Then it would be necessary for the Russians to concoct a story about how the *Discovery* was damaged by debris from the *Columbia*, killing us both. I prefer the original plan, but the choice is yours."

"Do you really think you can kill me with that butter knife, Klaus?"

"I don't want to," he said. "But have no doubt that I will. Emil is dead. Ilsa is dead. One more will not matter."

"Or two. What makes you think the Russians are going to let you live, Klaus? At the moment, the Americans have to blame the explosions on the Omega Alliance, even though they know the Russians are involved somehow. But if Klaus Dietrich—or Angelo Crespi—ever turns up alive, the whole thing comes unraveled. They can't afford to let you live, Klaus."

"They can't afford not to," Klaus said coolly. "I have taken precautions. If I don't return from this mission, certain information will be sent to the Americans. It will prove that this entire operation was engineered by the Russians. There is no Omega Alliance, Sam. They never existed. Terrorists who don't exist could hardly be responsible for bombing the Shuttles. If I die, the Americans will discover the truth, and they won't like it one bit. Who knows how they would react? They could even start a war, and that is something the Russians are not prepared for at the moment. No, Sam, I'm completely safe. You will be, too, if you make the correct choice. If you don't, I'll kill you right now."

I had no doubt that he meant what he said. Klaus's grand design was the only thing that mattered to him now. He had deliberately destroyed his own past in order to create the ultimate revolution of the future. I was the last remaining link with his past; when I was gone, he'd finally be free of history.

"I'll make you another offer," I said. "I'm going over to the squawk box. I'm going to tell Braxton to evacuate the *Columbia*. They'll come over here, and we'll all return to earth on the *Discovery*. When we hit the ground, Angelo Crespi can disappear. You'll have what you want—a Shuttle destroyed and a riled up American public. You'll get your space race and your colonies and your endless Revolution. There's no need to kill those people."

Klaus thought it over for at least two seconds.

"No," he said. "Klaus Dietrich is dead, and if Angelo Crespi disappears, who would I be then? I'd be hunted by both sides. I could accomplish nothing. No, Sam, we have to do this my way."

"I see. But let's just make it clear, then, that the

people who die up here will be doing it for the sake of your miserable ass. The Revolution doesn't demand their death, and neither does history. But Klaus Dietrich demands it."

"I do what I must," he said.

"Bullshit. You do what the KGB wants you to do. You're such a big fucking genius, Klaus, did it ever occur to you that the Russians aren't exactly stupid? You didn't count on them killing Ilsa, but they did. And Emil started the whole thing, to hear you tell it. He was Spartacus—and what good did it do him? They killed him and went right ahead with *their* plan, with the bombs and the letters and the rest of it. They'll kill you, Klaus. The minute this is over, you're cold meat."

"I told you, I have taken steps—"

"And so have the Russians. Can't you see that? It's already falling apart. You're going to manipulate history and civilization, are you? The great, visionary scientist? But when all is said and done, right now your glorious scheme depends on whether or not you can kill me with that knife."

"I will," he said, "if it is necessary."

"Klaus, I'm going over to the squawk box now. What happens after that is up to you."

I sucked in a deep breath and pushed off of the computer cabinet with my right hand. The squawk box was mounted on the opposite wall, about a dozen feet away from me and nearly the same distance from Klaus. I tried for a low trajectory, one that would keep my feet no more than a couple of inches above the floor.

Klaus waited till I was launched, then dived head-first to intercept me. He was in midair and committed.

I straightened my legs and kicked off the floor as

emphatically as I could. Klaus sailed beneath me, headed aft, unable to reverse himself. He waved the knife at me as he passed, raking the bottom of my left shoe.

I bounced off the ceiling, taking most of the impact with my arms and shoulders. There was no hope of controlling my flight now; I was simply a ballistic projectile, like a bullet or a Ping-Pong ball. I rebounded toward the port bulkhead, missing the squawk box by several feet.

I managed to snag an instrument cabinet as I ricocheted from the wall. My momentum caused me to swing around the cabinet at if it were a maypole and slam into another cabinet. Again I rebounded, but this time I was able to hang on and stabilize myself.

Klaus had soared all the way to the air lock. When I looked, I saw him trying to steady himself in the far corner. He was facing me, a deadly grin stamped on his features. He held the knife in his right hand, up and away from his body.

"That was a good move, Sam," he said.

We were still nearly equidistant from the squawk box, but we had switched ends of the Spacelab. I knew he wouldn't fall for the same trick again; he'd wait until I committed myself first. I could try to play a chesslike game of position and wait until the caroms and rebounds gave me an advantage. But God knew how long that would take.

There was nothing handy that I could use for a weapon, not even anything to throw at him. My tools were all packed away in their case.

Out of the corner of my eye, I saw something floating near the ceiling. It was Klaus's fake bomb, drifting lazily around its own center of mass, wires splayed out like the tentacles of a jellyfish.

I went after it, moving slowly and keeping within reach of the wall. I didn't want to give Klaus a chance to catch me adrift. I snared the bomb and turned myself around with a quick jackknife move. Now I was standing upside down on the ceiling. Physically, it made no difference, but seeing Klaus and the rest of the lab upside down was disorienting. I had to look for a second to find the squawk box again.

The fake bomb was about the size of a thick book. No way to tell its weight. The only thing I could do with it was throw it, and that wouldn't be easy. When you throw things on earth—darts, baseballs, rocks—your hand and eye automatically compensate for gravity. You know the thrown object will drop before it reaches the target, so you instinctively aim high. Here, I had to be dead on target all the way.

"It would take a very good throw, Sam," Klaus said. Upside down, it was impossible to read the expression on his face.

I cocked my arm, paused, then faked a quick throw. Klaus didn't go for it.

"A very American tactic," Klaus said, a hint of laughter in his voice. "Find something and throw it. We Europeans don't throw things so well. I suppose that's because we play soccer and you play baseball. We are, however, very skilled at kicking things."

By way of demonstration, Klaus unhooked his helmet from a latch on the air lock door and carefully placed it at his feet. He backed up a step, then booted the helmet with the precision of a penalty kick in a World Cup match.

If it's difficult to throw in zero-G, it is just as difficult to duck. I misjudged the helmet's trajectory, got my feet tangled, and moved the wrong way. It crashed into my right knee with enough force to throw me out of what passed for balance in orbit. My feet lost contact with the ceiling and I was left hanging in midair.

Klaus had rebounded from the air lock and was flying toward the squawk box in a controlled dive. Before I could get my feet back on the ceiling, Klaus had caught himself on the wall and was hanging onto the squawk box itself.

If I could get into the crew module, I could use the radio there. But to do it, I'd have to get through the connecting tunnel. It would be a good place to get a knife in my back.

I didn't know how much time we had used up, but however much, it was too much. I couldn't go on playing a cat and mouse game. Klaus knew it; he was anchored next to the squawk box, content to wait for me to come to him.

"You can't win, Sam. You might as well admit it."

I still had the fake bomb in my hand. The helmet was rattling around at the other end of the lab now. Klaus had nothing left to throw but the knife, and I knew he wasn't about to let go of it.

"Okay, Klaus," I said. "Here I come. Get ready."

"I am, believe me."

I let him get more than ready. I feinted with my shoulders and Klaus tensed his body, preparing to receive my dive. I gave him two more fakes, then fired the bomb right at his feet. I was already airborne by the time the device cracked into the wall. Klaus had lifted his feet and was moored only by his left hand, clutching the squawk box.

I curled into a cannonball before I reached him, then unfurled myself like an exploding party favor. I hit him feet first, kicking as hard as I could into his rib cage. Pinned against the wall, Klaus took the full force of the blow.

My knees buckled and I kept on coming. Klaus swiped at me with the knife and sliced through my golden coveralls, my quilted long johns, and a couple of inches of my left thigh. The blade was so sharp I didn't even feel it.

Instead of rebounding from Klaus's chest, I grabbed at him. Knees planted against his thorax, I clutched his hair with both hands and jerked. His forehead smacked into my left knee.

But his arms were still free. He released the squawk box and wrapped his left arm around my back. Together, we floated away from the wall while he jabbed at me with the knife. I couldn't get a grip on his right arm, but he couldn't get a clean stab at me. We spun around each other, grappling and flailing.

He nicked me again, this time actually grating the knife against my ribs. I noticed a nebula of tiny red globules floating along with us.

I let go of his hair and reached for his arm with both hands. He squirmed away from me. For a second we were out of contact. Klaus lunged at me. With nothing to push off of, all I could do was try to rotate around my own center of mass; it wasn't enough. The knife plunged into my left shoulder. This time it did hurt.

The corners of my vision turned hot and red for a moment. I felt Klaus jerking the knife free from my shoulder, saw him raise it again as blood splattered in every direction. A marble-size drop of it broke against his nose and disintegrated into a fine red mist.

He had to duck his head to keep the cloud of blood from getting into his eyes. I think, for a split second,

he was fascinated by the phenomenon; since it was
my blood, I couldn't afford that luxury. I grabbed his
wrist with both hands.

My feet brushed against something while I struggled to keep Klaus's wrist in my grasp. I risked a
quick look and saw my feet gliding into the interior of
the Crespi quark detector.

Klaus clawed at me with his free hand. He went for
my eyes and almost got them, but I managed to de-
flect him with my right shoulder. He rebounded and
floated away from me. I still had his wrist, holding
him at arm's length.

I hooked my feet around the quark detector, then
pulled. It was like throwing the hammer. Klaus flailed
helplessly, but there was nothing to give him leverage.
He sailed around me in a wide arc as I pushed against
the instruments. I swung him through a full one
hundred eighty degrees, picking up speed and momentum. He smashed into the floor headfirst.

The tension in his wrist disappeared and the knife
drifted out of his fingers. I released Klaus and caught
the knife before it floated out of my reach. Then I
turned myself around to face Klaus again.

But Klaus was floating listlessly a few feet above
the floor, like a wrecked ship in the tide. His eyes
were closed and he wasn't moving.

I unhooked my feet from the quark detector and
bent down to look at Klaus. He was breathing rag-
gedly and his pulse was weak. I didn't know if I'd
simply knocked him unconscious or broken his neck.

I noticed that it had begun to rain blood. A forma-
tion of droplets collided with my face and got into my
eyes and nose. I sneezed and found myself propelled
backward into the air, into another cloud of my own
blood.

My golden coveralls were soaked red from my left shoulder to my left foot. I told myself that it looked worse than it really was.

I let Klaus float free on the air currents and pushed myself toward the squawk box. When I tried to raise my left hand to flick the switch, it refused to move. I tried the switch with my right hand and got it.

"Braxton! This is Boggs!"

"*Columbia* here," Braxton said calmly.

"Braxton," I panted, "there's a bomb on the *Columbia*! You've got to get everybody off!"

"What the hell?"

"No time to explain, just do it! I think it's set to go off just before you reacquire Houston."

"Jesus! That's only fourteen minutes! Where is it? How do you know . . . ?"

"Crespi set it."

"Crespi?"

"He's really Klaus Dietrich. A terrorist."

A terrorist. That was what it came down to, in the end. His dreams of El Dorado in the sky would come true or they wouldn't. History would decide that, and even Klaus Dietrich couldn't change it. All he could do was fill the air with blood.

"Where is the bomb?" Braxton asked. "Maybe we can disarm it."

"I don't know," I said. "Just get into your suits and away from the ship."

"We've only got one maneuvering unit over here."

"Okay, then just get outside. I'll come over with the other units. But hurry, dammit!"

I dived toward the tunnel to the crew module, passing over the limp, starfished body of Klaus Dietrich. There was no time to bother trying to tie him up. I made my way through the tunnel, proceeding as well

as I could with only one functional arm. I came out in
the mid-deck and went straight for the locker where
my space suit was stored. I didn't even know if I
could get into the damned thing in fourteen minutes,
but there was nothing to do but try. I pulled open the
locker and had to duck as everything in it jack-in-the-
boxed all over the place.

I wasted at least a minute chasing after all the free-
falling paraphernalia. Once I had retrieved it, there
was no place to stash everything to keep it from floating away again. My left arm had gone completely
numb, although it seemed to be bleeding as profusely
as ever. By the time I had maneuvered myself into the
space suit, it was speckled with red and looked more
like a painter's smock than a sixty-thousand-dollar en-
semble by NASA.

I fumbled with zippers and snaps and prayed that
I'd gotten them all. If I hadn't, I'd find out quick
enough in the air lock. I pulled my gloves on, grabbed
my helmet, and dived back into the tunnel.

Klaus had drifted up to the ceiling, still spread-
eagled and limp. I wasn't even sure that he was still
alive.

In the air lock I slipped my helmet into position and
punched the cycle button. My suit ballooned up as the
pressure dropped, reassuring me that my fly was
zipped. The cycling seemed to go on for hours, although I knew it was only supposed to take about
thirty seconds. It must have taken me at least five
minutes to get into my suit, so there couldn't have
been more than eight or nine minutes remaining until
we reacquired Houston. And shortly before that happened, the *Columbia* would explode.

The green light came on and I opened the air lock
hatch. I stepped outside and looked around for one of

the two maneuvering units we had. We were in shadow, on the night side of the earth, and it was difficult to see anything distinctly.

I remembered watching Klaus on the television monitor. When he reached the *Discovery*, he had unslung the maneuvering unit and tied it to an antenna. I looked, and there it was. I gave myself a cautious push away from the air lock and floated, too slowly, toward the antenna. After several seconds I was able to grip the antenna with my right hand; the left was completely useless by now.

Untying the maneuvering unit, I worried that I'd have more problems with the contraption. There wasn't time for another giggly sky tour. And it was possible that the device itself was malfunctioning; I remembered Klaus zigzagging around the nose of the *Columbia* before he finally got things under control.

That suddenly struck me as curious.

I remembered I had radio. You are so isolated, so utterly cut off from the rest of humanity when you're wearing a space suit, that it is easy to forget that you can still talk to other people.

"Braxton, this is Boggs. How are you doing over there?"

There was a pause of a few seconds. Then I heard a voice that sounded like Hollings.

"Boggs, get over here with those maneuvering units. We don't have much time!"

"Hollings, is that you? Look, I think the bomb may be planted somewhere on the nose of the ship. Outside."

"Where?"

"Right on the nose, somewhere. Crespi was doing something there before he came over. I'm going to look for it."

"Well then, so am I. I'm closer. I'll be outside in another minute. So will the others."

. I didn't have time for another argument with Hollings. He might find the bomb, but I didn't think he'd
be able to disarm it.

I finished strapping on the maneuvering unit, then
pushed myself away from the ship. I didn't know
where the other unit was, and I wasn't going to waste
time looking for it. I didn't even stop to stare at the
incredible expanse of the Pacific Ocean beneath my
feet. I lined myself up with the nose of the *Columbia*
and pushed forward on the control stick.

This had to be an express run. I decided not to
bother with the turn-around maneuver. I'd accelerate
as long as I could, then come in with all jets blasting.
It was a risky way to travel, because if I didn't time it
right, I could make a rather large hole in the hull of
the *Columbia*.

Before I was halfway there, I could see that I was
going to miss my target by a good ten meters. I cut
my jets and tried to realign myself. I needed to go left,
but my left arm was dangling uselessly, like a sausage
in a delicatessen window. I'd have to go completely
around to the right.

I gave the right-hand control a short spritz, just
enough to get myself turning. I had to be a slow turn,
because I wouldn't be able to stop it with a counter-
thrust to the left. When I came into line with the nose
of the *Columbia*, I'd have to gun the jets and worry
about the spin later.

The *Discovery* swung lazily through my field of vision, then the earth, and then the bottomless blackness of outer space. Finally the *Columbia* was back in
view. I waited as long as I could, then jammed the
control stick forward.

It took a long burn. I began to worry that I might not have enough nitrogen left to decelerate. Throughout both burns I'd silently counted elephants. I reached nineteen of them before I felt comfortable with my new vector. That meant a deceleration burn of another nineteen seconds.

I was still spinning, and I'd keep right on spinning until I could find some way to fire my left-side jets. I could reach across with my right hand, but that shifted my body around so much that I was afraid my center of mass had changed. I was afraid to find out what would happen if I fired the jets while out of balance. The *Columbia* was getting bigger, now, and if I couldn't get the spin under control I was going to have some real problems.

I saw three small figures floating near the forward hatch of the Shuttle. I wondered if Mission Specialist Powers was one of them. There was no way to tell; they were still too far away, and anyway, they were upside down.

And that was my answer. I was still thinking in two dimensions, but three-dimensionally, it was obvious what I had to do. I found the correct control, on my right, fortunately, and gave the jets a quick shot. Immediately, I turned upside down. I fired another blast to neutralize the new motion, then lined myself up again. Upside down, my right-hand jet would negate my right-hand spin. I nudged the control stick and felt the gentle vibration of the unit for a second. My spin stopped.

"Boggs, this is Hollings. What would the bomb look like?"

"How the hell would I know? Just look for anything that shouldn't be there."

I saw someone, presumably Hollings, hovering

around the blunt nose of the Shuttle. He was wearing the one maneuvering unit left on the *Columbia*. The other people, five of them now, were simply floating next to the ship. They were going to have a hell of a time getting away.

"Found it!" cried Hollings. "It's small, about the size of a book. It appears to be attached to the skin just above the RCS fuel tanks. What should I do, Boggs?"

"Don't try to move it. I'll be there in another minute."

"Boggs, this is Braxton. We've only got about three and a half minutes before reacquisition."

"Then there's only about three minutes till it goes off. Maybe less. Get everyone away from the ship."

"You're coming in mighty fast, Boggs," Braxton cautioned.

"I know, I know." I was trying to estimate time and distance, but it's not easy in outer space.

"Boggs," said Hollings, "it's right above the fuel tanks. They're hypergolic fuels—they ignite on contact. If the explosion ruptures the tanks, they'll blow the whole nose off."

"Don't touch it! Just hang on for a minute!"

I counted seven space suited figures near the forward hatch, plus Hollings on the nose. Everyone was out.

I rotated to line myself up with the *Discovery*. I couldn't get exactly in sync, but this was no time to be a perfectionist. I fired the jets.

There was no point in counting elephants again. I'd know when it was time to stop firing; I'd either crash into the *Columbia* or see it as I flew past. There was no real sensation of deceleration, other than the muted vibration of the jets, but I trusted the laws of physics. I had to be slowing down. Had to be.

"You're high, Boggs!" someone shouted. Then there was an excited babble as everyone tried to talk at once. Braxton somehow raised his volume and told everyone else to shut up.

"We can't reach you from where we are, Boggs," said Braxton. "You're going to overshoot."

"Damn. No time for that."

"I can reach you," said Hollings. "Just keep sitting on those jets and keep your attitude steady."

"Roger," I responded. I felt like a Navy pilot trying to land on the deck of a carrier in dense fog. My instinct was to turn myself around so I could at least see where I was going, but Hollings had told me not to He was my landing officer, and I had to trust him.

"Steady," he said. "Almost here."

I tilted my head forward to be able to look down between my feet. I seemed to be coming in at an angle. The delta wings of the Shuttle swept into view, then out of it. I saw the pilot's windshield a few feet below me, then it, too, slid on by.

I felt somebody grab my left leg; it hurt like hell.

"Cut!" shouted Hollings. I released the control stick and looked down at Hollings. He had me in tow with his left hand while he jockeyed his unit with his right. We went into an odd gyration, oscillating through ninety degrees of arc while Hollings tickled the jets. Somehow, he got us under control. Hollings pulled me in. I felt my feet thump against the hull of the *Columbia*.

"Two minutes," said Braxton. "At one minute, you guys get the hell away from there."

"I hear ya, Brax," said Hollings. "Now kindly shut up!"

I oriented myself so I was looking down at the nose of the ship. Hollings pointed toward the bomb. It was a flattish, rectangular object about three inches thick, eight inches long. It was mounted a foot away from the three RCS tubes.

"I can't figure what's holding it on," said Hollings.

"See any wires?"

"None."

"Dietrich was only up here for a few seconds. He didn't have time to connect anything. Could it be magnetic?"

"Not on this hull."

"Then it must be stuck on with some kind of adhesive. Maybe we can pull it off."

"Let's do it, then." Hollings braced his feet on the sloping nose of the ship and grabbed hold of the bomb with both hands. I tried to get set from the other side, but my feet kept slipping off of the hull.

"Help me," Hollings grunted.

I regained my traction and tried again. In the maneuvering unit, it was difficult to bend forward far enough to get a grip on the bomb. I managed to get my right hand around the edge of the bomb.

"Use both hands," Hollings instructed. "This mother's really stuck."

"Can't," I said. "Got myself stabbed in the other one."

"Well, do what you can. Push in my direction."

I tried, but all I did was push myself away from the ship again. I pulled myself back in and tried to get my fingers under the edge. I couldn't; space suits don't come equipped with fingernails.

But I did have a knife. I'd stuck Klaus's butter knife in one of my pockets, just to get it out of the way. I was probably lucky that it hadn't sawed a hole in my suit.

I unzipped a pocket on my right thigh and found

the knife. It was too short to use as a crowbar, but I thought I might be able to wedge it in under a corner of the bomb.

"A minute fifteen," Braxton announced.

"Hang on," I told Hollings. "Let me see if I can pry up this corner." I caught a quick glimpse of Hollings; in the shadows, I could see the strained, determined look on his face.

The hull was slightly curved where the bomb was attached. Unless the bomb was precisely molded to match the contour of the hull, which I doubted, it couldn't be flush at all four corners. But the two corners at my end were tight and seamless. I pulled myself around to the front end of the ship, while Hollings moved to where I had been.

I found what I wanted. One of the corners was perhaps a centimeter out of line with the hull. I shoved the knife under it and tried to slash away as much of the adhesive as I could.

"One minute," said Braxton. "Get out of there!"

"Almost got it! Hollings, pull on it when I say go!"

Hollings wrapped his fingers around the forward edge of the bomb. I pushed the knife as far as it would go, till only the handle extended from under the device.

"Now!"

I pulled up on the knife, keeping my feet firm against the hull. I heard Hollings grunt as he pulled back on the bomb.

"It won't—"

Hollings's voice stopped short.

"It's coming!" he shouted.

Abruptly, the adhesive gave way. The bomb snapped up, into Hollings's hands, and I went flying.

"Get rid of it!" screamed Braxton. As I tumbled

away from the ship, I saw Hollings sailing off in another direction. He looked like he was trying to throw the bomb away.

I rotated away from him. I was out of control and couldn't see what was happening. Before I could get my hand on the jet control, I heard a weird blurt of static, then something slammed into my tailbone.

There was no sound, not even when the debris pierced my nitrogen tank. The jolt numbed my whole body, like an electric shock from a cattle prod. I was only vaguely aware of a sensation of speed.

"Oh my God!" someone shouted. I heard a half dozen different voices bouncing through my helmet, and none of them made any sense.

"Boggs!" Braxton's flat voice cut through the confusion. I saw the ship flash by me, and then again and again. I was spinning.

"Boggs!" Braxton repeated. "Can you hear me?"

"What?" I mumbled.

"Boggs, get out of that unit! Your tank is ruptured!"

I wasn't sure what he meant. I was spinning so fast now that everything was a blur.

"You're leaking nitrogen, Boggs! Unstrap the unit!"

The numbness was wearing off, but it was replaced by an unimaginable vertigo. I was spinning off into the galaxy, jetting around randomly like a balloon.

I had to stop the spinning, somehow. Braxton had said to unstrap the unit. I managed to slip my right arm through the straps, but the left still wasn't working. I shut my eyes and tried to do it by feel alone. It seemed to help.

I got my left arm free while still hanging on with the right. I opened my eyes again and saw that the spin wasn't quite as bad. Apparently some of the random motions had canceled each other out. I held the unit at arm's length while it pulled me along on its erratic course.

"Don't let go of it, Boggs!" Braxton shouted. "Try to get it under control."

"How?" I asked. I couldn't see a way to do it. The nitrogen was spurting out from three different places in the tank.

And suddenly, it stopped. The reason was obvious. I was out of fuel.

I waved my right arm and tried to turn myself around. Although I'd released it, the maneuvering unit continued to float alongside me.

I saw the earth again, immense and blue, sparkling, as the sun rose over its eastern limb. Then I saw the *Columbia.* And the *Discovery.* They were a long way off.

"It's stopped," I said. "Out of fuel."

"Christ," said Braxton. "Listen to me, Boggs. We can't reach you. You're going to have to figure something out."

"What about Hollings? He's got a unit."

There was a long pause that told me more than I wanted to know.

"He's dead," said Braxton. "The bomb went off before he could get rid of it. He's gone and so is his unit."

"I'm sorry, Brax," I said. "I mean about Hollings."

Braxton didn't linger on sentiment. "There's another unit on the *Discovery,*" he said. "Anderson is trying to make it across, but it's going to take a while."

"How can he get there? He doesn't have a unit."

"We're going to throw him at the *Discovery.* There's nothing else we can do."

"What if he misses?"

"Then you'll both have problems."

I stared at the two Shuttles, now the size of dime store toys. I couldn't estimate my speed, but it seemed to be considerable. Every second was taking me farther away. Already, they couldn't have been closer than a mile.

"Look," I said, "don't try it. Even if Anderson makes it, by then I'll be too far away to reach with the maneuvering unit. What about the ship? Can you come after me in the ship?"

There was another pause. I suspected that Braxton was talking things over with the others on a different frequency.

"Boggs," he said, "it doesn't look too good. We've got people scattered all over the sky here. Everyone is pretty close to the ship, but they can't get back to it. There are only three of us still with the ship."

"I understand. You have to pick them up before you can come after me. How long would it take?"

"I don't know. Twenty, thirty minutes. How's your oxygen?"

There was a small gauge attached to my belt. I tried to focus on it, but it seemed to swim in and out of view. I realized I must have been getting weak from the loss of blood. I shook my head and blinked several times. My vision cleared again.

"It says thirty percent on the gauge. How long does that give me?"

"About an hour, if you keep calm and relax."

"Make it forty-five minutes, then. I'm bleeding pretty bad, I think. I had a little barroom brawl over on the *Discovery.*"

"How do you feel?"

"Weak. Shaky. My heart is going a mile a minute."

"So is the rest of you, Boggs. I can barely see you."

"Can you get to me in forty-five minutes?"

"We can try," he said. He didn't sound very confident.

It was about time to think things over and take stock of my situation. The Shuttles were so far away by now that they appeared to be a single, misshapen lump. In forty-five minutes, I probably wouldn't even be able to see them. And they wouldn't be able to see me, because in forty-five minutes, we'd be on the night side again.

"I've got an idea," I said. "How about if I use my oxygen as fuel? I could blow myself back at the ship."

"Don't do anything now," Braxton said sharply. "I'm already in the ship. We'll get the others—"

"Forget it, Brax. You can't come after me first because if you do you could lose the others. And if you don't come after me first, you'll never find me. I've got to come to you. It's the only way."

"If you use your oxygen for fuel, what are you going to breathe?"

"I can plug the hose back in any time I need to take a breath."

"For how long?"

"As long as I have to, I guess." I wished he would just shut up and let me handle this. The whole idea was becoming less attractive the more Braxton talked.

"Be quiet and let me think for a minute," I said.

The *Columbia* wasn't exactly a motor scooter. Even if Braxton had the touch of a concert pianist, it was going to be a complicated task to pick up the four people who were nearby. The ship would have to do all the maneuvering, because those of us out here in the inky void could do none at all.

It would be a long forty-five minutes. The scenery was fantastic, but I wasn't here as a tourist. In fact, I was already feeling a strange, cold loneliness. Even with my radio, I was about as alone as anyone had ever been. I wanted to get back where the people were.

And if I was going to run out of air anyway, I might as well do it constructively. At this point, there wasn't a hell of a lot left to lose by trying.

"Braxton," I said, "I'm going to try it."

"Are you sure you know what you're doing?"

"No. But I don't have any other ideas. I don't think you'd have a very good shot at finding me forty-five minutes from now."

"It'd be tough," he admitted.

"Okay, then. I'll try to aim myself at you. If I miss, you'll have to track me down."

"We'll be here," he said. "Good luck, Boggs."

I took a deep breath—a luxury—and unplugged the oxygen connection at my waist. The hose was about an inch in diameter. I didn't think there would be very much pressure in so large a tube. I was right. When I pointed the hose away from me, I didn't notice any appreciable acceleration in any direction.

I tried cupping my hand over most of the opening to increase the pressure, like one of those people who play music on a vacuum cleaner. That seemed to help, but it was hard to be sure. I looked over my shoulder and saw the Shuttles gleaming in the distance. They were still miles away.

The mathematics weren't appealing. I'd need to generate as much total thrust as the runaway maneuvering unit, plus enough extra to get me back to the ship before my air ran out. I didn't know if I could do it even with a full tank.

The maneuvering unit was several yards away from me now. That was good. I could use it as a milestone.

The more I altered my own course, the farther away it would get.

I found I could still beathe even with the hose unplugged. There was enough air in the suit itself to keep me going for a while. The trick was to know just how long I could take it before oxygen starvation set in. It was a subtle way to die. I'd have to keep on the ball.

I plugged the hose back in when the air in my helmet began to remind me of my high-school gym locker. The cool, fresh oxygen was glorious.

"How are you doing, Boggs?"

"Just fine."

"Any problems?"

"No new ones. I seem to be making a little progress. I'm about fifty yards away from the maneuvering unit."

"You're still going away from us, though. What does your gauge read?"

I looked at it and tried to read the numbers. They didn't make much sense at first.

"Nineteen percent, I think." I unplugged the hose again and went back to work. Nineteen percent didn't sound like a lot. Maybe it was like gasoline. The thing to do if you were running out of gas, obviously, was to drive very fast so you'd get home before you ran out.

The west coast of South America was below me now. I'd come all the way across the Pacific in just a few minutes. I must have been going faster than I thought. The Andes looked incredible. I'd always wanted to see them. This wasn't what I had in mind, but you take what you can get. Maybe after I got home, I'd take a vacation in Peru. See Machu Picchu and the Inca ruins. I wondered if there had been an

Inca Klaus Dietrich, all hot and eager to change history. If there was one, he must not have done a very
good job. History was all through with the Incas.

History was probably all through with me, too. The
first man to make love in outer space was about to
become the first man to die there. No, the second.
Hollings had already claimed that dubious honor. If
he had performed badly during that long week of
waiting aboard the *Discovery*, he had redeemed himself in his final moments. I felt glad about that.

I remembered to plug the hose back in for a few
seconds. There didn't seem to be much point in checking the gauge again. You seldom find much comfort
in naked numbers, whether they're on a telephone bill
or a life support system.

After a few more sniffs of cool O_2, I went back to
my spaceship mode. The S.S. *Boggs* had covered several hundred yards of vacuum, judging by the distance to the abandoned maneuvering unit, but the
nearest safe harbor was still impossibly far. I felt like
the *Flying Dutchman*.

There were dense, gray clouds blanketing the Ama-
zon Valley. Hot and steamy down there, just as it was
getting hot and steamy inside my space suit. I'd always heard about the cold reaches of outer space, but
with no oxygen flowing into my suit, I was in danger
of cooking in my own body heat. Sweat was beading
on my forehead; instead of rolling down into my eyes,
it broke free whenever I turned my head, creating extremely local showers inside my helmet. Given enough
time, I'd either fry or drown.

I didn't think I'd get that much time. Curiosity
drove me to take another peek at my oxygen gauge. It
read three percent.

"Boggs," Braxton said, "we just picked up Powers

and Morley. Two more to go, then we'll come after you."

"Good, good," I said.

"How's your oxygen?"

"Gone."

Braxton didn't say anything for a few seconds. I didn't mind. Braxton wasn't a bad guy, but I didn't want to spend my last few minutes listening to him telling me what to do. I figured I could probably die without any help at all from NASA.

"Plug your hose in," Braxton told me. "Save the air you've got left. Just a few minutes more."

"Take your time," I said. "I'm kind of enjoying this. Hell of a view up here."

"Get that hose plugged in, Boggs!"

"Roger, Cap'n. Batten down the hatches." I held the oxygen hose up to my helmet and stared into it. I didn't see anything coming out of it. When I was a kid, one of my friends told me once that his garden hose was plugged up. He asked me to take a look and see if I could find what was blocking it. While I was looking, he turned the water on full force. I wasn't a very bright kid, I guess. But it was a hot summer day, and that water did feel good. I wouldn't mind feeling that way right now.

Although, really, I didn't feel that bad. It was hot and muggy, but aside from that I was lazy and relaxed. If I could just get this damned fishbowl off my head, I'd be able to get a little breeze on my face. A nice, cool breeze, blowing my hair around and drying the sweat. If I could just move my left arm, I'd be able to get the helmet off and feel the breeze. One-handed, I couldn't seem to manage it. The thing was stuck, somehow.

Someone was yelling at me. I wished he would stop.

I was getting awfully tired. Maybe if I slept for a few minutes, I'd be able to figure a way to get the helmet off and feel the wind in my face. I'd wake up cool and refreshed. God, that would be nice. So nice.

But first I really did need that nap.

CHAPTER 17

Someone was shoving something into my face. It was annoying, but I didn't seem to be able to do anything about it. I couldn't even talk; something was clamped over my nose and mouth.

I saw a big, round face looming over me. Heavy black eyebrows above a broad nose. He spoke to me but I couldn't understand what he was saying. It sounded as if he were trying to spit and clear his throat simultaneously.

He pulled the thing away from my face and said something else I didn't understand.

"What?"

He turned his head and said something to another person. Then he looked back at me and said very slowly, "Dr. Dietrich, can you hear me? How do you feel?"

I didn't think anyone had ever called me Dr. Dietrich before. I felt pretty sure that I was actually someone named Sam Boggs. One of us was making a mistake.

"I am Colonel Grigory Shlyapkin. We picked up yourself five of minutes past. How are your feelings?"

My feelings were mostly confused. Shlyapkin was speaking some strange language that even Henry Higgins might have a tough time identifying as English. Shlyapkin sounded like a Russian name. And if he was Russian, then—

Either I was in Marxist-Leninist heaven, or I was aboard the Russian Kosmolyot. Since I was too much of a revisionist to be welcome in Bolshevik nirvana, I decided the second seemed more reasonable. They thought I was Klaus Dietrich, making the rendezvous after completing my dirty work on the American Shuttles. Since both the *Columbia* and the *Discovery* were still in good shape the last time I saw them, the Russians might not be very pleased with good old Klaus. On the other hand, they'd have no use at all for Sam Boggs. If they wanted to think I was Klaus Dietrich, I'd play along with them.

Shlyapkin wanted to talk. I could barely understand him, and the questions I could understand, I didn't want to answer. I reached for the oxygen mask again, and Shlyapkin obligingly placed it over my face. Shlyapkin realized that conversation was going to be impossible as long as I needed the mask, so he patted me on the shoulder and floated away to tend other matters.

I didn't know how long I could get away with it. Sooner or later I'd have to take off the mask and say something. Maybe I could pretend that I'd suffered brain damage from the lack of oxygen; they wouldn't expect much conversation from a babbling idiot. In fact, maybe I really did lose some brain cells. How could I tell?

Even if my gray matter had withered away like the

perfect state, there was nothing I could do about it now. I felt tired and a little hazy, and my leg and arm ached, but beyond that, things seemed more or less normal to me.

I raised my head and looked around. I was still in my space suit, minus the helmet, and I had some kind of strap lashed around my waist to keep me from floating away. Around me I saw what seemed to be the crew quarters of the Kosmolyot, roughly the equivalent of the mid-deck of the Shuttles. The place had all the Spartan charm of a one-room flat in Leningrad; if the *Discovery* looked like someone's vision of the kitchen of the future, the Kosmolyot was more in the mode of a hydroelectric power station. If the Russians ever got around to building space colonies, Klaus's revolution would probably be led by radical interior decorators.

Shlyapkin floated back into view. His heavy brows angled together to form an angry V.

"You are not Dr. Dietrich," he said accusingly.

"I never said I was."

"Your name is Boggs."

"My name is Boggs," I agreed.

"We have radio contact to *Columbia*. Very much confusion is happening."

That seemed like an accurate assessment of the situation. Shlyapkin looked angry enough to dump me back into space. I tried to mollify him with a grateful smile.

"Thank you for saving me," I said unctuously. "*Bolshoyeh spacebo*."

"We are regrettable of the error," said Shlyapkin. "We are attempting for rectification."

If he considered saving me an error, I wasn't looking forward to any rectification. I was about to thank

him again when another cosmonaut approached
Shlyapkin from above, upside down. They conversed
rapidly, and neither one of them sounded very happy.
I knew a smattering of Russian, but not enough to follow what they were saying.

The second cosmonaut disappeared, and Shlyapkin
turned to me again. He was wearing a forced smile on
his broad face.

"Dr. Boggs," he said, "we are pleasing to inform
yourself that you will be returning again to your own
American ship. Note, please, that Soviet Union is
much in compliance with treaty obligations. Our pleasure is satisfied in servicing needs of brother cosmonauts. Knowing of emergency situation on United
States Shuttle *Discovery*, our duty is offering of necessary assistance. You will report this, yes?"

I caught his drift. My brother cosmonauts had cou-
rageously saved my life. They had rushed to the aid of
the stricken *Discovery* in a spirit of boundless good-
will and international cooperation. They were all swell
guys. Hell, it was almost true.

"I am very grateful," I assured him. "The American
people are also very grateful." I suspected that the
American people, if they ever found out what really
happened up here (which seemed unlikely), would
be mad as hell. But I was willing to play the game.

Shlyapkin smiled in relief and gave me another
comradely slap on my injured shoulder. I gritted my
teeth and smiled back at him. Détente was alive and
well in orbit.

I stayed aboard the Kosmolyot for another two
hours while Shlyapkin and Braxton worked out the
details of the exchange. The Russians wanted nothing
to do with me, but they wanted Dietrich badly. I

didn't know what Braxton wanted, and I didn't even care to think about what Houston would make of the situation. But it was clear that Shlyapkin wanted to get rid of me as soon as possible.

Two other cosmonauts, Chernik and Voloshin, helped me out of my suit and put dressings on my wounds. They didn't ask how I got them, and I didn't volunteer any information. The numbness in my left arm had faded somewhat, and I found I was able to move it if I didn't mind excruciating pain.

Chernik and Voloshin knew even less English than Shlyapkin. We chatted mindlessly for a while. They thought highly of the Soviet Olympic basketball team, and I told them about the Boston Celtics. They asked me if I owned my own automobile; when I replied that I had a Winnebago, communications broke down entirely.

The Kosmolyot maneuvered briefly, not long enough to produce more than a hint of gravity. Shortly after that, Shlyapkin came down from the flight deck and told me to get suited up. Chernik and Voloshin helped me get back into my gear, and we parted with handshakes and a promise that I'd send them some Elvis Presley records.

"*Columbia* is one hundred meters distant," Shlyapkin told me as I prepared to enter the air lock. "Easy jump will be sufficient."

"No maneuvering unit?"

"That is not permitted to be necessary," he said. "Air-lock door will remain in closed position until assurances of Dr. Dietrich's coming are visible. You understand?"

"You don't open the door until Dietrich is on his way."

"Very correct. Again, I personally tell you that we

of Soviet Union spacecraft are honored to have participated in rescue of yourself. American cosmonauts are like brothers of Soviet cosmonauts. We wish to you a safe return to your homeland."

I shook his hand. The bastard hadn't intended to save my life, but that's the way it worked out. He'd hear no complaints from me.

I lowered my helmet into place, then stepped into the air lock. Shlyapkin closed the door behind me. I felt the cool rush of air from the tank the Russians had given me; my suit ballooned up as the pressure dropped.

They let me wait there for five minutes. I began to wonder if Klaus really wanted to transfer to the Kosmolyot. The Russians certainly weren't going to be pleased with the way his little operation had turned out. I suspected that they might be a little reluctant to reward him with that important job in their space program. On the other hand, Klaus's future with the Americans would likely be limited to a cell in Leavenworth for the murder of Hollings. And if the Americans were unable to try him for a crime committed in outer space, the Germans would have no difficulty in convicting him on a basketful of charges. Any way you looked at it, Klaus's future was not bright.

At least he had a future. Hollings didn't. Neither did Emil Rothenburg. And Ilsa.

I could still feel a little sympathy for Emil. He wanted to change history, but he didn't learn from it. Long ago he thought he could survive by working for the Nazis; when he realized he was wrong, his escape cost him a leg. This time he believed he could use the Soviets for his own purposes. He was wrong, and there was no escape.

Emil's master plan made sense in the warped way

that grandiose plots always make sense, to someone. But the Russians had their own great plans, and Emil—and Spartacus and the Omegas—were never more than a convenient cog in the grand wheel of geopolitical destiny. Emil dreamed up a bunch of phantom terrorists who would hurt no one; but the KGB made them real. People died. Emil died. Ilsa died.

I was thinking of Ilsa when the outer door opened. I poked my head outside and saw the *Columbia* and the *Discovery*, lined up side by side as if on display in a used-spaceship lot. As Shlyapkin had promised, the *Columbia* was only about a hundred meters away. I saw two people floating outside the aft air-lock. One of them dived toward me.

I watched Klaus's progress for a few moments. I wondered what I should think of him now. My best friend, scientist, revolutionary, megalomaniac—and murderer. I didn't know what to feel. Then I realized that I was too tired to feel anything at all, for anyone. My heart was as empty as the vacuum around me. I just wanted to go home.

I pushed off the side of the Kosmolyot and began my voyage to the *Columbia*. I knew this was the last time I'd ever have the chance to float free and unrestrained, to sail the infinite deep. I should have been collecting impressions, storing up memories for the long earthbound years ahead of me. But all I felt was fatigue and the melancholy aftertaste of another dirty job.

Klaus and I were approaching each other. We could have talked, I suppose, but there was nothing I wanted to say to him. He was a few feet above me and to my left. As we closed to minimum distance, I saw Klaus raise his right hand and flip me a jaunty little salute.

I flipped him a salute of my own. Space-suit gloves are stiff, and it's difficult to move one finger independently of the others, but I think he got the message.

Then Klaus was gone, and only the *Columbia* lay ahead of me. The figure by the air lock lifted his arm and waved to me.

"Welcome back, Boggs," said Braxton.

I did salute Braxton. A real salute. "Request permission to come aboard, sir," I said formally.

"Cut the bullshit and get yourself turned around, Boggs. You can't grab me with your feet."

"Roger," I answered. I gave my body a little twist and started to turn upside down so I'd be able to reach Braxton. I timed it badly and was beginning another revolution when Braxton snared my left ankle. He reeled me in until I was able to get myself organized and stand upright on the deck of the Shuttle, a few feet aft of the air lock.

"How are you?" Braxton asked.

"Worn out. How the hell did you manage the exchange? Houston must have gone crazy."

"Houston didn't have anything to do with it. Neither did Washington. I told you before we lifted off, Boggs, you're part of my crew. My crew goes where I go. And I'm going home."

Braxton reached for the airlock hatch, but I stopped him. "Not yet," I said. "You'll be here again, but I won't be. I'd like another minute."

Braxton must have understood. He released his grip on the hatch and turned to look at the earth. Together, we silently watched the slow rotation of that immense blue ball. Somehow I knew I'd never be able to tell anyone about this, not simply because McNally probably wouldn't let me, but because the words haven't been invented yet. Someday, someone—probably one of those unborn rebels who will one day populate the skies—will find the right way to say it, and then everyone will know how it feels to stand atop Olympus and look back on the greatest mystery of all.

"Looks like a nice day on the Cape," said Braxton. He pointed toward the long, slender finger of Florida.

"Uh huh."

"It won't last, though," he said. "See that storm brewing down there in the Caribbean?"

"*Carib*bean," I said automatically.

"What?"

"Never mind," I said. "Let's go home."

Dell Bestsellers